A Left-Hander on Route 66

By

Michael Lund

BeachHouse Books

Chesterfield, Missouri, USA

Copyright

A slightly altered version of one chapter appeared previously in the Route 66 Federation News under the title of "Flights of Desire Along Route 66."

Graphics Credits:

Cover by Dr. Bud Banis. The front cover is composited from a photo of Route 66 courtesy of Tom Ferderbar [tomferd@wi.rr.com] and Dr. Bud Banis, photo Objects from Hemera Technologies (www.hemera.com) with text and enhancements by Dr. Bud Banis.
The Left-hander is portrayed on the cover by Jason McCoskey.
The twins in the womb graphic is an original creation by Loren Robertson, the sailplane illustration is by Mike Melton [Tallwalkervizns@aol.com]
Publication date August, 2003
ISBN 1-888725-88-5 Regular print BeachHouse Books Edition
First Printing, August, 2003

Library of Congress Cataloging-in-Publication Data
Lund, Michael, 1945-
  A left-hander on Route 66 / by Michael Lund.
    p. cm.
Sequel to: Growing up on Route 66.
  ISBN 1-888725-88-5 (regular print BeachHouse Books : alk. paper) --
ISBN 1-888725-89-3 (16 point MacroPrintBooks ed. : alk. paper)
  1. Left- and right-handedness--Fiction. 2. United States Highway
66--Fiction. 3. Judicial error--Fiction. 4. Prisoners--Fiction. 5.
Missouri--Fiction. I. Title: Left-hander on Route Sixty-six. II. Title.

  PS3562.U486L44 2003
  813'.54--dc22   2003017770

BeachHouse Books
PO Box 7151 Chesterfield, MO 63006-7151   (636) 394-4950
macroprintbooks.com

Praise for the Michael Lund's Route 66 Novel series:

"I finished your [first] novel . . . and was struck by how perfectly it seemed to encircle (of course) the world of childhood and its heady veering toward adulthood. It's a loving and funny book . . . and made me recall with mingled pleasure and embarrassment all the twinges and itches and passions of adolescence. Well done, and thank you for putting it into my hands."

--Carrie Brown, author of *Lamb In Love* and *The Hatbox Baby*

"A wonderfully well-wrought [first] novel, set in a place that's still the stuff of myth, about coming of age in a simpler time when sex was giddily mysterious and life was filled with endless possibilities."

--Bernard Edelman, editor of *Dear America: Letters Home from Vietnam* and *Centenarians: The Story of the 20th Century by the Americans Who Lived It*

"In *Growing up on Route 66*, Michael Lund gives us a loving look through the telescope of memory, resurrecting forgotten feelings in the idiom of adolescence sharpened by the lens of age--and wisdom. He takes us back to a time when the road ahead was a winding one, just right for joyrides, meant to be wandered, with curious roadside attractions and shady stops along the way. Reading [his] book is like returning to a summer night when you were young, when life was full of promise, mystery, and terror, that time at twilight, before your mother called you in to wash up and go to bed, when you were playing a leisurely game of kick-the-can and wished that the game could just go on and on. Fortunately, Lund promises that it will go on, in the second book in his series, *Route 66 Kids*, and, I hope, many more to come."

--Eric Kraft, author of *The Personal History, Adventures, Experiences & Observations of Peter Leroy*

For my equally wonderful left-handed son and right-handed daughter.

ACKNOWLEDGMENTS

I wish to express my sincere gratitude to Dr. Bud Banis, a publisher of the old school (an educated friend of the author) and of the new (a skilled man of business and technology). We have worked happily together on the basis of an electronic handshake, surely a modern-day miracle.

Robin Sedgwick has graciously offered editorial advice in the course of this book's production, and for that I am also grateful.

Any inconsistencies or errors remaining in the pages that follow are, of course, attributable solely to the author.

Prologue: Points of No Return

Scene: The Missouri River Valley. Time: thirty to forty years ago

You don't know about me unless you happen to have read a work by Mark Landon called *Growing up on Route 66*. In that book Mark was recalling a particular version of childhood a generation ago, remembering an almost magical neighborhood called "The Circle," where he grew up close to fabled Route 66. But even if you'd read his story, you might not have noticed me among all those future babyboomers.

You might even say I was "outside the Circle" anyway, for I didn't live on his street and never belonged to his social set, try as hard as I might to be accepted by America's rising middle class. In the Midwest in the 1950s there were many undistinguished figures like me filling in the background of the typical scene, dark figures missed by the bright light trained on the few who stood in the foreground. We lost souls weren't traveling down main roads (Route 66 was "America's Main Street," remember) but instead, if we were remarked at all, stopped, deer in headlights, wandering onto those throughways.

My name is Hugh Noone, and while Mark was trying to make time with Marcia Terrell on a high school hayride one fall evening in 1960, I *really* was making hay on the wagon right behind his. But, ironically, while Mark's failure to go all the way now makes him look noble, my success in achieving union confirmed me as socially second rate. Too, while this moment of non-climax was pivotal for Mark on his journey toward sexual maturity, the same date is not actually very important in my story. I was really just passing time on that Youth Fellowship outing, it turns out, waiting innocently until my life would suddenly take the shape it has now.

I say "suddenly" because I have become convinced that for each of us there is a single critical instant, a moment of choice and chance that fixes our individual history. And I will need to talk here about an event which occurred two years after those several dozen of us teenagers were taking a moonlit ride on the Roper farm. In the later event, the town of Fairfield, Missouri, where I grew up, suffered a calamity. I did not cause that disaster, but I was a party to it. And, as critical as the moment came to be for many citizens of our small town through the next three decades, I learned that my life too hinged on the moment when Billy Rhodes raced a hundred-car freight train to the Kingshighway/Route 66 crossing. That's when my life veered further from the "Mother Road" on a detour that ended in prison.

I have been obsessed with such turning points, those moments when a specific history, long toiling up some prominent hillside of causality, is at last propelled over the peak to race down the other side. Points of no return, I've called them--steps in grand processes after which no turning back is possible, where an inevitability settles over all those concerned as they move, often swiftly, toward an inescapable outcome.

I will want to consider that communal point of no return for the small town of Fairfield, known to adolescent wags as "Cross Rhodes." But I need, too, to focus more narrowly on the private turning point of my own little life. I found that moment, where, along the continuum of hours from birth to the present, things conspired to direct me to the place and condition I now endure. But sometimes I am not sure it all didn't start earlier. Much earlier. It may have begun in the womb.

I'm left-handed, you see, a fact that places one in a certain relationship to the rest of society. Humanity is, I have read, about 90 percent right-handed. But a consistency of handedness was even more evident in the remarkably straight, white, middleclass world I grew up in. In fact, so rigid was convention in those days that there were *no* left-handers! We'd all been made into regular right-handers by our parents, our teachers, and our employers.

I've learned recently that left-handedness occurs in the advanced development of the brain, that is, late in gestation. The left hemisphere of the brain is dominant in most people. And it controls the right side of the body. Sometimes, however, the brain is more symmetrical, whether through inheritance or through unknown factors involved in fetal growth. In such individuals the right hemisphere tends to dominate, and the person is left-handed.

Now, as a group, left-handed individuals tend to exhibit more varied traits than right-handers. Some think such variety is good, but I say that's why we don't fit in so well. Left-handers have too many rough edges to match up neatly with stereotypes. And rough edges tend to irritate.

Post-World War II left-handed selves were, as I said, gradually erased from view beginning even in infanthood. We all had to go down our roads, like Route 66, in the proper, prescribed manner--on the right. If I tried to eat Pablum with my left hand, my mother would transfer the tiny spoon to the other side. My natural instinct to throw a ball southpaw was sharply criticized by my father (my stepfather, actually--I'll get to that). Other lefties found themselves tearing colored

3

construction paper with scissors made backwards for them, sitting on their preferred hands as they tried to copy onto third-grade tablets script letters from blackboard models, coloring outside the lines because precision ran along paths foreign to their perspective.

It didn't take long for all the left-handed selves of those days to be disguised by right-handed toys (bows with arrow guides on the right side), hidden in conventional positions (on the third-base side of the plate at bat), lost in schematic diagrams (sixth-grade square dancing, for instance) of standard movement (grab your partner, do-si-do). But, of course, they were never destroyed completely. Some lingered out of sight and out of mind until certain moments of destiny when they would leap out and demand recognition. It happened to me. It happened at that moment I want to tell you about.

Modern science is beginning to recover those left-handers, I read, as psychologists and sociologists are taking the old meaning away from "sinister" (dangerous, but deriving from the Latin for left-handed). Soon left-handers may get to be themselves.

If you had pictures of infants in the womb, you'd find that some of us can be seen sucking our left thumbs. It's natural; it's ordained. That's an image of me you have in your mind's eye right now, in fact. The real me, Hugh Noone unshaped by right-handed norms, all happy potential to become a self I never did become, at least until today.

I'm in jail right now, by the way--one of the reasons I have plenty of time to research matters like handedness. And I've been given, by the state judge hearing my appeal, the opportunity to write down this account of my past, a confession of sorts.

The way I see it, a right-handed version of me, convicted of a crime I didn't commit, has put the left-handed me behind bars. I believe, with my lawyer's appeal (she's another left-hander), I'll be out of here very soon. But in the meantime I have some things to say to you as well as to the judge, all the world's right-handers and all the world's left-handers masquerading as right-handers. That story proper begins in the next chapter, and it may in the end prove that the world isn't completely rigged against left-handers. They too might somehow follow Route 66.

There is, however, a preliminary event from my early childhood to consider, a moment which I remember as emblematic of my lost identity. It is a brief appearance of that shadowy womb self, the real me.

By the way, I have also sometimes wondered if I'm not a twin, the left-handed self of a right-handed brother (or sister) who would have done so much better in the world. He or she might have been lost somewhere in development, perhaps not long after we (once one cell?) divided into two organisms. Again, a picture at one time early in our mother's pregnancy might have shown the pair of us, perfectly balanced in amniotic fluid, a yin and a yang making an ambidextrous wholeness. It would be no wonder I've had a hard time since, that perfect companion lost and my left-handedness coming on so strong without him/her.

Some restraining influence like a companion soul was, however, absent at one critical moment early in my life. I couldn't have been more than four or five years of age when I accidentally saw my mother nude.

Grownups in those days were very careful to keep themselves covered, especially in front of children; so you should understand that this was quite a shock to me. Around our house bathroom doors were consistently locked, and people changed clothes within the privacy of bedrooms.

One day, waking up from an afternoon nap, I didn't see my mother immediately. She was not in my room, not in the living room, not in the kitchen. So I pulled open the bathroom door and walked right into her breasts.

She stood as if she might have been on her way out the door, except that she was bent forward at the waist, and her arms were spread as her hands rested beside the door frame. Her blouse was unbuttoned but still tucked in her skirt, hanging low from her hips. She had no brassiere on.

My stepfather was standing behind her, but from my low level of vision I didn't at first see beyond my mother's startling, naked form. And those large, swaying breasts took my entire attention. They were somehow appealing.

Not that I recalled being nursed. I had been formula fed, like most of my generation. Mothers were enjoying the advances of science fueled by the war effort of the previous decade. I was weaned from the bottle at the earliest possible date

So I don't know what inspired me in appreciation of those breasts. Surely not desire at that age. Maybe only curiosity. Whatever feeling I had, though, caused me to reach a hand out for them, a smile, I'm sure, on my child's innocent face.

I don't remember my mother's reaction to my appearance, or to my reaching out for her. I suspect she so little anticipated anyone's coming into the bathroom at that critical moment--for reasons I suspect you now can guess--that a look of stunned surprise was probably frozen on her face.

Before I could touch a breast, I learned that my stepfather was in the room too. He reached around my mother and slapped my hand down.

I cried out in pain, as he had hit me hard. But I also cried out in fear, for the look on my stepfather's face, appearing over my mother's shoulder, was angry, livid. I had done something terrible; but, as is so often the case in childhood, I didn't know what.

What I'd done that so offended this man, my mother's second husband of two years, was not touching her breasts. It was reaching out to do so with my left hand.

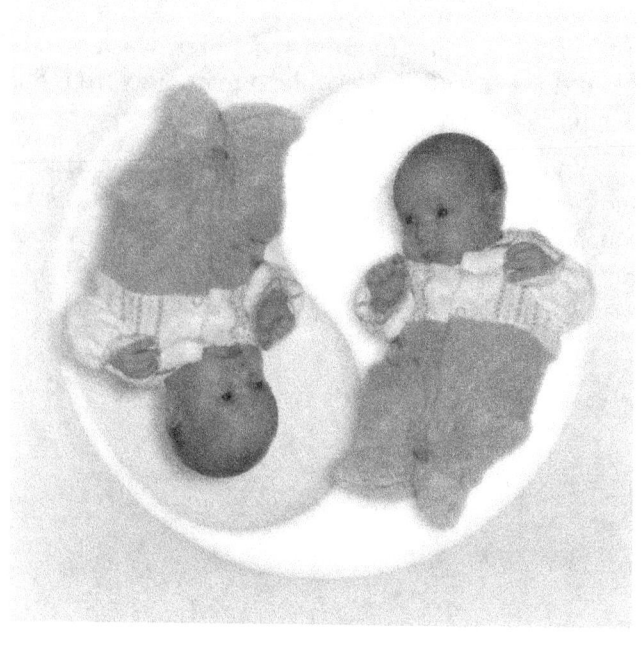

Part One:
Killer Instinct: Chapter 1

I wasn't exactly sure how Linda got on top of me, but it didn't worry me too much. I knew I was strong enough to reverse our positions when I wanted to. And right now, being on the bottom was kind of fun.

For a boy just turned sixteen years of age, and coming more or less from the wrong side of the tracks, wrestling with this particular young lady was a social accomplishment. But I also liked the feel of her rump resting on my stomach, and I enjoyed watching those far-better-than-average breasts press against her blouse as she leaned forward. She was trying to hold my wrists flat on the ground with her hands.

"Give. Or I'll use the Indian torture," threatened my attractive opponent. What we called "Indian" torture in those days involved thumping on your victim's chest with the tips of your straightened fingers. It might not have hurt much the first few times, but if you kept it up long enough, your victim would "give." It was the principle of water dripping on stone.

To succeed, though, as torturer, you had to achieve the superior position: sitting on the victim's torso and pinning his upper arms to the ground with your knees. This left your own arms and hands free for thumping. Linda had achieved that position with me.

What were we doing rolling around under the apple trees in her side yard on stately Missouri Avenue one warm fall afternoon in 1962, you ask? Well, of course, mostly this is boy-girl stuff, ways of touching and exploring without committing ourselves to any arrangement beyond the temporary. We're certainly not on a date, not Hugh Noone and Linda Roy. We had just happened to arrive at her house from downtown because we had been headed in the same direction after school. (Well, I had taken some deliberate pauses and strategic detours to make sure I was walking the way she was.)

There's also the sports thing at work. The system in these days requires of me and all boys at least casual acquaintance with the standard high school varsity sports. And this particular high school junior *girl* is also inspired by varsity competition. She's not wrestling at school, as we're well before that phase of women's liberation. But she is a tennis player, and a darn good one. Her drive to win (that famous killer instinct) carries over even to friendly, and sexually charged, battles with boys her age.

"Give?" she demands again, thumping on my sternum. The Indian torture is beginning to hurt a little.

"No," I answer, and reach up with one leg, trying to hook her head and pull her backward. But she's wise to that old move, and ducks down close to my face, her head out of my leg's reach. I don't mind, as her breath, sweet as the apples in the branches above, warms my cheek. And those breasts . . . soooo, so close, sooo fine.

At the time I was in high school, by the way, the late 1950s and early '60s, boys in America did not face a decision of whether or not to go out for sports: of course, we went out. The only question was which sport we would compete in. I had chosen tennis, for reasons I'll explain shortly. But that's how she knew who I was, how I could joke with her on the way home, how we could come to be casually engaged in a little mock wrestling.

10

I wasn't really in her set, you understand. The Roy family was part of Fairfield's upper crust. That doesn't mean the millionaires one might find in larger places like St. Louis, but the doctors (in her father's case, dentist), lawyers, successful businessmen who could afford private music lessons, expensive sports outfits, and large homes like the one to my left as I lay on my back in the Roys' beautifully manicured lawn.

I, on the other hand, lived in a nondescript neighborhood off Highway 00 on the west side of town. The bungalows and Depression era houses that lined several blocks not directly connected to famous Route 66 were mostly owned (or rented) by men who worked at the shoe factory or for the highway department. The mothers in these homes cleaned the houses of the better-to-do, or worked late shifts at the grocery stores and weekends at department stores downtown. Their children took a lot of shop at the high school, or home economics, and never considered college.

I didn't believe I really belonged in this group, but no one in any of the other groups at school--especially people in Linda's class--saw me as quite their equal. With a stepfather who worked nights as a security guard at South Central Missouri State College and a mother who took in washing, I just wasn't up to the standards of Fairfield High's high society. (My real father, by the way, died overseas in the military, never having seen me in this world. I'm sort of half orphan, or feel that way most of the time.)

Sports were the most recent arena in which I hoped to prove I didn't belong "on Black Street," which was how everyone referred to my neighborhood, despite the fact that there were half a dozen streets crossing that thoroughfare (and I lived on Cedar). I particularly liked tennis because the court offers no bias toward right-handers, which is not true of all sports. Try to find left-handed golf clubs sometime!

About my only option to sports as an avenue to distinction would have been the Fairfield-Phipps County 4-H Club. Members were easily identified by their blue corduroy jean jackets worn every day at Fairfield High School. But people like Karen Murphy, a girl I'd gone out (and more) with, were somewhat beneath the social class I aspired to.

I had a dream of becoming an actor, going to Hollywood. But I didn't know how to get started. The few times plays were put on in school, the usual class leaders ended up with all the parts.

I might, now that I think about it, have been able to endorse an amended version of the 4-H's stated goals if I couldn't find a theatrical troupe to join. That is, I wanted to use my *head* to figure out how society's *heart* worked so that I could get beyond where my old man was. And I was pledging my *hands* to better service in grabbing *healthy* Linda.

My hands weren't doing much right now, though, as she had the weight of her body in those knees on my biceps. This did, of course, make her vulnerable to the second standard counter against the Indian torture: a sudden upward thrust of hips that topples your opponent forward over your head. You have to do some squirming after that to get completely free of the body on top of you, but it generally takes the pressure off

I considered this maneuver for a moment, but decided to wait just a bit longer. Linda's thumping on my chest was kind of exciting. And, when she paused to give me a chance to surrender, she treated me to a very pretty smile of satisfaction.

There would be little argument that this is one of Fairfield's most beautiful sixteen- (or is it seventeen?) year-olds. She is tall (five feet 7 inches, I happen to know) and slender. But she has, all the boys agree, the breasts of a larger woman. They're not too big, unnatural looking. And there is absolutely no extra flesh around them. They stand out like the breasts of a magnificent Greek goddess sculpted by Michelangelo.

This idol of Fairfield High also has a characteristic gesture that undoes me. She has the habit of shifting or shrugging her right shoulder, as if her clothes on that side are binding. It's a motion some tennis players develop as part of their service rhythm. It frees the arm from the sleeve so that no hitch occurs in the swing.

I, however, have come to believe that Linda shrugs that shoulder unconsciously in order to shift her brassiere strap. Her breasts, I am convinced, want to be free of unnecessary restraint. They are so perfectly formed, so firm, they need no support.

So whenever she gave that little hitch, which she did right then in preparing to resume the Indian torture, and I thought of that breast slipping free of--what?--a C cup? I was too excited to stay still.

I humped up quickly, jerked my arms down to my chest, and rolled over from my back to my stomach. I didn't even rely on the trick I generally resort to in fights with boys, using the unexpected strength in my left hand. Since most boys were right-handed to begin with--or had learned to box and wrestle as if they were-- they were often caught off guard by a left-handed move. I'd used this technique to turn the tables in many losing battles. But the standard humping maneuver proved to be the turning point in Linda's and my little tussle this afternoon. As soon as I executed it, I knew I had won.

13

Taken by surprise, she found herself on all fours on the ground just behind where I had been. Though she turned quickly to get on top of me again, I had already risen to my knees. From there I caught her by her shoulders, rolled her to her back, and swung my leg quickly over her legs.

She is far less comfortable now that I have suddenly popped up in the superior position, straddling her hips, grabbing both wrists. Those breasts, not at all flat even with their own weight and showing taut nipples, are too conspicuous in both our eyes.

"Let me up," she says. She seems to have forgotten that she started this contest, daring me first to arm wrestle, then to leg wrestle. As we all know, such adolescent games can begin innocently, just for fun; but there's a powerful eroticism present from the start. And I know she's experimenting with me because she thinks I'm too small to be dangerous, that I'm intimidated by her princess status.

"Give," I demand, wanting just a bit more from this encounter I have worked fairly hard to engineer. "Or I'll give you the Cowboy torture."

I have no idea what the cowboy torture might be. I have made it up on the spot.

"Let me up, Hugh Noone," she says again, angry now and squirming. But I think I see tears starting to form in the corners of her eyes, and I know she's losing confidence. And I want something from her, some kind of recognition.

I lean forward slowly, gazing deep into her eyes. It looks as if I might lean down and kiss her, though I only want her to see me--to see me, I now realize, as a potential future date.

Maybe that's the cowboy torture, I think, kissing until you give! Until you say you'll go out with me.

"I give. You get off me, you. . . . " She can't think of what to call me. I pause to let her think. And then wish I hadn't.

"You little *twerp*," she says.

2

Of course, that got to me, and I let her up immediately.

I didn't know then--and I guess I don't know now-- what the dictionary definition of "twerp" is. But I don't think there's any way it can be complimentary. The "erp" part doesn't sound good, and "tw" precedes too many words like "twinkle," "twiddle," "twitter." But linking that word with a reference to my size hurt the most--"little" twerp.

Linda herself seemed a bit embarrassed that she'd spoken so strongly and, as soon as we had scrambled back to our feet, she joked that that cowboy torture had really worked! But we both knew this afternoon's play was over, that it was time to reinstate the fine line between a country club family and someone living on Black Street, between the world of Route 66 thoroughfares and society's back alleys and dead end streets.

We saw each other the next day, of course, passing in the hall at school, and later we were on neighboring courts at tennis practice. But we acted as if we'd never touched each other. And my project, given impetus during that roll on her side yard, of earning the right to go out with this popular young lady entered a new, more dedicated phase.

I was not, thanks to Karen Murphy, a virgin. I had learned some months ago that having sex isn't so hard. Once you get started, things can take care of themselves. I'd also found that there is a place you can touch a girl and she loses all control. I figured that once I got to that spot with Linda, there would be no stopping.

The whole wrestling affair reminded me, though, that I was interested in Linda Roy not only because she was beautiful, everyone's dream date. I was also in competition with her on-again off-again boyfriend (now off--a recent fight, I'd heard).

Robert Paterson was a natural match for Linda Roy, tall and good looking, favored by the gods of money and status. His father, brother-in-law to Fairfield's mayor, was director of our most prosperous bank and a member of the town council. As a consequence, Robert was--I'll admit it--where I wanted to be, recognized as one of the town's elite, a regular Route 66 guy. He was also number one on the varsity tennis team.

I wasn't sure which I wanted more, to beat Robert Paterson at tennis or to win his girl. But I knew these two challenges were the focus of my life at the beginning of my last year in high school. And, although I didn't know it at the time, my wrestling bout with Linda Roy would prove to be the first step in reaching one of those goals.

Let me explain my sports rivalry with the "Favored Son" (as I had nicknamed him in my thoughts). Paterson had gotten his growth early, and with it the attention of junior high and then high school coaches. While he had lettered in multiple sports for two years, tennis became his specialty. In my (unbiased) opinion, however, he had reached a plateau last year as a junior. I felt he was ready to be dethroned.

Against his size and power, I brought primarily determination. I was five foot seven inches when I stretched, but I had pretty good quickness on the court. My hero was the emerging Australian star, Rod Laver, who, although only my size, had just won tennis's Grand Slam. I envied in particular his reputation as a spectacular shot maker, and I spent many lonely hours every day practicing against the backboard on the town courts. (Paterson, of course, had taken lessons at the country club from an early age.)

Just two days after being pinned by and pinning Linda Roy, I resumed my pursuit of Robert's position as Fairfield High's best singles player with a challenge to his ranking. After two years of varsity tennis, I had risen this season to second seed. And players could challenge the next highest player to a one-set contest for seeding at any time.

"Don't make me beat you again, No One," gibed Robert, using his favorite nickname. "You don't have the game to win against me." We were facing each other on opposite sides of the net.

"Maybe not, maybe so," I countered feebly, trying to stare him down (though I had to look up to do so).

As he laughed and spun on his heel to begin play, I noticed something odd about big Bobby Paterson: he had bad breath. Oh, it wasn't terrible, overwhelming; but it was there. And it was a striking contrast to the breath of Linda, dentist's daughter whose mouth was a shrine to cleanliness. How odd, I thought, for one so well bred to be careless about personal hygiene.

I had nothing new to try against Robert's big first serve and powerful overhead. But I had to vent my frustrations against him anyway. I also knew that the girls watched challenge matches. So, even if I lost, I'd have Linda's attention.

As I played, I tried to think of myself as Rod Laver. Years later, in jail doing research, I've learned part of the reason it was so easy for me to think of Laver as my hero. The whole idea of Australia as "Down Under" reflects an Old World perspective on the earth, the idea that Europe is on top where it belongs. All the maps and globes of past centuries were not made with England-France-Germany at top-center by accident. Those countries of empire believed all other places were removed from the heart of the universe.

And Australia was even worse than the lesser countries of the Northern Hemisphere; that colony (actually, until the end of the nineteenth century, colonies) was founded by convicts shipped from England, criminals who represented the opposite (antipathy/antipodes/antagonists) of the good, the natural. That's why they had to go where everything was popularly thought to be upside down, backwards, inverted from the natural order.

In my terms, of course, this meant they were all left-handers.

Rod Laver himself was left-handed. And, although I had been taught to play right-handed in a town parks program, I secretly modeled myself on the Rocket (Laver's nickname) and played left-handed at school. Some of my success on the team, I'm sure, was owed to this unorthodox style, as I came at my opponents from an unexpected angle. Laver's triumphs at Wimbledon and elsewhere had convinced me that even my alien nature might one day succeed within a right-handed world. If I had enough determination, if I refused to give up. A scrappy alley cat might one day get to travel down Route 66.

So I played with fury that day at Fairfield High, with the other members of the boys team and most of the girls watching. And I might have beaten my nemesis except for one crucial accident. I made the mistake, I'm sure, because of a failure of concentration. As I played against Robert Paterson, I began to rethink my bout with Linda Roy; and I began to imagine what I might have done while I was on top of her.

When your opponent has more power than you do, your best hope is to extend play, not try to match strength with strength. If you can keep the ball in play, he'll get frustrated at not winning points quickly and then either tire or make mistakes. Playing Favored Son, then, I took the pace off my returns and tried to run down everything.

Instead of threatening to kiss Linda, I could have leaned far forward, put my head on her shoulder, let my chest press against that magnificent bosom. It would have been a good first move.

My strategy had an effect. While Bobby reeled off the first three games of the set, I settled down to win my serve; and then he lost his serve. (Remember that the first to six with a lead of two wins the set.) We stayed on serve until the seventh game.

I could have pretended her efforts to throw me off unbalanced me, my hands holding her wrists accidentally brushing those firm breasts. I might have slipped into even more contact, contact she couldn't resist.

Most tennis experts believe the seventh game of a set is crucial. It's a measure of concentration after both players have been feeling each other out in the early games; and the winner of game seven most often goes on to take the set. So I gave everything I had in that important game, telling myself I had that extra desire to win, the killer instinct.

I could have released her wrists, suddenly cupped her face in my hands, kissed her tenderly, said she was the most beautiful woman in the world. I could have tried a little tongue.

Although my serve wasn't a weapon that won points, I had calmed down enough to avoid double faulting. And Favored Son had become a bit more cautious in his returns, giving me the chance to place the ball better, keep him moving, and eventually to score off his errors.

If I'd slid back when I was on top, my rump would have pressed against the tops of those long, muscular legs, even that place of desire all women had.

When it was advantage-Noone (my chance to win the crucial game), though, I'm afraid I panicked. Suddenly, I wanted it over with, the game (and set) decided right now. So, uncharacteristically, I followed my serve to the net, intending to make a crisp volley on his return, put the ball out of his reach to win the point, the game, the set--on to Wimbledon!

If I had followed my instincts, pressed home my advantage, would her squirming have become responding, that arching a reaching?

Apparently, Robert also had decided things were coming to a head and that he had to change his tactics. No more tentativeness, he crunched my serve with a powerful forehand. The ball came right at me as I crossed the end of the service line at the middle of the court. All I could do was try to get my racket out in front of my body, block the ball back at him.

No, I realized; Linda would have stopped me before I could get where I wanted to be. Because she didn't know me well enough yet, she would have thrown me off her, gotten up, and, when I was down, she might have kicked angrily. . . .

Wham! the ball ricocheted off the end of my racket and into me. Into that part of me men never want to be hit. I went down in a heap.

I survived, of course. The blow was not dead on target (if that had been, as I suspected, Paterson's aim), but it would take me several minutes to recover. And a

21

blow of that nature does something to your killer instinct. I lost 6-2.

As bad as losing, of course, was knowing that Linda and the rest of the girls team had watched me rolling on the court, all doubled up. It was a lot worse than the cowboy torture.

I swore revenge on Robert Paterson.

3

I was consoled by Billy Rhodes, one of the team's last alternates but perhaps my best friend at school. Billy lived on the Circle, but had the most eclectic group of buddies from many grades and across all the neighborhoods of town.

"Good match," he exclaimed as I sat slumped by the fence afterwards. Everyone else had gone home. "You had him up until the seventh game."

"Yeah," I sighed, trying to copy his optimism.

"What you need to do is talk to Doc Garnet."

"Why Garnet? Has he got a cure for this?" I said, cupping my groin.

"No, stupid. He's played professional."

I knew who Doc Garnet (retired) was from the pool hall downtown. With several old cronies he regularly played three-rail billiards at the big table near the entrance. A cigar stub clamped firmly in one corner of his mouth, he bent his short, portly old body over the rail and scored point after point at a very difficult game. I couldn't believe this ancient guy could ever have played tennis.

Still, something, anything was needed to give me the edge over the Favored One. I decided I'd talk to the old doctor. I also decided all of a sudden that I'd just ask Linda for a date! No more accidental wrestling encounters, no more public efforts to get her attention, but a planned formal date.

Arranging dates in those days, of course, was a nerve wracking experience for both sexes. Boys did the calling, girls the waiting. I'm sure it was hard on the adolescent females whose phones never rang; but I still break out into a nervous sweat today remembering how difficult it was to pick up that receiver.

What should you say first, for instance? You can't just start off with "Will you go out with me?" But it's not easy small-talking for half an hour either--"Could history class be any more boring?" Often there's a single right thing to say ("You're such a good dancer") that, once delivered, guarantees success. But if you make the wrong move, the whole project can be doomed.

There can even be problems making contact in the first place. Her mother might answer and want to know who this is, why you're calling. You could unexpectedly hear the father on the other end, and he *claims* she's not home, but you wonder if he's not just screening the field of her admirers. The brother takes your call, and now everyone in school will know you've been turned down.

In my case, such calling was even harder. I refused to dial right-handed (unless my stepfather was around). This is the pre-touch-tone phone era, of course. And, guess what, right-handers? It's not as easy pushing that ring clockwise as it is pulling it along behind you with your index finger. Try it sometime. If you're so nervous your hand is shaking already, you've got a good chance of misdialing. Or simply giving up on the whole idea.

And there was one last thing about calling Linda Roy in particular: that super-sweet mouth of hers. Now, I know you couldn't smell through the phone lines in those days anymore than you could see the party on the other end. But I could never think of Linda without knowing that her father was a dentist, that he required all his children to brush after every meal (and snack!), and that, as a consequence, Linda's breath was springtime itself. I'd been close enough to her, wrestling, to confirm that.

Even now, years later and in a place where sweet smells are rare indeed (prison), I don't hear violins when I imagine talking with the Fairfield princess. I smell fresh flowers. And when I wanted to call her after losing to Bobby in the challenge match, I had to brush my own teeth and swig some of my stepfather's rarely used Listerine before I could approach the phone.

Before I finally got up the courage to speak with her, in fact, I had met twice with Doc Garnet. How Billy knew this guy had played tennis, or even how he knew the doctor in the first place, was a mystery, but he was always like that. While Billy went to school with the rest of us, joined the Boy Scouts, worked part-time at Phipps County Lumber Store, he also seemed to have time to roam about town and meet odd characters.

Doc Garnet hadn't practiced medicine for ten years, though he had been a public figure for over thirty. And Billy was right about his tennis past. Though the professional circuit early in the century barely paid the players to tour, he had traveled the country for about five years, seldom winning but placing high enough to earn expenses and a bit more. More to the point of my own story, what Doc Garnet taught me over the next few weeks dramatically changed my approach to the game and gave me a strategy for beating Bobby Paterson, which was, remember, one of the two goals of my life.

The way I saw it, I was at a crucial point in the trajectory of my tennis career, a place from which I would shoot forward to a serious career in the sport at college and beyond, or else peak at this high school level and slide downward to nothing. In one sense, my whole life was at stake here. I couldn't miss this opportunity.

To my surprise I learned that Billy's pool hall acquaintance could still beat just about anyone in town. I later saw him win several matches with guys who played for the college team. He did it not with power or speed but with accuracy and consistency. Over and over again, Doc put the ball exactly where he wanted it, and that always gave him time to be where his opponent would put the ball next. Each exchange moved the other player farther and farther out of position until, eventually, he could not make a play on Doc's shot.

Doc was completely unlike the high school coach, Mr. Womack, who loved the serve-and-volley game. Coach had tried to convert me from the left-handed style I'd developed playing on my own, but I was beating everyone but Robert Paterson and could resist this pressure. Wanting for myself the flash of big serve and punishing ground strokes, I didn't necessarily want to emulate Garnet's whole game. But I still hoped I could learn some things from him, especially about the serve.

The key to a good serve, Garnet told me, almost in passing, is the toss. "It should be straight up above your head," he insisted. "Like the sun at high noon." He threw the ball, his body with a discernible pot belly standing perfectly vertical beneath it.

This toss didn't increase power. For that you wanted to throw the ball ahead of you, out into the court, so that your body's forward motion drove the ball down and across the net. But the high toss advocated by Garnet inspired accuracy; and, with my small size, I would never have an overpowering serve anyway.

Doc Garnet combined his high, vertical toss with a special racket grip, twisting the handle past a traditional backhand position. The turned racket struck the tossed ball right at the moment when the player's wrist snapped from a cocked to an extended position in the natural motion of swinging. And that snap imparted spin to the ball without one's having to work very hard.

"See," said Doc, the ball arcing over the net. He did it all with arm and shoulder, his body straight up. And he insisted that the precision required of this serve would improve other parts of my game. Master this motion, he said, and I would be better than anyone else my age.

That ball above my head, then, motionless at the very apex of its journey, became my symbol for success in tennis. At that point the ball should be struck, the game engaged, insisted Garnet. With such a serve, victory was the inevitable outcome. And I believed that it was so.

It took me longer to perfect the telephone call to a girl.

"Hello, Linda?"

"No, this is her mother." Social secretary for the country club, former Women's Club president, altar guild at St. Mark's Episcopal Church. "May I ask who's calling?"

"Um, Hugh Noone, ma'am." Then I delivered the lie I'd prepared in advance for this situation. "It's, uh, about tennis practice. At school."

"Oh, ok. I'll get her."

I was ready to lie myself, but I had not anticipated Linda's doing the same thing. When I finally got my conversational ship past the surf crashing on the shore to calmer waters out in the bay, her smooth responses always pushed me gently away: "That's the night of my church youth group"; "I really wish I could, but my parents are taking everyone out to dinner that evening"; "Oh, if I just didn't have so much homework!" She was by far the better actor, despite my belief in my own potential.

I realize now that I was blinded by desire. These references to family, school, and country club were just the signs I was supposed to pick up on that she didn't want to go out with me at all. She had decided to avoid hurting my feelings with a sudden, absolute rejection. I had not done any dating at this social level, though, and believed it was just my bad luck that she'd agreed to attend the Pep Band's homecoming float planning meeting on the very night I wanted her to go to the movies.

I must confess she delivered these little disappointments to me as sweetly as she breathed over those brushed, polished, mouthwashed teeth. Each rejection hurt, but I never understood that the pain came from this beautiful creature who shrugged shyly (lifting and dropping one magnificent breast) as she said "no" one more time. It was as if someone else were knocking me back to Black Street, to Karen Murphy, to the life of the son of a night security guard and a woman who took in laundry.

"Would you like to walk home with me after tennis practice tomorrow?"

"You're so nice to ask, but my dad wants me to stop by the office for x-rays."

"Again?"

"Last week's didn't turn out."

Whenever she felt unexpectedly cornered, she resorted to an unchallengeable excuse.

"I thought I might go bowling on Saturday night. Are you free then?"

"On Saturday? Oh, shoot. I have to . . . uh . . . I can't . . . um."

"What?"

"It's embarrassing. It's my. . . . I won't be able to. . . . I'll be having these terrible. . . . "

Finally she whispers the secret word.

"Cramps."

4

While I worked on my tennis game in order to beat Robert Paterson and my conversational skills to woo Linda Roy, I was not free of other responsibilities. I went to school all week, of course, and I had the regular chores of a teenager on the weekend: cutting the grass in season, cleaning my room, and taking on little tasks my parents deemed within the range of my skills and I usually found well outside the reach of my interests.

In addition to household chores, I also had a part time job at Rexall's Drugs downtown. I generally worked two evenings during the week (6:00-9:00) and an eight-hour shift on the weekend. With tennis practice every day after school and matches that went from 4:00 to as late as 7:00, then, I was actually a rather busy boy in those days.

Naturally I resented any extra demands on my time. When my stepfather asked me to wash the garage floor one Friday in the midst of my campaign of calling Linda for a date, you can understand, I hope, my frustration.

"Not tonight!" I protested.

"Get it done before I get back from work," he commanded. He generally had the midnight-to-eight shift, so that meant I would have to stay in that evening or get up early in the morning. He would be going bowling before work.

"I should be practicing," I argued.

"If you're playing football, sure." He thought tennis basically a sport for sissies.

"Really, Pop," I said, using the name he insisted on. "Couldn't I do it tomorrow after I get back from work?"

"And make sure you get in the corners."

As I told you earlier, my stepfather married my mother when I was barely out of infancy, and I'd known no other father. The man I believe my mother truly loved (they had been childhood sweethearts, she a war bride) left for the Pacific when I had just grown bigger in my mother's womb than the gleam in her soldier's eye.

He never came back, of course. Well, he came back to be buried, an event my mother never referred to. In my first year in high school, introduced to library research skills, I had traced in the *Fairfield Mirror* the story of Richard Noone's unspectacular career: drafted, trained, shipped, killed before he turned 21. It wasn't clear how much of him lay in the flag-draped coffin she had followed that dreary November day to Fairfield's one cemetery.

I believe my stepfather, Henry Maas, might have been a friend of my father's, but I only knew for sure that they were contemporaries in high school. Maas, too, served in the Army, as a military policeman at Fort Dix, New Jersey. Bad knees kept him out of the infantry, and his veteran status helped him to a secure position as night watchman on the campus of South Central Missouri State College. As far as I knew, he took two strolls around campus on his shift and spent the rest of the night listening to sports on the radio--delayed broadcasts of football, baseball, boxing.

Six feet tall and heavy, Maas towered over me and my mother. Through the years she had put on weight, but she was not a large person. I had her height and my father's slender build, so it's no wonder that Henry took up four-fifths of the space in our little house on Cedar Street--sleeping all day so that we had to be quiet, and absent all night while we slept. Of course, I resented the ways he squeezed me and my mother into the corners of his life, into the nocturnal rhythm of his plodding existence, into the distant background of his relentlessly right-handed world. It was as if we had been flattened under the slabs of mighty Route 66.

Our five-room house on Cedar Street had a detached one-car garage in the back. Henry's aging Buick leaked miscellaneous fluids at a slow but steady rate out there, staining the porous cement floor and, over time, leaving a layer of greasy residue made up of about equal parts oil, dirt, and dog hair (my stepfather loved big dogs, and, at this time, we owned a sometimes dangerous boxer).

Now, my mode of transportation at this time added nothing to this mess on the garage floor, but removing that sticky layer of goo seemed nonetheless to be my job. I rode an old motor scooter, not one of the sleek Japanese models that would become popular in another decade, nor the peppy Italian vehicle seen in films about European vacations (Cary Grant, Deborah Kerr), but a much worked on Cushman, heavy and slow. I parked the scooter in the yard, covering it with a tarp in bad weather, but the garage floor was still my assignment.

As I watched Henry plod through the kitchen on his way out of the house, my anger rose and I almost said something I would regret. Something about how, if we had a newer car, if he had a better job, if we lived in another neighborhood, the floor wouldn't need to be cleaned. But my mother and I knew well not to cross this large man.

When I had pulled the garden tools, old paint cans, unused pieces of lumber out the garage and filled the bucket to start scrubbing the floor, Billy Rhodes showed up.

"Party at Karen Murphy's," he informed me. "Wanna go?"

"Can't 'til I get this done. You got your car?"

"Yeah. Goin' to be beer. And maybe Tip the Scales." This was the latest kissing game.

"Hm. Who else is going?"

"Tommy Stoltz, some people from football." That would mean cheerleaders like Patty Simpson. That might mean Linda Roy.

"Why don't you help me here?" I leaned on my mop.

"I'll watch. You're doing fine."

One of the things I hated about this chore was that it was hard to predict when I would be finished. The floor was so deeply stained that, scrub as I might, there would always be a darkened area at the center, fading the farther you moved out but never completely disappearing. Pop could use that fact to keep me working as late as he wanted. I longed for a clear line to cross in the whole operation after which I knew I would eventually be done.

"Know what I heard?" Billy said as I filled a second pail with sudsy water.

"What's that?"

"Paterson got in trouble last weekend."

"With who?"

"His parents. They found a rubber in his billfold."

"Big deal! Haven't you got one on you?"

"Sure. But I don't show it to my parents."

"My parents could care less what I got in my wallet."

There was a possible advantage here, though: if bad-breath Paterson was grounded, I might have more room to operate. A picture of Linda resettling that perfect breast with a hitch of her shoulder bloomed for a moment in my mind's eye. I looked around to see if I could call the garage floor clean.

Still I hesitated. I didn't need a confrontation with my stepfather. Our relationship had become precarious in recent weeks. Training hard for tennis, I was getting stronger and cockier; and I had begun in little ways to challenge this man's authority over me.

Even with his size advantage, Maas must have realized that a day would come when he couldn't expect to control me. There would be a moment when I knew I had gained the upper hand. It was probably some months off yet, but he knew and I knew that at some point my life would go forward on my terms, not his.

Then Billy decided for me: "This floor looks good. Come on."

"OK. Let me put this stuff away." The lumber, cans, and equipment had already been returned to their places, but I had to take the mop and pail into the pantry off the kitchen. Stepping away from that closet, I saw my mother standing in the doorway.

"Mom," I asked. "You OK?" Her eyes were blank, and she stood motionless with one hand on the doorframe. "Mom?"

"Hmm?"

"You OK?" I came over closer to her.

In the last year I had gotten used to looking down at my mother, as she was now several inches shorter than I was. I probably wasn't conscious of it exactly, but she had also begun to look older than her thirty-six years. It was not just the added weight slowing her movement, but a growing carelessness about appearances that aged her. She didn't put her hair up as often, and her clothes, increasingly out-of-date, sometimes needed buttons replaced, a hem resewn. She looked tired in the face.

"Henry's gone?" Whenever he was there, she referred to him as "Pop."

"Yeah. Bowling. What are you doing?"

"Oh, watching TV. There's some ironing." While the washing machine with which she made extra money for the family was in the basement, she ironed in the kitchen, using a board that folded down from the wall.

"I'm going out. With Billy."

"You did the garage? You know how he is if you don't do a good job."

"Sure. It's good. You need anything from downtown?"

"No. I've used up my allowance anyway." Pop gave her the money to buy groceries and pay bills on the first of each month.

Still, she was standing there with a faraway look in her eyes. She puzzled me. It had never occurred to me to wonder what went on her in her mind, what she was thinking. She was just there, cooking, cleaning, seeing that I was ready for school or work. And for a moment I might have felt sorry for her, sorry for her alone on a Friday night with nothing to do but laundry.

Betty Maas--once Noone, once Morgan--had few friends outside the immediate neighborhood; and most of her family were dead. She was not generally a church person and didn't have time for things like PTA. Her life went forward inside this Cedar Street house.

As I looked at her motionless there in the doorway, her eyes not focused on anything, I wondered perhaps

35

for the first time in my sixteen years about the quality of her life. Had she once had dreams, aspirations? Did she still recall my father, lost Richard Noone? What did she think now of slow moving, slow thinking Henry Maas? Had she invested all her hopes in me, her single offspring? (Henry had never wanted a child of his own.) Would I ever do anything to make her proud?

A final question occurred to me: was it possible Betty Morgan had begun her life left-handed?

5

This brief hint of concern for my mother vanished, I'm sorry to say, the moment I walked out to the street to climb into Billy's partially restored '49 Ford. Friday night: party time.

The object of my desire, as I've said, was Linda Roy, lovely, sweet breathéd, sweet breasted one. But I knew there would be problems making contact with her tonight, beyond the apparently busy life that had been in my way previously: I would not be meeting her on neutral territory. The high school crowd was gathering at Karen Murphy's; and that young lady had certain desires in which I held a prominent place. So my evening might have to involve some tricky maneuvering.

Karen Murphy was shorter and heavier than Linda, but not at all unattractive. Though she would grow too plump early in her twenties, right now her full build inspired open-mouthed admiration from males in her vicinity, especially when she wore the tight skirts that were her trademark. Her reputation had been slightly tarnished by rumor, stories that included my name. But though she had gone farther than most girls in our school, she'd kept it quiet; and so had at least one boy who'd enjoyed her willingness to experiment.

Like me, Karen suffered from having parents of low social standing. Her father clerked at the Rexall's where I worked, and her mother cleaned homes. Fervent members of the Church of Christ, they lived in a deluxe mobile home just beyond the east edge of town. The carport on their lot was where Karen often hosted parties for her teenage friends.

When Billy and I got there, it was nearly 11:00, the time things tended to get interesting. There were several dozen kids on and around the carport, which had a row of tall storage cabinets along the side opposite the trailer. Some of the partygoers had beer hidden in their cars, and there was a stash just beyond the reach of a light mounted on a pole beside the carport. The Murphys had helped Karen maintain her popularity as hostess by agreeing not to emerge from the trailer until 1:00 a.m., the official end of any party.

Billy and I were just in time to join the game. Tip the Scales must have been a local variation of Spin the Bottle, as I've never heard of anyone else playing it.

Those willing to play gathered around the lid of a metal garbage can turned upside down on the carport floor. While not without some dents and scratches marring its surface, the convex lid balanced neatly on a point at its center, its two handles 180 degrees apart. One player began the game by placing the beer he or she was drinking somewhere along the edge of the lid, causing it to dip to the floor at that point.

The object was to restore the lid's original balance by perfectly countering with your own beer can the weight on the opposite side, the beer put there by the last person. The previous player was the one you wanted to, as we said, "tip the scales" with--that is, go off into the bushes for a period of brief or sustained necking, depending on how attractive the pairing was to both parties. If you failed, then the next person tried to balance the lid to earn the right of tipping the scales with you.

There were obvious dangers to this game. Often the one you wanted to try making out with wanted to make out with someone else; so the order of play involved some competition. You would also have to guess how much the person before you had reduced the weight of his or her beer by drinking some of it. And placing your can at the right distance from the edge was crucial to sustaining the overall symmetry. Since we all kept drinking while we played, the chances of balancing tended to go down the longer we were at it.

My goal tonight was to wait for Linda to place her beer, then right the garbage can lid myself with a perfectly weighted and positioned counterpart. I felt I had to seize the moment in order to alter my relationship with this society belle, this local beauty. If I could just get her starting necking, even in a party game, I believed she would find me irresistible. The more I drank, of course, the more convinced of this I became.

Also around the lid, however, was Karen Murphy, who raised her beer and nodded to me as I joined the circle.

"Hi, Hugh," she said. "And Billy." He was going to play too. There were probably a dozen kids milling around the can, waiting for the right moment to make a move on someone.

The advantage to Tip the Scales, you see, was that you could sneak into a very brief experiment with someone, learn if you (and she) liked it. If things clicked, formal dates and more could follow. If no violins sang, the pair could separate easily, go their own ways. I was gambling that tonight Linda wouldn't be afraid of me, fellow tennis buff, former wrestling opponent, small, polite Hugh Noone from Black Street.

Linda had come with her good friends Susan Morrison and Janet Cottingham, country club buddies, members of the tennis team. Half a dozen football players had come too that night, but not Robert

Paterson. The circumstances, I told myself, were favorable.

As often happens, of course, I was repressing knowledge of two key features of the situation: chance and right-handedness. Chance not only took Linda from me, but put her in the arms of someone I never thought could be so lucky.

Full of my daydream that she wanted me, I was thinking only of the move to make *after* Linda had had a turn. But her play also had to come after someone's, and I had completely forgotten that this person had at least an equal chance of heading off into the dark with Linda. That chance was simply dumb bad luck for me.

Eight or ten cans into the game, the odds become very much against someone finding just the right spot with just the right level of beer in a can to bring all the others to harmony. It was at this normally tipsy point that Linda set her can down on the lid almost randomly.

I know now, years later, of course, that Linda might just have wanted to show that she was willing to play that night and was hoping her can would balance or be balanced by no one's. A large part of the game's appeal, after all, was the thrill, feeling the riskiness of random pairing; but only a few players went on to tip the scales.

Linda's play, however, done casually, without any real thought, perfectly balanced the lid. The previous player? My best friend, Billy.

All three of us were taken completely by surprise: Billy with joy, Linda with amusement, me with consternation--followed immediately by a sense of complications. Someone else, it turned out, was not surprised at all.

This is where the right-handed universe came in.

You see, most of the players milling around the lid were waiting for their turn to play. Turns moved back and forth across the lid, since you could only balance someone from the opposite side, and moved from boy to girl to boy to girl. But play also moved around the lid in two-turn steps.

And which direction did the turn go after every two moves? Clockwise, of course. Or, for those of you who haven't thought about it, from left (bad) to right (good), as the hourmarker moves (in the northern hemisphere) on a sundial or other primitive clock, the order right-handers think natural.

Since I had wanted to team up with Linda, I had kept to the other side of the lid from her. The rest of the players, following internally the clockwise pattern of plays to that point, fell back to give space for the obvious next player--me. I had, in fact, been waiting so eagerly for Linda to make her play that I had stepped up to the lid and reached my beer can out so far that I couldn't have pulled back if I'd wanted to.

Intending then to hold myself in reserve for Linda, and Linda only, I found myself instead, according to the world's relentless right-handed bias, offered up to the next player. And Karen Murphy took me. Her can, perfectly placed, restored the lid to balance. Our beers were as neatly paired as the lid's handles.

She pulled me behind some trees out beyond the other side of the row of cabinets that made one wall to the carport. I cast a longing look back in the direction of Linda and Billy. I tried to believe that she was disappointed. Perhaps she was even jealous?

But I could not think about her now, as Karen put her arms around my neck and pushed me back against a sturdy oak.

"It's been a while since we did this," she observed, kissing me almost fiercely on the lips. It made me think of the killer instinct I had associated most with sports.

"I do remember how to do this," I agreed and kissed her back with at least an equal intensity. Though I couldn't be with Linda tonight, it didn't mean I shouldn't enjoy myself! I'd never dated Karen steadily before and wouldn't have to after this night.

"I have something I want you to see," Karen said, pulling back a little, taking a deep breath. We still had our arms around each other and were pressed together at the hips. There was clear evidence of my excitement.

"Mmm?"

"Something important. Wait a minute." She unbuttoned the top of her sweater. I could see a gold chain around her neck, something dangling from it between her breasts.

It's embarrassing for me to admit even now, when I'm a grown man, a man in jail, how quickly lust changes its object for a teenage boy. Just moments before I didn't want anyone but Linda Roy. But now, with real live Karen Murphy in my arms, I had almost forgotten about the distant princess. Here was this other girl about to show me her breasts!

She pulled on the chain, getting it, I assumed, out of the way. I pushed one hand under her sweater up the back, searching for the magic clasp that would free her gifts for appreciation.

"I've missed seeing you," she said, hesitating and looking at me intently.

"Hmm?" Did we need discussion here? As I breathed in the smell of shampoo and perfume, felt the taut muscles of her back, looked down into rich cleavage, I experienced a tremendous rise of desire.

"Hold this," she whispered, guiding my free hand to her chest.

"Yes, *yes*," I agreed, but felt, instead of warm flesh, a hard object poking into my palm. I looked more closely. It was a cross, a little gold cross. What did *this* have to do with anything?

6

It would be a long, long time before I fully understood this encounter as critical in my life's journey. It was not so much what I did (or, in the end, didn't do) with Karen Murphy, though that can't be discounted as a link in the lengthening chain of circumstances that concludes with me here in jail. But Billy's thirty minutes of pleasure in the arms of Linda Roy also shaped one element of my history from this moment on.

Of course, it was some weeks later before I learned for sure what he had done with her. And I need to be clear about what Karen was offering me first and how that also affected future events.

I should acknowledge, by the way, that the hand which held her cross was my left hand. In the dark-- where no one would be watching--and in the heat of the moment--that is, without thinking--I had used the hand that came naturally. It's a miracle, in fact, that my hand stopped when it encountered something other than its goal.

My instinctive reach cooled quickly, however, when I realized what I had. "What's this?" I asked.

"My cross. It's new."

"So?" I, of course, saw only surface, a necklace, an ornament. I was about to learn that she actually referred to its spiritual context.

"Mr. Drinkard gave it to me, our preacher."

"Um-hm. It's nice. Now, let me. . . . "

"Hugh, wait. I want you to know, this is important."

44

I began to understand what was going on here: she was using this moment of intimacy to testify. I couldn't believe it!

Karen and I had had sex, pure carnal delight. The frameworks of affection, love, respect had been nowhere in sight. We were two young animals discovering a new level of pleasure. While I knew vaguely that her family was religious, I never thought that fact would affect our relationship.

"I understand," I offered, hoping to get past this religious obstacle and on to the shrine where it had so recently, so warmly nestled. I leaned forward and nuzzled her neck.

"I've rededicated my life to Christ," she responded. "I want you to know."

But she didn't pull away from me. In fact, while she leaned her head back to see into my eyes, her hips were pushed forward against me. And with my back blocked against the tree, my front distinctly liked that pressure.

"OK. I get it," I admitted. The formulas were recognizable from my many unhappy experiences of Baptist Sunday School (I had refused to go once I was in high school) and rare summer revivals. My parents seldom attended church, but occasionally my mother would get religious and drag us all to a week of hellfire-and-brimstone services. Then we fell back into sleeping late on Sundays, at the most tuning in to whatever local church was featured on Fairfield's one radio station.

"But we're supposed to be Tipping the Scales here," I insisted to Karen. "You know--party rules?" This time I kissed her, but gently. I was willing to take some time.

"Oh, that's fine. We can neck. We just can't . . . you know . . . do the other thing . . . unless. . . . "

A dull ache spread through my groin when she said this, as I realized that my present arousal would have to fade instead of continuing to its appropriate culmination. That always left me depressed, even sore. Still does, now that I think about it.

"Unless . . . ?" I questioned.

"Hugh, I shouldn't, unless you want to . . . to talk about *us* first."

Whoa! Us? There was "you," and "me," sure. But, so far at least, no "us." I certainly saw myself as a long way from marriage, if that was what she was thinking.

"You know graduation is only eight months away," she continued. "Don't you want to be on your own when you get out of school, do what you want to do?"

I wanted to do more of what I was doing right now (I had both hands on her rump, and she was rubbing up against me). But we didn't need to follow her fast road to emotional adulthood.

I believed, of course, that if I could keep her here a bit longer, she would have to give in. Her firm bottom was in my hands. And she was beginning to respond to my hips' movement. Had she passed the point of no return?

Why girls can't understand a boy's need to finish what he's started in this department, by the way, I never could figure out. Once he's got the machinery in motion, there's a natural inevitability to the whole process. And my desire on this particular night had been mightily primed by the hope of getting Linda Roy in my arms again.

Girls, of course, can go forever without finishing and still be happy. Karen was completely content cruising along at one speed. I wanted the accelerator to the floor.

But she wouldn't leave off about whether I really wanted to be with her after the sex, whether I was ready at least to go steady, if not become engaged.

I stayed in the dark with her as long as I could stand it. When we finally made our reappearance among the partygoers on the carport, I was physically whipped. I also felt more reason than ever to go out with Linda Roy. If fun with Karen was going to be complicated by church, of all things, I would probably do just as well in the country club set!

The dissatisfaction I was feeling was made even greater by the goofy look Billy sported when he returned from the dark with the girl I desired. What had they been doing out of the reach of light? I was sure I didn't want to know, but I also suspected I would find out.

At 1 a.m., when the Murphys popped out onto the stoop of their trailer like coo-coos in an old clock, the partygoers went their own ways. Linda left with Susan Morrison and Janet Cottingham, Karen waving to us all from the stoop with her mom and dad. Billy and I climbed into his '49 Ford and took off down Old Farm Road.

"Where're you headed?" I asked, for we were going away from town.

"Just feel like a drive. It's a great night, great party."

"Take it easy," I advised. Billy loved to drive, sometimes to drive fast. We'd both had some beers, and I suspected he was high on Linda Roy too, though I didn't see why she'd given him as much time out there in the dark as Karen had with me.

Still, there was a full moon. The countryside of open pasture and stretches of deep woods fit our mood, arguing that we were free spirits in open territory. We weren't headed for Route 66, of course, not in Billy's rattletrap. That was a road for better cars and better citizens.

Old Farm Road went east of Fairfield on a straight line for a number of miles. Though blacktopped, the county road rose and dipped over rolling hills at steep grades. Driving it at high speed was a favorite activity for local teenagers, giving us the thrill of nearly flying when we crested a sharp rise, then feeling extra gravity as we swooped down across a creek bottom before climbing the next hill.

Few cars had seat belts at this time, but, of course, we gave little thought to danger. The road was straight. So what could happen? I didn't realize how each successive up and down taxed Billy's powers of concentration, even the strength he could call up to hold the wheel. There could come a point when he would lose control.

As Billy drove this roller coaster ride that Friday night, I did try to make sure he didn't forget what he was doing. I also kept trying to get him to say what had happened with Linda.

"So, how'd it go with you and Tipping the Scales?"

"Oh, we were just talking about tennis."

"Yeah, sure!"

We shot over a hilltop at about 80 miles per hour, feeling our bodies lift from the seat. We had to shout, as the windows were open on both sides.

"Hey, this isn't an airplane, you know."

"Right." He might have slowed a fraction.

"So, you and Linda?"

"She's not going with Paterson right now, you know."

"I know. Was she willing to neck, then?"

"Well, I shouldn't say, really."

We swept downhill, through a low stretch, up the next hill, pulled down toward the road by centrifugal force. Billy's face had a rapt look.

"What about you and Karen? You still together?," I asked, trying to nudge Billy out of what I considered my territory.

"We've never really been together. We're just friends. Maybe we go out now and then."

"Yeah, sure!" I said, as we popped out of a wooded part of the road onto a flat stretch. The moon lit the way, and I could see Billy pushing the Ford toward 100.

How easy it seemed to cover the landscape, while I could make no advance on Linda. I had horsepower on loan, but no command of the heart. Only later would I learn that my love life *was* racing along at a similar speed. It was just that--like being the passenger in Billy's car--I wasn't doing the driving.

The car now shot downhill again into a stand of tall oaks whose branches blocked the moonlight. Billy hit the brakes hard.

A car was pulling out of a lane up ahead, fortunately on the other side of the road, but coming toward us. The driver had swung wide in pulling out and come across the middle of the road, apparently not seeing us approaching.

We could guess who this was, not the precise persons but the general class: two lovers out parking. That was the other thing Old Farm Road was famous for, lots of little turnoffs and short drives where teenagers went on weekend nights.

"Watch it!" I yelled, though Billy had seen them before I did. My arms braced on the dashboard. My right foot pushed an imaginary brake pedal.

"I am, I am!" He was braking hard, but still trying to avoid losing control. He hit the horn.

Then three things happened at once: the other driver gunned his engine and swerved back to his own side of the road; we went squealing by, unable to stop before we had passed the same spot; and I recognized the driver, whose image in the car window, as he gave us the bird, burned itself into my memory.

7

"Follow that car," I shouted, punching Billy on the arm.

"Gotcha!" he replied, cranking the steering wheel to get us turned around so we could give chase. The parked car was racing away back toward town.

"Who were they?" Billy asked.

"You didn't see?"

"I was trying not to hit them!"

"Yeah. Well, it was Paterson."

"No! He's grounded."

"Maybe so, but he got away long enough to go parking."

"Who with?"

"I wish I knew. I couldn't make her out, and that's why I want to catch up with them. Now where'd they go?"

"They gotta be up here somewhere."

We were bouncing over hilltops, bumping across small bridges. I could no longer see taillights ahead.

"Slow down, slow down. We've lost them."

To my surprise, Billy cut back to something close to the speed limit. We were at the town line anyway.

Once we were under streetlights and among houses, Billy said, "Well, that's that. We've got a couple more beers. Wanna go someplace and finish them?

"OK. Where?" Paterson and his date could be anywhere by now, so we might as well finish our night of partying.

"Vacant Lot. You can walk home from there." This was an undeveloped plot on Limestone Drive, Billy's street. Nearby families used it to park the second cars that crowded their own driveways. My house on Cedar was a five-minute walk from there.

Once we'd eased in beside the Morgans' old De Soto, popped a couple of Falstaffs, and settled back to gaze at the stars, I realized I had renewed optimism about my two current life goals: winning Linda Roy and challenging the top seed on the tennis team.

General opinion in the school held that Paterson was trying to get back together with Linda. He just didn't want to appear desperate, so he was holding out as long as he could before he went begging. Now he'd been spotted with another girl at a place where he could only be doing one thing, one thing Linda wouldn't be happy about (should she happen to hear).

It couldn't have been Linda he was with on Old Farm Road, as we'd seen her leaving Karen Murphy's with her girlfriends not fifteen minutes ago. So Robert was seeing someone else. Somehow escaping his parents, he was also cheating--well, sort of--on his longtime girlfriend.

Ah, I thought, Linda would be more ready for me now when I made my next move, sweet kiss planted on that heavenly clean mouth, strong arm enfolding that lovely shoulder as it shrugged to settle her magnificent breast.

And Robert would *not* be ready for me when I made my next move, new Doc Garnet-inspired kick serve that would knock Favored Son off balance, destroy his confidence. His bad breath meant sourness within, I concluded. I would win the girl and the game.

"What're you gonna be when you grow up?" asked Billy in the midst of my ruminations.

"Hm? Oh, professional tennis player, I guess."

"Ah. Me? Astronaut. Going to fly to the moon." While Americans were still struggling to overcome the embarrassment of Sputnik's having beaten us into orbit, Kennedy's enthusiasm for the space program was inspiring my entire generation.

"Sure you'll be an astronaut. You and Superman." I took a drink from my beer.

"I'm serious. You know, you don't have to burn fuel all the way to get there."

"In your rocket? To the moon?"

"Right. Rocket just has to escape earth's gravity. Then it coasts." He tipped back his can, then studied its label.

"I see."

"There's a point out in space where, once you pass it, you're free of earth's pull and you'll end up on the moon."

"The way you were sailing off those hilltops on Old Farm Road?"

"I'm not going fast enough, yet. My old Ford needs a bit more power. But I'm getting there."

"You know, astronauts have to study, physics and stuff. Way more than college."

"No!" This seemed a genuine shock to Billy. He tried to drink, but found that his beer can was empty.

"Oh, yeah. Right now, in fact, if you're planning to be an astronaut some day, I think you'd better be passing algebra with Miss Timmons." Few of us were passing math at this point, as our young teacher was just out of college and very intense.

"Give me another beer!"

I checked the bag. "Sorry, Billy, we're dry."

Bending down to look for beer, though, I discovered something else: I was drunk! I had forgotten my own theory about drinking: there *is* such a thing as "one too many."

I had based this theory on the behavior of my stepfather. But I had also tested it once or twice myself.

When Billy and I decided to get out of the car and head toward our respective homes, I learned that he too had gone to the point of one too many. I found him tumbled onto the grass beside the driver's door.

"Billy! Get up." I reached down to help him and found myself neatly stretched out beside him.

"Get up yourself," he urged, looking me in the face as we lay side by side in the grass.

"I'll get up, but you've got to carry me home."

"Where is home?"

"Follow me."

We managed to pull ourselves to our knees and peer down the hill toward his house, just two doors away. After several minutes of intense study, we thought we could make it, following a path of trees, mailboxes, and yard furniture for support.

Perhaps thirty minutes later we had gained Billy's stoop. But there we encountered a further obstacle: Billy's spaghetti fingers wouldn't hold the key he needed to open the door. Perky volunteer, I claimed I could handle this task.

Billy slumped at the bottom of the steps as I fumbled at the lock. He began to tell this joke about a shy society boy, Reginald, who wanted to lose his virginity. Reginald's friend Jack had fixed him up with a bar waitress so willing to have sex, all he had to do was bring up the topic. Reginald arranged to take her horseback riding.

I took Billy's key and studied the situation. Doors, you know, are generally made for right-handers.

Reginald's idea was to bring up matters reproductive when he and the waitress were alone out on the ride. Still, he was so shy he couldn't speak directly about sex. He'd have to find some way for the subject to come up naturally.

Now, I realize, doors are in one sense ambidextrous. That is, the knob is on the right side going one way, on the left coming back. So right-handers find the knob on the convenient side going, say, in; and left-handers, coming out. But the side you need to use a key on--the outside side of the door--much more often has the knob on the right, where a left-hander has to reach across his body to unlock and unlatch.

Reginald decided he could turn conversation with his date, the bar waitress, in the right direction by spurring his horse, a proud stallion, ahead at just the right point. Seeing his mount from the rear, tail held high, she'd have to comment. From there, he figured, it would all be downhill to the sack.

But they went the whole ride without incident. He showed her the horse, who was, in fact, handsomely endowed, and waited for comment. Nothing.

Not only are outside doorknobs generally placed poorly for left-handers, but turning them is also done more easily with the right hand. Like dialing a phone, it's hard to twist clockwise with your left hand. Check out the wrist action on this one. Now, it's true that many knobs can go either way, but some--like Billy's that night--require a left-to-right motion.

Reggie complained to his friend Jack that his date had not taken the hint. Jack said, "No problem. Just paint the horse's privates green. She'll have to notice that."

OK, thought Reginald. And the next time they went riding, the horse's genitals matched the full leaf of summer. But, again, the girl, who commented on all of nature around her, seemed never to notice this one conspicuous item.

I was having a little difficulty that night with a doorknob on the right side of Billy's door. I had to find the elusive keyhole, insert the slippery key, and turn things in an unnatural (for me) direction.

Reginald complained to Jack, who advised, "Just increase the hint--paint the whole back half of the horse green!"

So, on their next outing, Reginald rode his stallion of two sections, the front deep brown, the back bright green. But one more time she declined to notice.

I wanted to get down on my knees and look closely at this situation of keyhole, doorknob, entryway. But to do so comfortably in my left-handed approach, I would have to step off the stoop on the right side, because the stoop was no wider than the doorframe. But I knew if I once got off the stoop, I'd never get up there again. Billy had been unable to rise from his slump, though he continued his joke manfully.

56

By now Reginald was going crazy. She was a beautiful girl with a beautiful body. "Paint the whole horse green!" cried the eternal optimist, Jack. His hope fueled by desire, Reggie did.

They rode down the trails, at this point intimately familiar. Reginald turned his horse this way, then that, watched the girl's eyes for any flicker of interest. As before, nothing. If she would just make one comment!

After I had puzzled long over this predicament of wandering lock and key, Billy somehow managed to gain his feet and stumble up the steps. He skipped the preliminaries of inserting the key, turning it, cranking the knob. He went directly to pushing the door, which opened easily, and Billy fell into his own house. I guess it had not been locked in the first place.

Finally, in the stables after the ride, when Reginald and his date dismounted, the beautiful and beautifully built waitress suddenly said: "Hey, that horse is green."

"Yes," responded Reginald elatedly, "Let's screw!"

8

You know how it is when you stay up too late at night and then are awakened early? You have no idea where you are, sometimes who you are. Especially if you are being rudely awakened, say, by a loud noise or an angry person. Or both.

Your body--and your mind, too, I suspect--has been cheated of its complete cycle of rest: lying down, drifting off, unconsciousness, gradual waking, rising. We're used to this process in all its stages, and breaking things off after you've gotten into it past a certain point causes pain. We yearn for that uncompleted portion of the natural sleep rhythm.

The morning after Karen Murphy's party, when she and I and Billy and Linda had Tipped the Scales, and when Billy and I had finished our beers out in the Vacant Lot, I was jerked from a deep sleep by my stepfather, big Henry Maas.

"What happened to that garage?" he thundered, though it sounded to me, hung over as I was, more like, *Whop 'em tharge!*

He had flung open the door to my bedroom, just across the little hallway from the one he shared with my mother. Our only bathroom was at the end of the hall.

"Wha'?"

"I thought I told you to clean the garage?" *I thigh chewing charge.*

"Huh?"

"Get out here." *Growl ear.* He grabbed one of my feet sticking out from under the covers and yanked it toward the floor. I swam more completely up from the state of suspended animation I'd been floating in. I was home, home in bed. But Henry was mad.

Ah, yes, then it came to me. It was Saturday, Saturday after Friday night. This was going to be a long day, especially as it was starting at 8:30!

Staggering out to the kitchen, I also began to remember the details of the night before the morning after: Billy coming to get me, going off into the dark, the fast drive across country, the car in the middle of the road, a face in the window.

"I come in after a hard night's work, and what do I find?"

Now I was hearing Henry's tirade clearly. Of course, I'd suffered this and others like it many times before. Something was not done well enough. It wasn't done on time. It wasn't done at all.

I remembered Billy and me drinking in his car on Limestone Drive, the effort to unlock his front door. Somehow I must have made it home from there, though that part of the night was even more hazy.

Now the indelible stain in the garage's cement floor would tie me down all day, a day in which I had hoped to put in several hours of good tennis practice. Henry would point to the darkened center of the floor as evidence I hadn't done what he'd asked, no matter how much I explained that that mark couldn't be removed.

"Let the boy have some breakfast," my mother pleaded with Henry. Henry took a glass from the drying rack beside the sink and poured an inch of whiskey in the bottom. He kept the bottle in a cabinet above the refrigerator.

"He can eat after he does his chores," Henry responded. But he sat heavily in a chair at the kitchen table, opposite to where Mom had put a glass of orange juice for me.

"I did clean the floor," I offered quietly. I didn't want to get my stepfather mad, but I knew that I had made an effort.

"I work all night at that damn college," he went on, raising one of his favorite themes--how those professors sat on their butts all day reading books. "And this is what I find when I get home. You think I went out to parties and left the cows unmilked when I was a kid?" He had grown up on a farm and was, in fact, never very comfortable in town. His family had lost the farm in the Depression, slowly and steadily falling into hopeless debt. His father had committed suicide in the end, never recovering from the moment of eviction.

"I know, dear," said my mother, trying to placate Henry. "I told him to do a good job. You have something to eat and then get your rest." Mom fixed dinner in the mornings for Henry, getting up well before dawn. She and I ate it warmed over in the evening.

"Ah," Henry said, resignedly. He leaned forward on his elbows, looked into the glass. "I need to sleep. Old man Pritchard's been hounding me again." Pritchard was the head of the grounds department, and he sometimes checked in on his night personnel.

By this point, I had finished the juice and the bowl of cereal Mom had put out for me. I was beginning to gauge the trajectory of Pop's anger.

Pop's rages followed a familiar pattern. They began with an explosion, brought on by some immediate stimulus. Then one of two things could happen:

continuing escalation to violence, or a sinking into torpor. Mom and I had gotten to be pretty good at distinguishing between the two.

"You go on out to the garage," advised my Mom. "Clean that floor." But I could tell from her look she was predicting escape.

The moment to watch in my stepfather's rages was the end of that initial outburst. There was always a bit of a lull, to catch his breath, to feel the depth of his own anger. Then the fit went on to new heights or it sank down into gloom. But you had to be right about that key point where the complete pattern could be measured--on to danger, or back to an uneasy stability. Mom was predicting calm.

She was wrong.

Oh, things looked good for a while. I moved some stuff around in the garage, inspected the spot and the rest of the floor while Henry ate in the kitchen. I'm sure Mom tried to distract him with other subjects.

The floor looked to me about the same as it always did after I'd washed it. I went back to the kitchen for the mop and pail anyway, playing it safe. If I stayed busy, and Pop kept eating and drinking until he got sleepy, I might get away by mid-morning.

I also hoped that, if I stayed out of sight and out of mind, he'd focus whatever was left of his anger on Pritchard. This retired Army master sergeant generally ran a slack operation. But lots of clues told me Henry was doing less and less on his shift. He was going to go too far one day and get himself fired.

As (bad) luck would have it, I banged the metal pail against the pantry wall on my way out. (No use blaming that right-handed door construction, I suppose, but it did make removing things from that small space awkward.) Henry rose up from the table.

"God damn it, boy, quit making all that racket." Drink in hand, he followed me out the door and across the yard to the garage.

I was determined to keep quiet and let his anger subside. Inside the garage, I plunged the mop into the pail, slopped soapy water over the dark stain, and began to scrub away at the cement.

"You've got to bear down on it," he complained, punching me on the shoulder.

I exaggerated my motions, but he was right there beside me, breathing hard, still drinking. He was nearing the boiling point.

"Elbow grease! That's how you get something done," said the man I'd never seen employ his own principles.

"It's getting cleaner," I offered, hoping to turn his attention from me, the culprit, to the stain, an inanimate object. "Look." I stepped back, resting a moment on the mop handle.

Mentally I reviewed my options for what was likely to happen next. He would get rough, and I would need to get out of there. To my dismay, I saw Mom coming from the house. She should have gone to their room. Or locked herself in the bathroom.

"It's dirty as hell!" screamed Henry and kicked the pail, sloshing water but not turning it over.

"Henry, you didn't finish your dinner," called Mom from the doorway.

"Dinner?" He looked at her.

"Go ahead, Pop. I'll work on it 'til it's clean."

It was the wrong thing to say.

"Oh, like hell you will," he roared, turning on me. "I've heard that line before."

I stepped away, still facing him. But he came on, backing me up against the far well.

"'I'll mow that lawn, I'll put away dishes, I'll clean the gutters,'" he continued in a whiny tone. "But *Pop* ends up doing it all."

By now I was getting angry too. Damn it, I had done this job, and plenty of others. And I didn't want to spend all day going over and over this same spot. Trapped as I was, frustration made me answer back: "I washed this floor!"

Henry looked behind him at the stain, then back at me. Then he grabbed me.

It was better than hitting first, but I knew I was in perilous trouble now. Henry was slow, but his massive body contained great strength. He lifted me by the front of my shirt and banged me against the garage wall.

"Henry!" pleaded my mother. "Put him down."

"He needs to remember who's boss around here. What I say goes." He thumped me against the wall a couple of times, but he wasn't completely out of control yet.

I had grabbed his wrists when he picked me up, so now I was holding on, looking for any opportunity to get away. He'd have to sleep this one off before I'd be anywhere he could find me. If I could somehow escape.

"You want me to scrub this floor with your ass, boy," he threatened. Our faces were so close I felt I was drinking whiskey along with him. Not a good thing for someone who'd had one too many beers the night before. Pop's breath reminded me of Paterson's breath, all of a sudden. Do you suppose *he* had been drinking before our last challenge match?

I wasn't saying anything. It could only infuriate Henry. So I hung on where I was, but this seemed to make him even madder. He began to punctuate his threats by banging me into the wall.

"You want me [thump!] to wash this floor [thump!] with your ass [thump!], you little *twerp*?"

At that point something snapped inside me. Instead of pleading or just trying to keep quiet, I released my hold on his wrists and grabbed the front of his shirt. I pulled my face even closer to his.

"I want *you* to put me *down*," I said in a voice that surprises me even in memory, for it was level and calm.

9

I think all three of us were quiet for maybe ten seconds. And each expected a terrible escalation to follow, Henry completely out of control.

But, holding me there against the wall for perhaps ten seconds longer, he looked in my face as if, for the first time in weeks, months, he actually saw me, Hugh Noone, there before him. And then he let me go.

"Hell," he said, turning on his heel. "I don't care what you do." He walked through the door back toward the house.

Mom looked at me in bewilderment for a moment, then followed her husband. Still woozy from beer, sleep, fear, I wondered what sort of miracle had happened to spare me a beating.

But I didn't question Providence. I went at that floor with genuine energy, making plenty of noise moving things around so that, if Pop had been listening, he'd believe I was doing something.

At first, I assumed that some change had occurred in my stepfather's slow-moving mind. Perhaps he had seen a younger version of himself in the boy who felt he was being wronged. Or maybe his wife's entreaties had actually broken through his anger. It could even be that, frustrated himself at the tasks he had been set by Pritchard or others, Henry realized he was making unreasonable demands on me.

As I mopped, however, I replayed this incident some more. I thought of the rude awakening, the hurried breakfast, the being picked up and jammed against the wall. And I concluded that perhaps *I* had something to do with this confrontation's ending peacefully.

Why, after all, hadn't I been blubbering as he banged me around? It had certainly happened before. And I had been decidedly unhappy.

Another thing kind of pleased me: my voice. A boy's voice drops in early adolescence, you'll recall. And I had glowed when, several years ago, people began to be confused by my voice on the telephone. They thought they'd reached Henry or a wrong number.

Still, in moments of panic or excitement, my voice, like most of my contemporaries' voices, tended to break. That shout of pleasure you use to cover a buried fear-- say, on an amusement park ride--could crack right in the middle. Your cry of surprise when, caught off guard in the high school locker room, you get goosed can go embarrassingly close to a feminine shriek. Or riding with a careless driver who runs a stop sign into moving traffic, you stomp the imaginary brake on the passenger side and let out a high pitched yelp. In these moments you realize you're not yet fully a man.

I had always believed, however, that a day would come in my life when my voice would stay at that low, manly level. No matter what the provocation, strength, composure, and fearlessness would govern my actions and my speech. And at least on this occasion it had happened.

Unfortunately, I can't say the opposite never happened again. In fact, you'll hear me squeal more than once before I get you all the way to my present place in life, the Missouri State Penitentiary in Jefferson City. But on this memorable occasion with big Henry Maas, I stayed true to my image of myself.

I felt so damn cocky, in fact, that, as soon as I had put away all my cleaning equipment--checking to be sure Henry had gone to bed--I went to the phone and called Linda to ask her out one more time.

"Uh, Linda? Hugh here."

"Oh, hi there. Are you calling to tell me our practice time has been changed?"

"No, I. . . ."

"Because if that's all you have to say, I'm going to be disappointed."

"What?"

"Yes, disappointed. Because I happen to have next weekend free, and I was hoping, you know, that you might be going to ask me out."

"I . . . I was!"

"OK then. Where are you taking me? I want it to be special, something I've never done before. So our first real date will be one I remember."

This was tough. The choices I had were movies, bowling, and roller skating. Wait a minute, though, I did have one more idea.

"Linda, I want you to go to a dinner theater with me."

"Oh, that sounds wonderful. What exactly is dinner theater?"

"Well, you have a dinner, see. It's in an old converted barn north of town, out toward Vichy. And then, after you eat, the waiters and the cooks and all become actors and put on a play."

I had heard about this at my job, as one of the soda jerks, a college student, had a bit part. And, as I've mentioned, I had always been interested in acting myself, in the movies especially. That may be where I found my models for rags-to-riches stories, coming from the other side of the tracks to make it big.

Anyway, the local amateur company was doing "My Fair Lady" in order to raise funds to pay for improvements in their barn theater. And Linda thought this was a great idea.

"Well, I'll see you at tennis Monday," she said as our conversation drew toward a close. "Aren't you challenging?"

"I'm going to. But how did you know?"

"Oh, I just thought it was time, I guess, since the last one."

I didn't need to be reminded of that double blow to my manhood, so I got off the line as quickly as I could. Of course, I was elated. I had the date of my dreams. And I knew I could beat Favored Son with my new serve, with Doc Garnet's winning strategy.

It's amazing how high my confidence ran about becoming number one on the team. Even when the coach approved Paterson's odd request for the time of the challenge (during the lunch hour on Tuesday), I remained calm, assured of success.

Paterson said he had to play at noon because of family commitments, but eventually I learned that wanting to play at midday was part of his strategy. He had other ideas too.

When he won the option of serving or receiving first, he decided to let me serve, giving up the advantage of his power game. Why?

I certainly had no idea that these odd requests added up to clever strategy. I was also distracted by the two other students who used their lunch hour to watch:

Linda Roy and Karen Murphy. I wasn't surprised to have Karen rooting me on, though I didn't want her thinking she had any rights to me beyond a general friendship. I assumed that Linda was there for Robert.

Karen called out to me while we were warming up, "You can do it, Hugh!" I nodded, but tried to keep my focus on what Doc had prepared me to do--the high toss, the twisted racket grip, the snap imparting spin to send the ball deep to the service court.

Linda waited until I came over to get a last drink and review my game plan a final time. She shrugged her right shoulder as she walked, as if she too held a racket and was preparing to serve. From the other side of the fence, she whispered: "You can beat him, Hugh. I *know* you can."

Well! I knew she was going out with me the next weekend, but I didn't think we were that close yet!

"OK," I responded with a confident smile. I saw that beautiful breast rise and sink as she rotated her shoulder again.

I decided she was primarily encouraging me as a fellow tennis player, someone who just wanted to do his best, rise as far as he could. She would probably go over on Robert's side when the match started. But she didn't. She called out to us both to play well, but she watched from my side of the court.

I played very well, by the way, the best I had ever done. All the instruction from Doc Garnet and the hours of practice on my own had really sharpened my game. But Robert Paterson had, as I said, a few surprises for me.

Somehow he knew I had developed a better serve, one with a high kick and deep placement. So he wanted an extra chance to get used to it over the span of the match. He gave up the advantage of serving first and, in fact, lost that first game. But over the course of the match that opportunity to gauge my serve made a difference. He learned to take it early, before the kick could put it up high where it was hard to return.

And playing at noon? Well, I bet you've already figured that out. As you remember, my goal was to throw the ball straight up over my head, let it hang there like the sun. When I did that at midday on Tuesday, I didn't see the ball. I saw the sun itself! I not only failed to hit the ball cleanly, I was blinded for several seconds by that bright orb.

Of course, I adjusted after a while, throwing the ball a little to one side so that I could keep from looking directly into the sun. But that took a little off the power Garnet's grip and toss had given me. The serve generally went in, but it had just enough less speed to give my opponent another tiny edge.

In other words, Paterson knew about my whole game. And he was ready with a perfect counter strategy. How did this happen?

Well, it was Billy. Not that my best friend meant to betray me, but remember his time Tipping the Scales with Linda? He wasn't making out. He was talking tennis, jut as he said!

Billy had even told me that's what they did when we were riding out Old Farm Road together. But, so hot to trot with Linda myself, I couldn't believe anyone would be in the dark with her and not enjoy the situation. Just appearing interested in tennis, Linda had gotten from innocent Billy everything Robert might need to know. And then she fed it to Robert in time for him to think up the best defense for my offense.

I learned, then, something from both Robert and Linda about killer instinct, that drive to win that pushes some individuals past normal limits, the urge to dominate that stops at no point on the way to conquest. I learned first from Robert, who played that challenge match with ferocity, his jaw set on his bad breath. I lost the match of my career, 6-4.

I didn't know about Billy's inadvertent blabbing for a long time, of course. I just assumed Paterson outplayed me fair and square, and that the match meant the end of my dreams of a professional career.

There was, however, a lot more than I knew going on between Linda and Robert. If I had known everything, I don't think I would be where I am today.

10

You would think that, with my interest in the theater, I would remember more about the production of "My Fair Lady" Linda and I saw on our first (and, it turns out, only) official date. But what happened after the play was so momentous that the acting out of Eliza Doolittle's transformation from street urchin to society lady faded almost immediately from my consciousness. Almost everything in my mental record of that night jumps from first meeting Linda to our making love.

I do remember seeing our algebra teacher in the lobby of the Barn Theater during the intermission. Puffed up at being out with my high school princess, I had hoped others from Linda's set might see us together, recognizing my particular achievement in this date but also acknowledging a new status for me in general. But dinner theater, it turned out, was not where teenagers generally went on weekends. So the only person from school I saw was Miss Timmons, who was surprisingly interested in us.

"Hugh," she exclaimed, beaming a broad smile at me. "And Linda. How *are* you two?"

"Why, um, hello, Miss Timmons," I offered. "Fine." I did like the sound of "you two."

"Hi, Miss Timmons. Isn't the music wonderful," added Linda. A small combo--piano, drums, clarinet-- played overture and accompaniment, though I had paid little attention to their performance. I didn't know, of course, that Linda's comment was one of those rehearsed pieces she had learned in attending many musical events.

"The music is grand, though the tenor isn't up to some of his pieces. How do you like the play, Hugh?"

Again, I'm not sure I had noticed anything going on on stage. I was completely intoxicated by Linda--her perfume, her clothes (another of those expensive sweaters that followed the perfect contours of her body), her practiced, cheerful patter that had begun when I met her at her house. And, let me not forget, that recurring shrug of the shoulder.

Linda had offered to drive, by the way, which had solved a major problem for me. Pop rarely let me use the oil-dripping Buick. And I certainly didn't want to have the most nearly perfect woman's breasts I knew riding behind me on a dilapidated motor scooter. I would have preferred to be the driver of a fastback Mustang coupe, but I accepted easily the passenger seat in Dr. Roy's Lincoln Continental as a more realistic alternative.

"The play is good," I finally said to Miss Timmons. But I was unable to come up with anything more to sustain our conversation. Why was she quizzing me, anyway?

Fortunately, this eager young teacher seemed to sense my awkwardness and began explaining that the play's many twists of plot would all lead to a logical conclusion after this break. It turned out she knew most of the local players and a lot about traditions of the stage. And shortly she left us, to "powder her nose," I guess. I do remember that she gave me a little squeeze on the arm, a warm look of encouragement. I had no idea at the time why she was solicitous, but I would learn later in that school year.

What I learned with Linda is more to the point right now. And that's what I remember from my date with a town belle, a member of the senior prom court, the class's "most likely to live out her dreams."

After the play, she drove me down Old Farm Road, not home. I hadn't dared to think it could happen. I had assumed the most I could hope for would be a few minutes parked out in front of my house when she dropped me off, perhaps the shyest of good night kisses. I'd never given up my belief, though, that if she started making out with me, she'd never be able to stop. I had faith in my sexual prowess, in the ability to carry a girl past a certain point to wild desire.

Linda pulled off on a hilltop lane and began explaining how I should have won my challenge match with Robert Paterson.

"You were playing so much better than I'd ever seen you. I think he just got lucky in the seventh game."

"Well, I did think I was going to win this time."

"I never saw a serve bounce so high. And you seemed to do it without straining." She shrugged her own shoulder, as if about to serve.

"I *have* been practicing."

"And you'll win the next time."

"Coach says I have to wait a month, that I've had my chances this season."

"That's so unfair." She put a hand on my arm, showing, for all I could tell, genuine concern.

"*You've* sure got a good game," I offered, trying to be complimentary as well. "Maybe you should practice more with me."

"Maybe I should practice some right now."

All the time we were talking, she had been moving closer to me. And I had been moving closer to her. Our faces by now were inches apart. We kissed, her mouth sweet and pure even after a Coke and candy bar at intermission. (What *was* it about a dentist's daughter?) When we broke, we were both gasping for breath.

"Get in back," she said with a surprising simplicity. I looked at the plush cushions of the back seat, its expanse of leather comfort.

"OK!"

I wasn't sure how she got on top, though I wasn't complaining. We had begun with traditional necking, me leaning over her as she slumped back into one corner. Then I leaned back to the middle, and she came across with me, making sure our lips never parted. And then I slipped or was pushed down the back of the seat until I was looking up at the little light (off) in the car's ceiling and Linda was massaging my thigh.

This is amazing, I thought, I haven't even gotten my hands on her spots of desire! It's true that I had had one palm cupped around the fabulous breast that had risen and fallen in her sweater with the grace of a goddess's. And my hips had pressed against her hips as I'd leaned across the car seat to kiss those willing lips. I thought I was good, but was I this good?

And then for a while things got fuzzy. We were kissing and holding and rubbing and pressing. I had a vision of a completely left-handed world. My mother wiped up the milk I'd spilled as a toddler with her left hand. My real father came back from the dead to give me a left-handed handshake. All my friends were left-handed, Billy and the rest of the tennis team, even Robert Paterson. TV anchormen, cowboy heroes from the movies, world leaders of the past and present, future astronauts and sports figures, all were left-handed like me. They were even driving down Route 66 on the left side of the road!

And then I realized that my pants were down and that Linda's black panties were hanging from the rear view mirror. Her magnificent breasts hung in her brassiere (why hadn't I gotten that off?) as she arched above me, a wild look in her eyes.

Hey, wait a minute, I thought. Who's running this show?

I tried to roll her off, get the upper hand. But she had one hand braced against the back of the front seat, the other on car's ceiling. And her knees dug into the seat on each side of me. She had me.

It wasn't her hand that had me any longer, but her woman's very self. She was rocking and rolling, calling and crying, lifting and lofting. Killer instinct!

And, all of a sudden, it struck me that this wasn't right, it wasn't right at all. It had been too easy and had happened too fast. I wasn't breaking through her upper-crust aloofness with my charm and earnestness. I was pinned in the back of her car, Black Street toy of Missouri Avenue debutante. I had to get out of there!

However, by this time something irreversible had also begun within me, something only part of me wanted to stop. All the rest of me wanted to rush before this wind.

You know, of course, that there's a point in a male's sexual excitement where climax becomes inevitable. And we can feel it, know what will come next, the sensation of pleasure which, even when you relax all muscles, make no move at all, rises and intensifies until the explosion begins. I didn't know I was that close to it until I was there, past the point of no return.

I tried desperately to heave my hips up, to throw Linda off somehow. But she just rode me back down into the seat, my bare bottom bonded to leather. She loved the thrust I gave and humped in exited response. It drove my own desire forward even more.

As all the blood in my body, it seemed, dropped below my waist, my oxygen-deprived brain had a different vision of the future, not at all the left-handed paradise I had thought of just a few moments earlier.

In this world I was the victim, used and abused, taken and discarded. Darkness spread over all the land as my seed was cast into desert ground.

Then desire won out and I rode that wave on to light. Though I had been frozen in place for some seconds, we were now bounding in tandem, banging and bumping without restraint. Let me tell you, there wasn't any Indian or cowboy torture!

And soon this became one of those times I told you about earlier, where my deep masculine voice broke and I squealed on a high note. . . .

Well, I remember more of Billy and me drinking the last Falstaffs in his family car than I do of the final phase of my great date with Linda Roy. I guess it's a blank because not much was said on the way back to town. There was certainly no talk of affection, of companionship, of our future.

Of course, I read all the signs of this night incorrectly. I assumed Linda was quiet because she was ashamed of what she'd done, that I had more or less seduced her. Sure, at times it looked as if she'd been the aggressor, taken the lead. But in my day boys didn't believe girls could do that. I had to take responsibility for what happened. I was the one who was supposed to stop.

By the next morning, and in the weeks that followed, my pride at having gone out with the girl of my dreams was mixed with a terrible feeling of guilt for having taken her virginity. My schemes to distinguish myself at school and in Fairfield had to take a new turn. And that's how the idea of building my own airplane, which eventually caused me even more trouble, got started.

Part Two: Flights of Desire

If you think a sixteen-year-old's dream of building an airplane unreasonable, consider the circumstances. America has always been an improvisational country, a tradition defined by its frontier origins. (This is something else I've learned from years of reading in the prison library. We don't *all* spend our time with law books and court-clogging appeals, you know.)

The 1950s, you should also remember, was a great time for build-it-yourself kits, from relatively small things like short wave radios, model ships, and pin-hole cameras to larger items such as carports, bomb shelters, and outside storage sheds. With an expanding post-war population, but industrial output driven by a Cold War military buildup, people filled many of their consumer needs through purchase of raw materials for home assembly. All sorts of plans were advertised in magazines available in Fairfield's downtown public library.

True, it may take some strain for you to imagine Billy and me behind the little garage at my Cedar Street house stacking up ten-foot-long one-by-twos to build the basic airplane frame; four-by-eight sheets of one-inch plywood for cross-sectional supports; rolls of canvas that would be used to cover the fuselage and wings; and cans of waterproofing that would shrink and cure the canvas. (If you're thinking such schemes can only end in disaster, you are, unfortunately, not far from the truth.)

But Billy and I are there nonetheless, contemplating these supplies a few weeks after my crushing defeat on the high school tennis courts and my hard-driving date with Linda Roy. With a bit of natural skepticism, Billy is asking, "Where do you get the engine for this thing?"

"There's no engine." I toss him a catalog, *Sailplanes and Gliders*. It had just come through the mail in response to my filling out an advertisement in *Illustrated Mechanics*.

"How do you stay up in the air?"

I go over the basic principles of gliding, thermal updrafts and the use of aerodynamics, concluding with what I know will be convincing: "There's a seat for you." I point to the illustration, which includes a passenger right behind the pilot.

"For me?"

"Of course. I've got to have a navigator. And a spotter."

"Ah, so we're going to spot the girls from the sky!"

"You bet. Not only that, I'll charge for a ride in my sky machine. It'll be more than a little kiss . . . for girls."

Billy laughs at this light allusion to homosexual activity. In these days no one talked openly of that culture.

"No kidding," he says. "This is going to be great for your reputation. Everyone will want to go out with you."

That is the point, of course. In a post-Linda world, I need some hot new prospects. After my one date with her, I had called Linda repeatedly, asking her to go out again. But she had reverted to her old tactic of always being busy--extra Sunday School classes for the Advent season; art lessons given by a retired instructor from the state college; many doctors appointments.

I tried to talk with her about what had happened on Old Farm Road, but she was amazing in her ability to evade or perhaps even forget: "I just loved 'My Fair Lady'"; "I'm so glad Daddy let me borrow the car that night because I had to be in right after our date"; "I would have liked to, you know, have spent more time with you. Of course, I never kiss on a first date."

If she was going to pretend it had never happened, what could I do? I didn't want it known all over town that I'd had sex with Linda Roy in the back seat of her Daddy's luxury car, though I was happy I had at least done it once with her. But I was baffled by her apparent amnesia and at my consequent inability to score again. I still believed, you see, in a girl's essential vulnerability to desire. Once she'd crossed the line to have sex, she'd want it more and more. Linda was just resisting nature.

I, of course, had yielded to another compelling drive, social ambition. One taste of the stature I felt when taking Linda Roy to the Old Barn Theater had only whetted a growing appetite. I wanted to move in circles higher than the one I had been relegated to--living "on Black Street," never quite one of the in-crowd at school, set off from those who knew what clothes to wear this year (penny loafers, Oxford shirts with button-down collars).

But I had the idea that, always the left-hander, I would have to use twice as much energy as everyone else running around social barriers to get where I wanted to be. Or I would need to do something stupendous to vault over the obstacles of class and status to land among the Patersons, the Roys, and the Simpsons.

Ah, Patty Simpson, the next girl of my dreams! She was a cheerleader at school, blond and energetic. Not so well off, perhaps, as Linda and her family, but in the same set because her father owned Fairfield's classiest clothing store. Patty cemented her place in the upper echelon by talking Daddy into giving discounts to her "best friends."

Although Patty was at most an average student who avoided advanced classes in math or science, she had an interesting reputation as a bit of a daredevil, a risk taker. The cartwheels and splits she performed as cheerleader were faster and flatter than anyone else's, and she would climb to the other girls' shoulders for spectacular jumps. At this stage in my life, that appealed to me.

Hugh Noone, aviation pioneer, fighter pilot, stunt flyer--it sounded good to me. And I was pretty sure it would sound good to her. I needed a way to show her I was the character in my flights of fancy, however. And I couldn't do that on my motor scooter!

Part of the idea of building a plane in the first place had come from my intimate relationship with Black Beauty, the motor scooter I had purchased eight months before I turned sixteen, before I could even legally drive it. Its tiresome attachment to the ground had inspired dreams of speed, even flight.

"Show me the picture again," says Billy, thumbing pages in the catalog from which I had ordered the plans.

"Here, page 57. Right by the *IM* girl." The *IM* girl was a scrumptious model who appeared in every issue, featuring a new tool or product. While I took some interest in the latest vise clamp or capacitor she posed with, it was usually her skimpy outfits that attracted my gaze. This week she was demonstrating a new synthetic drive belt for a bench saw. She'd put it around her middle and was acting as if the motor would spin her like a top. What an attractively flat stomach she had!

Patty Simpson had a similarly remarkable waist, the center of the hourglass our generation had selected as the perfect female figure (36-22-36).

"Move those two saw horses out from the garage, Billy."

"Uh, I've got to go now, I'm afraid. Going to wash my car."

Oh well, I needed more time to study the plans, anyway, making sure I knew exactly what I was doing. I wasn't fooling myself about the size of my ambition here. The plane would take months to construct. And even if I did get it built, I'd need to arrange for flying lessons. And I wanted an experienced pilot to check it out. That had to be Gary Hamilton.

Gary Hamilton was a man to be admired for flying and more. After establishing half a dozen still unbroken running records at Fairfield High School, the six-two, crewcutted Hamilton had joined the Air Force and served in Korea. He started his own air charter service when he returned a decorated veteran. And he remained one of the town's most eligible young bachelors, despite stories of occasional heavy drinking.

Hamilton's mother (a World War II widow with two younger daughters) had brought cleaning to my mother for years, but I knew who Gary Hamilton was from Ray's Racks, the downtown pool hall, where he regularly held the challenge table in eight-ball against all comers. It's the same place Doc Garnet and his cronies could be found.

Although eight ball was the established game at Ray's, Gary actually preferred call shot, where you had to identify before your turn both the ball you would sink and the pocket it would go into. The game was to 50, so you had re-rack the balls after fourteen had been sunk. The idea was to leave the single ball remaining from the original rack of fifteen in such a position that you could sink it and break up the new rack of fourteen at the same time, giving yourself more clear shots. A good player would run more than one rack per turn, leaving his opponent too far behind to catch up.

All of us highschool onlookers knew the secret to winning call shot, though we couldn't always command it: patience. You had to wait until you could see a potential run set up on the table. Until then you played safe, leaving no good shot to your opponent. But once you saw the opening and made the first ball in a run, it was all downhill. Of course, if you missed the key first shot, your opponent then had the advantage.

One Saturday when Gary was defeating challenger after challenger at table number one, he did something that convinced me he was a man to model myself after.

As generally happened when one of the local champions was on a run, a ring of spectators had gathered around the challenge table. This table was close to the bar behind which Ray and his wife served soft drinks and snacks (no alcohol, as Phipps was a dry county back then).

I was among the observers, as was a very good looking young woman. I had no idea who she was, still don't. But I recall her figure, accentuated by tight new blue jeans and a long-sleeved man's shirt with the tails tied together at the waist.

Apparently Gary thought she was standing too close to the play area, for he turned to her at one point, leaned his cue stick against the table, and said, "Darlin', we need just a bit more room here."

And then he put two hands around her waist and lifted her as easily as if she'd been a doll and set her on the bar. He did it so smoothly, returning to pick up his cue and take the next shot, that she didn't spill a drop of the Coke in the glass she'd been holding. A bright flush of pleasure spread up from her neck.

I noticed something else: held as she was at the middle, the young woman's tight jeans slid down her tummy a little as she first stood on tip-toe, then was lifted off the floor. And her shirt rose up just a bit as she put her arms out to balance her drink in front of her; and I saw her navel nested in soft, sweet flesh. I couldn't erase that picture from my memory, nor, in my imagination, take my own hands away from Patty Simpson's equally spectacular middle.

12

Our 1950s cheerleaders, you see, wore skirts that were tight around the hips and then fell in pleats to just above the knee. Their sweater tops came down to waist level. So in certain routine maneuvers--jumping with an arched back, for instance, feet kicked up behind and arms thrown overhead--a tantalizing bit of flesh was revealed to the eager boys crowded near the sidelines of the football field or along the edge of the basketball court.

To my mind, the bare midriff was a fine sight indeed.

Don't forget, too, that in those days, girls seldom exposed anything more scandalous than their calves above bobby socks. Perhaps, with formal dresses, shoulders and the soft area above a low neckline might be visible. While bikinis could be worn on the French Riviera, you wouldn't see anything but the standard one-piece swimsuit, snug down on the thighs, in Fairfield's summer. So whenever I caught a glimpse of navel, I had a predictable, measurable response.

I watched Patty Simpson run, jump, and play at every home basketball game of Fairfield High that winter of 1962-63. And her navel winked into view far more frequently than did those of Mary Hawkins, Jane Koch, Charlotte Jenkins, or Ann Robinson. Ooh, the center of that hourglass middle! I had almost become obsessed with it.

Possession of such an attractive prize, I had concluded, was to come through daring. I would lure her with Hugh's High Flyer, then win her with Hugh's Hungry Lips.

Of course, at the moment I was earthbound on (or saddled with) Black Beauty. And, for the time being, I was having to imagine Patty swinging a leg over the back of my motor scooter and pressing her middle up against me from behind as we went for a joy ride on the pavements of Fairfield.

Black Beauty was the product of one of my earlier obsessions. Well aware that I would seldom or never drive the family car when I became old enough to get my license, I had fallen in love with the idea of a motor scooter in my sophomore year. It was better than the traditional bicycle, which others in my socioeconomic class had to use if they didn't want to walk everywhere in town. The mechanics weren't so complicated that a teenage owner couldn't work on it himself, and the cost of operation was within the budget of a boy working fourteen hours a week at Rexall's Drugs.

There were, I believe, in all of Fairfield in those days only two motor scooters, little changed in appearance or function as they were passed down from one generation of high schoolers to the next. Black Beauty was fifteen years old when I bought it for $175 from Jimmy Coughlin, who had paid the same price to Pete Harding, who had shelled out slightly more to Michael Wheeling.

Oh, each owner made minor changes: a new seat cover, a better headlight, a fresh paint job (Pete who gave it the three coats of black that inspired its current name). But it was a town fixture for many years before sleeker Japanese versions revealed its obsolescence to Dick Elliot, who had bought it from me.

While they couldn't go cruising down Route 66, motor scooters were thought, by those of us who could never afford cars, to be babe mobiles. Girls wanted, so our mythology went, to press their bottoms onto the broad metal body above the rear wheel, experience the titilating vibrations coming from a suspensionless ride, have their voices drowned out by the single-cylinder engine mounted beneath the driver.

"Why not borrow the Petting Machine?" asked Billy when I was contemplating my Patty Simpson campaign. The pointy-nosed '49 Ford was a classic model, but Billy's needed considerable work.

"Have you patched those holes in the passenger side floorboard yet?"

"Hey, she can prop her feet on the dash like everyone else."

"Have you found a way to keep the gear shift from popping out of third?"

"I just rest one hand on the knob all the time. It's no problem."

A theory entertained by some of Billy's friends asserted that he would transform this jalopy into a thing of beauty, and he worked on it steadily. But, as far as I was concerned, he was forever on the upward slope of this project, with more things on the "to do" list than in the "done" column.

"Well, you'd probably need it the one time I get my date with Patty." Billy was going out regularly, but with different girls. After Tipping the Scales with Linda, he'd called her several times. But for him too she was busy. Right now he was headed for a third date with Karen Murphy, which pleased me, as it kept that earnest churchgoer out of my hair.

Still, Black Beauty had its own appeal, I knew that. It was through Black Beauty that I had first got to Karen Murphy, in fact. I'd offered her rides home from school. I hadn't minded a bit her hands holding onto my hips. And when she'd rested her head softly on my shoulder as we pulled under her parents' carport, I'd known I had a chance with her.

But I was past Karen Murphy and moving beyond Black Beauty now, I thought, ready for the greater challenges represented by Linda Roy, Patty Simpson, and who-knows-else. I didn't have a finished airplane, of course, but I had enough material to begin the campaign. And if Patty would ride over to Cedar Street on Black Beauty with me, I thought I could inspire her imagination.

My plan was to be in the right place to offer her a ride and then, in a friendly detour, show her what I had. It was before work one early winter afternoon that I had my chance.

I had to be on the job at 6:00 on many weekdays, but I had taken to cruising downtown on Black Beauty as early as 5:00, hoping to see Patty going to or coming from her father's store. Everyone cruised Main Street, of course, in cars if they had them. So I wasn't conspicuous. But I hoped I was noticeable enough that Patty could be tempted to go for a ride with me.

She had no regular boyfriend, though she dated regularly. Her father discouraged any long term relationships in high school, insisting that she would go off to college to find Mr. Right. So, many a hopeful caller had the pleasure of coming to take her to the movies, to one of the school dances, or to a friend's party. But they all went right back out the revolving door of her house off 10th Street.

The unimaginatively named Simpson's Clothing Store was across the street from the Rexall's where I worked, so it wasn't hard to be in the neighborhood. In fact, I often parked in the town lot behind Simpson's store, though there was more than enough room for Black Beauty in the alley beside Rexall's.

Of course, what I needed was some sort of daredevil display to get Patty's attention, to convince her I was more than somebody who lived "on Black Street," a little guy who hung around the pool hall. No, I was someone who didn't drive a car because a motor scooter was more exciting, more dangerous!

Alas, Black Beauty wasn't going to take me, Evel Knievel-like, up a ramp and over fifteen cars parked side by side to land at Patty's feet. It's top speed was probably 35 mph going downhill. And acceleration, with its slip clutch, was unremarkable.

With Billy's help, I had been working on a possible maneuver: if you turn a scooter sharply enough to one side as you approach a stop and then brake at the same time, you can slide to an impressive halt, a lot like a skier finishing a slalom run. Your speed has to be just right, and you need to lean the scooter into the slide, wheels coming first as you lean your body back toward the direction you've come.

If you've let your speed move up past a certain point, however, you're going to be in trouble. Your forward momentum will overcome the limited restraint of the tires' traction, and you'll go through your parking spot and crash into whatever lies beyond.

Still, if you've recognized the precise limit beyond which you shouldn't pass, your machine can put out an impressive screech of tire on pavement and the unsettling smell of burning rubber. If you're in complete control, you can, with one foot, flick out the kickstand and park that baby right as it comes to a stop!

I came slashing into the parking lot and stopped in style right in front of Patty one Wednesday afternoon when my airplane parts had become a fuselage frame spread out on three wooden sawhorses. The project was something to show a girl who might be impressed.

Patty was holding a dress box in her arms, propped on her tummy. Since she didn't have a coat on, I figured she was probably taking it out to a customer's car.

"Oh!" she cried, jumping back. "Hugh! What are you doing?"

"Parking. What does it look like?"

"That fast? And you could have turned over."

"Nah. I know what I'm doing. These things have a lot of power, but you can learn to control it." Cranking the handlebar throttle, I revved the motor.

"Really?" She looked the scooter over.

"Here," I said. "Sit on the back just a minute. Feel this thing humming."

She sat, but sideways, tentatively. I goosed the engine again.

"It's warm," she noted. The motor, air cooled, does heat up when you're not moving. I sit on a sculpted, spring-loaded seat right above the engine. The seat is metal, but encased in a padded vinyl cover.

"It cools off when I get her up to speed. Wanna ride?"

"Can't. I'm working. Maybe later."

"Sure. Just let me know."

Well, it was a start at least.

I cut the motor off and pocketed the key. Better not to linger, I thought; it would make me look eager. I walked out of the lot, not looking back.

It was still only 5:30, so I didn't need to start work. I could go down to Ray's Racks, just see what's going on.

Twenty minutes later, coming back to Rexall's from Ray's, I walked down Main Street and glanced over at the lot where I had parked. To my surprise I saw Patty astride Black Beauty. She had pulled the scooter upright off the kickstand. She gripped the handlebars, twisting the throttle with her right hand, and her legs were spread wide for balance.

Above her shapely hips on the seat I had warmed only one half hour earlier her straight back rose from that thin, thin waist.

Rhrhmm! Whose engine is that I hear warming up?

13

I took the sight of Patty's alluring figure on Black Beauty as an omen: I would be going out with her soon. And I was right. It all began on the Saturday after that same Wednesday when she agreed to take a ride with me.

The Spirit of St. Louis II's recognizable airplane shape could be seen from the street that ran along the top of Piney Ridge on the western edge of town, crossing Cedar a block off Highway 00. Stopped there to admire the general view of Fairfield, I was able casually to draw attention to my backyard project. And Patty wanted to see.

We cruised down Cedar and up my driveway to take a closer look. My plan was working to perfection, though there was one tickle of doubt in the back of my mind. It came from the discussion I had had the day before with my math teacher.

I'd met Miss Timmons as she was coming out and I was going into Rexall's.

"Hello, there," she said brightly. "If it isn't my favorite algebra student." I knew I wasn't her favorite. That had to be the brains, Mark Landon and Larry Thornton. But I had been doing better in her class this term.

"Oh, hi, Miss Timmons." I stepped back to let her pass.

"Haven't I seen you here before?" she asked, looking past me into the store.

"Yes. I work here. Stock boy."

"Ah. Is that how you earn your tickets to the dinner theater?"

"Well, yes, it is."

"I haven't seen you with Linda recently, though. Are you two still seeing each other?"

"We just had the one date."

"Ah. So, who's her lucky successor?"

I didn't respond right away, and she figured things out. "Ah, you're surveying the field for right now. Good. That's good. It leaves more time for math."

I chuckled.

"You're doing the right thing, though. Take your time. And do classy things, like take your date to the theater. Most boys your age are too eager. All they want is. . . ." She hesitated, but I knew what she meant.

"I . . . um . . . I have to go to work now. But it was nice seeing you, Miss Timmons."

I liked Miss Timmons, though I couldn't figure out why she was interested in me. And I was embarrassed not to be able to name Patty or someone as my current theater partner. I also played over in my mind what she was saying about what girls liked. They wanted to go slow?

Patty was not a bit slow in admiring The Spirit of St. Louis, which certainly pleased me.

"Oooh, it's sleek, like a missile," she said, looking down its ten-foot length.

"The wings are really long. That's how it stays up on the air currents."

"Where does the pilot go?"

"Right here. The bubble cockpit gets added later, but it's small, just enough for his head to poke up. The pilot leans way back, he's almost lying down."

"How does it take off?"

"We pull it behind a car on a long rope. When it reaches a certain speed, the car stops quickly and the cable drops off a hook under the nose." I knew I would need some help at this stage, either borrowing the family Buick or getting Billy. But I figured when I got that close, enough people would be interested to get me airborne. (It never occurred to me, of course, that an airplane tied to a moving car was certain trouble.)

"Hmm," said Patty. "Do you have a parachute?"

"Oh, no. You just glide in to land. There's no engine failure without an engine."

"It reminds me of the vault."

"The vault?"

"You know, the routine the girls want to do. With a trampoline?"

I didn't want to reveal that I had no idea what she was talking about here, because that would underscore how little I was included with the in crowd.

"Somebody was telling me about that. You're using a trampoline. . . ?"

Trampolines, by the way, had been a fad in Fairfield a few years back. One of Mr. Simpson's competitors, a Mr. Charles who ran the Sears catalog store, dug deep pits in the lot behind his building. Trampolines were stretched across the pits and, for a few months, teenagers paid something like 75 cents an hour for the privilege of bouncing up and down.

Charles had gambled that initial enthusiasm would pay off his investment and bring him to the point where every bouncing kid was pure profit. But, as you might guess, the fad had a short life, and Charles later had to sell the equipment at next to nothing.

"You know," Patty continued. "At the start of the basketball games, I want to jump through a paper-covered hoop with a Fairfield eagle pictured on it held high by the other girls. But we need permission to use one of the little trampolines to vault from. I'll be over six feet in the air."

I could see her excitement as she described this maneuver. It would be impressive. I imagined her cheerleader sweater rising up as, arms held high, she burst through the hoop.

"Oh, yeah. And old Bluenose wouldn't let you do it?" "Bluenose" was our name for the principal, Mr. Sanders.

"Right. But I've been practicing. Want to see me vault?"

"Sure. At the school?"

"No, at my house. Come on." She turned back to Black Beauty, swung a leg over the back, and patted the seat in front of her for me to get on. I wondered how I was supposed to follow Miss Timmons's advice and go slow with this girl!

I do need to go slow in my telling of the story for just a minute here, acknowledging one of the admirable features in the basic design of a 1945 motor scooter. (You'll see why I linger over this detail shortly.) I liked the simple mechanics of the slip clutch, which served as the vehicle's transmission.

A slip clutch works on centrifugal force. The end of the engine's spinning crankshaft throws spring-mounted curved plates outward inside a cylinder. Once enough friction between the plates and the inner walls of the cylinder is established by the increasing centrifugal force, the cylinder turns, transmitting power via a heavy link chain to the rear axle.

There's a bit of delayed reaction from throttle to motion with Black Beauty, but I always know that, once a certain rpm is reached, we will move. And any time you cut back the throttle, you're actually disengaging the drive mechanism, so the scooter coasts easily and economically.

Yes, a motor scooter that's running is a fine thing.

It's getting it running that's not always so fine. Especially when you're in the middle of a campaign to impress a girl who sports a superior navel.

Black Beauty had, like most of its contemporaries, a kick starter. A metal crank angled up from near the floorboard at the bottom of the engine with a rubber pedal two inches square on its upper end. At the base of this crank was a toothed wheel about three inches in diameter, which engaged another, smaller toothed wheel on an extension of the crankshaft. When the kick starter is depressed rapidly--by driving it down with your foot, often resulting in your own rising up over the scooter's handlebars and seat--the engine turns over and, in theory, starts.

The larger drive wheel on the kick starter turns the littler wheel on the drive shaft about two and a half revolutions. A magneto, also spun by the starter's kick, generates a spark, which should ignite the gas drawn into the chamber by the moving piston. But with just a couple of revolutions for the crankshaft provided by the single kick, there's not much room for error.

When it works, though, a boy has wheels! The cost of gas is so low in those days (less than thirty cents a gallon) and the mileage is so great with this engine (more than 40 miles a gallon) that I can cruise the town for weeks on a tiny portion of my pay from Rexall's. Yes, the moment Black Beauty's engine roars into life is the point where magic begins. I go from ordinary mortal to exotic traveler with rides to give. Patty snuggles up behind me right now, arms around my waist, ready to be transported.

Of course, if you haven't given Black Beauty enough gas when you attempt to kick start it, the engine will sputter and go still. Give it too much gas with successive kicks, the engine floods. When the engine's cold, it can be hard to catch the single spark. If it's hot, the gas vaporizes quickly and all you get is a giant backfire.

Most of these problems, of course, increase with your scooter's age. If, for instance, your scooter is as old as Black Beauty was at this time, it might well be missing one of the teeth in the wheel turning the engine over. Thus, the owner's kick produces less than the full revolutions designed for the machine. And, too often for complete peace of mind, the motor coughs or hiccups but fails to start.

That's what it did when Patty was ready for me to take her home, ready for me to show appreciation and support for her cheerleading skills, ready for me to watch her fly.

I set the throttle (no choke since the engine was warm), flipped the kick starter up, planted a foot on the end, gave a hop to get the maximum leverage, slammed the pedal to the floor.

"Kchung, pfft," said Black Beauty. Then silence.

I should also mention that of course the kick starter is right-handed. That is, the position necessary to adjust the throttle, hold the scooter up, and kick all at the same time is more comfortable for those who approach things naturally with the right hand first. So, on top of all the other handicaps I faced with this particular aging machine, I had to try to start it from a position that was to me awkward.

"What's the problem?" asked Patty innocently enough.

"Kchung, pfft," said Black Beauty.

"Uh, just a minute," I said. "I need to check a connection." I fiddled with the one possible connection, magneto to spark plug.

"Come on, let's go," said Patty leaning back on the scooter, spreading her arms wide. "I want to fly!"

"Oh, Lord," I said to myself, "Give me wings!"

14

God was not merciful (or, if so, His ways were mysterious).

The last thing I wanted here was for Patty to look closely around her at things other than my sailplane in the making. I knew our house was old and small compared to hers (she lived in a new development out past the hospital). And neighboring houses, though well kept up generally, provided additional evidence that I belonged in one socioeconomic group, she another. Bringing her here was a risk I had had to take, but I hoped that all eyes would be on The Spirit of St. Louis II.

To make matters worse, however, not only did Black Beauty refuse to start that afternoon, but while I was kicking and sweating, a train roared through the neighborhood, making it seem as if Patty and I were in the path of a tornado.

Our house on Cedar Street was a hundred yards up the hill from where the tracks ran east and west across Fairfield, parallel to Business Route 66. But we were still close enough that the sound of a train, augmented by the tunnel effect caused by a slight ravine in the side of Piney Ridge, was deafening when those engines thundered past.

Fairfield sits on a plateau in the northern reaches of the Ozark foothills. And trains coming from Oklahoma, Texas, and the West Coast have to climb laboriously up from the Gasconade River twenty miles away to reach it. (Going the other way, of course, westbound trains coast easily down the lengthy decline.) The town is the high point, and eastbound trains are usually up to speed when the caboose pulls out of Fairfield and into the countryside.

I guess about the time Patty had been first stroking the long slim body of The Spirit of St. Louis II, a pair of giant diesels pulling a hundred freight cars coast to coast were struggling up the last few miles of the rise. The noise of the two straining locomotives grew in a steady crescendo.

"What's the matter, Hugh," asked Patty, her voice already louder than normal. "Won't it start?"

"Rrrumbble," said the train in the distance.

"It's just flooded. We need to let it sit a couple of minutes. Hey, tell me again how your trampoline will work. Maybe I can help make you go even higher." I was stalling here as much as Black Beauty!

"Well, we've got the hoop. Jane and Charlotte made it by joining two hula hoops." She half sat on one of the sawhorses holding my plane, an arm thrown over the tail section. She had warmed to her topic immediately. I warmed to the attractive picture she made by The Spirit, like one of the pin-up girls posing by a fighter plane in WWII.

The hula hoop, of course, was another fad of the times, like trampolines. Though also shortlived, it has returned fairly regularly in successive decades, though I can't understand why. You just twirl the hoop around your hips. There's no goal to be reached, no reason to keep doing it that I can see.

"But the hoop is covered in paper, right? So, you can't see where you're going?" By now I was close to shouting, but I wanted to keep her attention on her own schemes, not turn it to the fact that I couldn't start my scooter, that I lived in a lower-class neighborhood, that I had no close involvement with anyone on the cheerleading squad of Fairfield High School.

"Of course. That's part of what makes it fun. I have to trust what's on the other side." She had leaned closer to me so that I could hear as the train entered the neighborhood.

"Rrroarr!" said the approaching Missouri Pacific locomotives.

"Do you land on a mat, or just the gym floor?"

"The floor. Though I'm thinking about using a mat so I can land and roll, or maybe do a cartwheel."

Of course, that's what *I* would want, a cartwheel that showed her bare middle as her feet passed over her head.

"That's a good idea."

The cartwheel is still my favorite cheerleader stunt. It has such a precise cycle: a beginning (she throws her lead arm down toward the ground, the other following like the second stroke of the letter "V"); a middle (her lead leg rises past the high point, bringing the other along to make a second letter "V"); and an end (arms and legs return to their original positions--up and down).

In the middle of the cycle we see the middle of her body and the stunt's center of gravity--the navel. The raised arms pull the sweater one way and centrifugal force swings the skirt the other. It's as if she is a spinning wheel, her bellybutton the axis. And Patty, as you can guess, has a great axis!

I sniffed the motor for gas, thinking it might be ready. "OK, let's see if we can't get going here."

"Kchung, pfft," said Black Beauty. I could barely hear it at this point, of course; the passing train was so loud.

102

"RRUMBBLERROOAARR!" said the Missouri Pacific.

Then, in a final blow, fate sent my mother out of the house to see what was going on. She had probably spotted us from the kitchen window. I didn't see her (or hear her, of course), or I would have signaled that I was fine, stay inside.

Generally she knew I wanted to be left alone with kids my own age, especially girls. And she had that typical mother's pride that said all the girls wanted to go out with me. But I was clearly having difficulty.

"Hugh, what's the problem? Not starting? Hello, um...?" She had to come right up to me to be close enough that I could hear. She practically shouted in my ear.

"Mom, this is Patty," I screamed, gesturing.

"What?" asked Patty. Or at least that's what I assumed she said, since I couldn't hear her at all.

The three of us waited a few minutes just looking at each other. Patty had a puzzled expression on her face, but Mom and I were used to such gaps in conversation. Trains passed through the neighborhood regularly, perhaps four or five times a day. And when you've lived in such a place all your life, you accommodate to the interruptions.

"Patty," I said again after a few moments, completing my introduction.

"Ah, Patty," said my mother. "Well, if you need a ride, Hugh, I guess your dad is getting up now. He might take you and your friend wherever you're going."

"It'll be fine, Mom. Just flooded, I'm sure."

"I do need to be home for dinner soon," realized Patty.

This was about as bad as it could be: Patty had probably already seen that my mother didn't shop at her dad's store (Mom's clothes were Sears mail order or homemade). And next my father would lumber out of the house unshaven and bleary eyed from having been in bed all day. What else could go wrong with my scheme to earn a date with the daring young girl who flies through the air with the greatest of ease? Perhaps one of the many loose dogs on Black Street would come by and bite Patty on the ankle!

And then a miracle did occur: my good buddy Billy pulled into the driveway in his '49 Ford. Karen Murphy was in the front seat with him.

"Hey, there's Billy," I announced. "Come on, Patty. He'll give us a ride."

I was a little uncomfortable being with Karen, but this was far preferable to hanging around my house any longer. And since she and Billy were cruising, they didn't mind dropping Patty off at her house. I walked her to the door.

"I enjoyed riding on your motor scooter--when it ran!"

I chuckled, trying to brush off my failure.

"I guess that's why I need an airplane. I could have flown you home. And I *would* like to see your vault."

"Well, I can't right now. . . ." Her hesitation seemed a signal.

"Would you like to go to the movies next weekend? I could see it then."

"OK," she said brightly, and I gave a mental jump for joy myself.

Of course, in the back of my mind I also knew that she probably saw me as one more in the series of local escorts her father would allow before she went on to more serious dating in college. But, maybe, following Miss Timmons's advice, my slow approach would allow longer relationships than those of my predecessors.

Back in the car I remarked that Billy had made some improvements in his own mode of transportation.

"Billy, there's a back seat back here!" Before, a worn and sagging love seat with its six-inch legs removed had bounced around behind the front seats.

"Yeah. I finally found an old seat in a junk yard down by Newberg. It's even bolted to the floorboard. Now I'm working on the motor."

"The motor?"

"He's going to replace the carburetor," Karen explained. "And get new rings put in." The old Ford burned oil at a tremendous rate, and the loss in compression made acceleration seem as if the car had a slip clutch worse than Black Beauty's.

"Billy, you'll be breaking your speed record before long."

Although it was slow to get going, Billy had pushed the six-cylinder engine close to 100 miles per hour.

"If I'm going to get you airborne in Spirit, we need full power in this old baby." He patted the dash.

If you're thinking that having this boy attempt to launch a homemade sailplane with this car is about as foolish as taking a homemade barrel over Niagara Falls, you're not far from the truth. (In the end, that part of the operation succeeded--I got airborne. The disaster came after I began my ascent into the clouds.)

Right now, though, I thought I had things in their right places. My plane was abuilding, my co-pilot assistant was readying the tow vehicle, and I had secured a first date with the shapely girl whose eyes would be wide in admiration--and in rising desire.

There was work to be done, sure. I was going to have to approach Gary Hamilton about some flying lessons soon. But lumbering Black Beauty was clearly proving to be a transitional vehicle, a stage along the way from a boy's walking to a man's flying. In fact, today might mark, I thought, the midway point in the development of my modes of locomotion, a moment of exponential acceleration.

The big immediate challenge was keeping Patty's focus on the daring of this scheme, on the man who would have wings rather than the environment from which he arose.

15

When I left the Uptowne Theater on my first date with Patty, I concluded that I had had the one outing her father allowed most beaus. She had taken advantage of her night with Hugh Noone to try something new, at least new to me. And I assumed it had to be a one-time event!

My timing had been good in setting up this first date, as Billy let me borrow his Ford. For a while I worried that he'd ask me to doubledate, but apparently Karen was busy that night and he'd agreed to my offer of Black Beauty for his amusement.

Fairfield's lone movie theater had two main seating options: downstairs for those who actually came to watch the "News of the Day," cartoon, and main feature; and the balcony, for those who were there primarily to neck. Talking your date into sitting upstairs was a delicate art, one I considered myself a master of. You were not "cool" in those days if you had to sit with a girl in the full view of older and younger patrons on the main floor.

From the moment I picked Patty up, I was at work convincing her we wanted to be in the balcony. Not that I meant to do that much up there, again following Miss Timmons's advice. But I wanted to establish the fact that we could be a hot couple, that dating Hugh Noone was not without risks.

"Where's that trampoline?" I asked after I'd met her parents and we had stepped onto the front porch to leave.

"It's around back. Wanna see?"

"Of course," I said, eager to please, eager to praise. "I bet it's great."

"Oh, you, you with your own airplane!"

The trampoline had a circular metal frame about ten feet in diameter and stood perhaps two feet off the ground. Patty, wearing a short skirt that looked to me as if it might belong to one of her cheerleading outfits, sprang up easily.

"You too." She had shrugged off her jacket and was bouncing lightly, her skirt rising and spreading, sinking and collapsing.

"I'm not jumping through any hula hoop!" I tried to stay out on the edge and avoid bouncing.

"I don't even have it here. But this is how the trick is supposed to go."

She moved to the edge beside me, took a little hop toward the middle of the trampoline, then a bigger leap midway to the other side and off on a horizontal flight out into the yard. Her arms were high, her legs tight together, that thin, thin waist outlined by a light behind her garage. Out on the edge of the trampoline I rose and sank in reaction to her jumps.

I was impressed with the mover as well as the move. Patty had her trajectory figured out and knew how to land. I was also seized with a desire to hold her by that waist, to hoist her for some kind of jump or catch her in a graceful landing.

"Hey! Way to go! Old Bluenose *has* to let you try it."

"You really think so?"

"*I* would. I would. . . ." I hesitated as an idea began to take shape from the back of my mind. "I would . . . I could . . . you know, stand out front and make sure you came down all right."

108

It was one of those promises you make on the spur of the moment which you suspect almost immediately you'll later regret. But, at the time, I was in the midst of an ongoing campaign, and I repressed any feeling that I might later look back on this sudden idea as a pivotal mistake.

Remember that there were no male cheerleaders in those days. The girls were decoration for the boys' sports. But I kept seeing my hands around that waist.

"Hey, maybe he would like that. You'd be my safety net!" And then she took my hands and put them right where they longed to be--on both sides of her then hidden but much contemplated navel. "Ooh, you have strong hands."

"I. . . ."

"But we'd better go, so we'll get good seats."

"Go . . . ?"

The Uptowne probably resembled most other movie theaters in small-town mid-America of those days. A ticket booth separated two doors to a small lobby, at the back of which sat a refreshment counter. On either side of that stand, where you could buy popcorn (15 cents), bottle cokes (a dime), and candy (a nickel), were the two doors to the main floor of the theater. And on the sides to the right and left were two small staircases, each turning once off a landing halfway up. In front of the stairs on one side was the manager's office; on the other, the restrooms.

There was a crucial moment, then, in the structure of a movie date where its fundamental character might be determined. When you stepped away from the refreshment counter, you started either down the gradual incline of one of the two aisles or you turned to the side toward a set of stairs. Down meant movie watching and respectable conversation about school, family, friends. Up meant an arm around the shoulder, handholding across the armrest that separated seats, and--if you worked it right--kissing whenever the movie's plot took its characters into the dark.

When we turned back to the steps that night, I had no idea that Patty's intentions were bolder than my own.

We went about midway up the balcony's rows, staying to one side but not quite on the aisle. Farther up, by the way, I saw Robert Paterson and Linda Roy. I guessed they were dating again. In fact, from the way they were leaned up against each other, I wondered if they weren't getting together again in more ways than one!

With what I know now, of course, I see that I might have put two and two together better in this case, tracking Linda and Robert's continuing relationship. But I was so focused on getting up the social ladder that, when one rung broke beneath me, I just put all my weight on the next. Linda was over; Patty was here.

I was a little unhappy at first with where Patty and I ended up sitting because I was on the wrong (that is the left) side. I preferred to be on the right, where all my moves could be conducted with the left hand. But I had had to let her lead from the popcorn stand, and she'd come up the left stairs (as you look from the front). And letting her go first, as a gentleman must, I sat to her left.

The movie? A Western, which was also unfortunate in that all those outdoors shots were in bright sun. The reflected light illuminated the couples upstairs. The greater distance from the screen made the balcony darker than downstairs, of course, as did rising smoke (people smoked in theaters--and everywhere else!--in those days). So there was some cover for smooching, but more rigorous necking would be a bit too obvious even for most of us veteran balcony sitters.

Both these factors, I later realized, encouraged control of the date to slide from me to Patty. She was pretty much ambidextrous, so being on my right didn't hamper her left-handed activities. And the continual glow kept me in check, while what she had in mind doing had other cover.

I don't remember the title of the movie we saw, but I believe it starred Alan Ladd, famous to all of us for his shortness even though it was carefully disguised in filming. We'd heard he had to stand on a stool to kiss the schoolmarm. (A part of me kept thinking of him as left-handed, never quite in the right position or relationship to others.)

But other parts of me were paying no attention to what was going on on the screen.

Patty had taken her jacket off when we first took our seats, folding it on her lap. Once the movie started, she spread it out across her, pulling it up around her neck as if she were cold.

This is a great excuse for me to reach around her shoulders and help adjust the jacket. My arm remains on the back of the seat, my hand cupped around her shoulder. I avoid the temptation to reach under her arm to the side of one breast, a well-known maneuver. She snuggles close, her cheek against my shoulder.

Even as we extend our contact with each other, we pay enough attention to what is happening on screen to comment occasionally. You can deduce the typical plot of the Westerns of those days from these whispered observations, separated by substantial periods of silence:

111

"Oooh, he's cute."

I squeeze her shoulder. *"He does have the white hat. . . ."*

"That guy needs to shave." Her left leg rubs against my right. *"How often do you shave?"*

"Oh, every day." This was true. My beard is dark and grew quickly even at sixteen. My leg returns her pressure. . . .

"Doesn't she know to stay away from him?" Her left hand, under her jacket (which has slipped over the armrest onto my side) squeezes my right wrist. I'm holding the popcorn box on my thigh with my left hand.

"Her father's going to need some help." I stroke her hair where it lies on her right shoulder. . . .

Somewhere in here I begin to realize that Patty knows as much as I do, maybe even more, about balcony technique. Her hand goes under my wrist to the inside of my thigh. I am excited.

"Why don't the rest of the people in town help?"

"They should have done something when he killed the sheriff. Now it's all inevitable, until the end." I go back to squeezing her shoulder. I don't want to go too fast, I remind myself. . . .

"She never should have stayed on the ranch. Now he's going to take her with him." Her hand slides up my thigh to my crotch.

"It must be uncomfortable, thrown over the saddle like that." I try not to squirm, but under cover of her jacket she's starting to rub. . . .

At times like this, I've learned, you should try to think of something else, anything else. Otherwise a natural cycle is going to take you along against your will. I don't want to appear squeamish here, or unappreciative. Still, the situation is ticklish, to say the least.

"*You . . . you want some candy*?" I try to imagine myself going back to the refreshment counter, getting goobers.

"*Watch the movie. . . .*"

Her rubbing is pointed. It can't be the first time. I picture myself working on the Spirit of St. Louis II, carefully stretching canvas over frame.

"*When's he going to come to the rescue*?" She kisses my ear, the lightest touch of tender lips. Her other touch is firm.

My mind races down Black Street, across town, through the wild, wild West. "*You can always . . . tell from the . . . music. It's been build . . . ing. There . . . he . . . comes!*"

16

I hoped my stoic posture in the Uptowne's balcony disguised what was happening from our fellow couples, certainly my masculine comrades. Perhaps they were all just as busy with similar maneuvers up there in the smoke and dark, but it was not a desire to imitate short (and possibly left-handed) Alan Ladd that led to my walking so stiffly to Billy's Ford parked along the street in the next block!

And, as I said, I was sure Patty's little trick meant my relationship with her would be, like that of my predecessors, a one-time event. If anyone was only going to have a single date with Hugh Noone, she had had about as much fun as she could.

To my surprise, she was cheerful and chatty on the way home and asked me to come to her house for a meeting with the other cheerleaders that coming Friday. She appeared to be calling me on the promise to be her "safety net."

I spent most of that week looking forward to my next meeting with Patty and working on Spirit. I also was looking out for a chance to approach Gary Hamilton about flying lessons. One afternoon, when I did not have to work, I found him again holding the challenge table at the pool hall. Again, he was playing eight ball.

I also saw my tennis mentor Doc Garnet that same day, patiently scoring at three-rail billiards against another old-timer, (Ret.) Colonel Wright. Doc had conferred considerable dignity on me at Ray's Racks by nodding in recognition whenever I came past, as few boys were even noticed by the half dozen old fogies who whiled away late afternoons and early evenings at this fading pastime.

Apparently, I had not disappointed Doc in losing to Robert Paterson some weeks back. He had told me I just needed to keep working on my serve, on that perfectly vertical toss, in order to be the best tennis player my age in town. I wasn't sure I'd ever play again, however, feeling that I'd missed the big chance of my young life and that it wouldn't come again. Still, I liked my association with an accomplished tennis and billiards player.

Today, though, it was Fairfield's flying ace I wanted to talk to. I was making steady progress on my sailplane, having completed the framing of the wings. So that you could transport the glider from garage to launch site and back again, the wings were designed never to be permanently attached to the fuselage . A complex set of bolted supports held them in place once you were ready to take off.

If you're thinking of this as an impressive construction effort, by the way, I should probably admit that what I had here was an elaborate soap box derby racer with wings. While the racer gives itself to the pull of gravity down a long slope, the sailplane lets itself be carried aloft by updrafts off flat fields warmed in the sun. The first seeks a peak speed, the other an ultimate height from which to glide back to earth.

Since there's no engine or propeller or drive system to worry about, the main challenge in building is to follow directions. To be aerodynamically sound, each part has to be precisely shaped, all joints exactly fitted. For once, my stepfather was a help.

Henry had worked on farm machinery all his young life. And he'd learned to jerry rig solutions when replacement parts were not available. He also had a friend at the college's physical plant who made some of the more difficult cuts for me. Happily, he seemed to think I was doing something worthwhile.

He did not know how to fly, however. So I needed Gary Hamilton for the next phase of my operation.

The way to get to talk to Gary, of course, was to challenge, that is, put my dime down at the end of the row of coins holding places for the next games at table number one. (The winner uses the other's dime to pay for the table, thus playing free until he loses.) I am good enough at this game to be a legitimate challenger, but I'll need a lucky break to win.

It will be after my game that I find out why Gary is a little more boisterous than usual, almost careless with his shots, though he continues to win. He's drinking a Coke from a bottle and smoking a lot of cigarettes. What I don't know--but learn later from Billy, who always finds out such things--is that he's slipping rum into the Coke from a backpocket flask. I don't notice that he takes many trips to the bathroom.

"You're building a plane?" Gary snorts when I tell him what I want. His break, privilege of the last game's winner, sinks two solid balls (which are numbered one to seven). To win I need to drop the stripes (nine through fifteen) and the eight ball before he finishes off the solids and the eight. I only hope the break isn't simply the beginning of the end for me.

"Just a sailplane, a glider."

"Yeah, well, that's no toy either. It's got to be done right. Who's helping you?" He banks a ball off the rail into a side pocket.

"Ah, no one. Well, my Pop some. But I've got the directions."

116

"Hoo! That's great. Directions. Where you gonna fly this thing?" He makes a tough shot on a combination. I haven't even had a turn yet.

"Down by Devil's Elbow. There're some good cliffs along the river."

Devil's Elbow was a hairpin turn taken by Route 66 as it climbed up the cliffs on the west bank of the Gasconade. I had scouted out an abandoned runway once used by a crop duster where I could make the launch.

"Well, that might work, but you know you need to wait for summer?" He's left himself in perfect position for the next shot, which rattles into a corner pocket.

"Right. For the heat."

"You also need to test fly it, which can be done any time. Know how to do that?" His last ball is blocked by some of mine--not surprising as all seven striped balls are still on the table. He has to play safe, leaving the cue ball up against the rail with no clear shot left for me. This is probably the only chance I have to win, and I can't make a single mistake.

"Um, test fly it. No."

"I could help you there. If you'd do me a favor." I miss a difficult angle to the far corner.

"Sure. If I can."

"Oh, you can, all right. You let me know when the plane is ready to try. And I'll tell you then what I need you to do." He makes the six and the eight. I've lost a dime, but made a deal. I hope it isn't a bad deal.

Meanwhile I have at least established contact and set in motion what I'll need in the spring and summer to take The Spirit of St. Louis II out over the Ozark valleys.

I am also at work on having an admiring spectator for my derring-do, athletic cheerleader, Patty Simpson.

I have taken to cruising her neighborhood on Black Beauty. I try not to be too conspicuous, but I hope for accidental sightings, the remote chance I can take her for another spin.

Her house is on a corner in a new development, perhaps a dozen brick ranchers on large lots. I can see the backyard with the trampoline from the side street as I go by. That's not where I see her next, however.

Patty is taking geometry, which most of us finished in our sophomore year. And I find her talking with Miss Timmons in the hall outside her classroom.

"Hugh," calls Miss Timmons. "Stop a minute. You know Patty, don't you?"

"Sure. Hi, Patty."

"She could use some help with her geometry. Could you be a tutor?"

Talk about things falling in your lap!

"Sure. What are you working on?

"Points. She has trouble understanding that they don't really exist on their own, but only as aspects of things like intersections."

I thought of the parallel lines coming together at infinity, the center of the circle, the crossing of the x and y axis. We agreed that I would come over on the weekend. We could work out the details Friday, when I was supposed to see her anyway.

As I stood in her backyard that Friday, watching her go through some preliminary bounces while the other girls checked the status of the giant hoop, I had a vision of me and Patty's bellybutton.

Now that her hand had traveled across the theater seat, I tried to imagine which way my hand had a right to move in response: up or down from that superb navel? I believed we were approaching a crucial moment in our relationship, and I didn't want to make a mistake.

I know, of course, that the navel is in one sense the center of a material self, the link to the mother's body from which we all develop. That old phrase for meditation--"contemplating your navel"--makes sense if you see it as a search for the beginning. We go back to the point of origin to find what we are elementally.

(I'm not fond of the phrase "contemplating your naval," of course, because that's what those of us in prison have so much time to do. We'd prefer to take action of almost any kind rather than search for some ideal definition of the self. But the appeals judge wants the full story, so that's why all this stuff is put down here.)

Contemplating someone else's navel is different, I suppose, especially the way I was doing it that winter in Fairfield. A girl's flat tummy is attractive because seldom seen, alluring in its centrality to all the desired parts of the rest of the body. If I could just get to Patty's, I think, there would be no stopping my slide up or down to enjoyment. Pleasure would come to her too, of course, leading me to the heart of someone atop the social scene, giving me an identity away from Black Street.

And I really want that, the sense of belonging at the top, or at least near the top. I don't have the luxury of questioning the direction America is moving in the early 1960s. I simply want to get out from under the wake of those in the front, become one of those leading the way, wherever it is we're going.

119

Ah, but go slow, said Miss Timmons. And I respect her advice. I will circle around Patty's bellybutton, then, for a time. And when I actually make contact, even slower I'll go. After all, I realize at some point, maybe I can do to her something like what she did to me!

/ 7

I took my place in Patty's world, then, in two respects. First, I became an unofficial member of the cheerleading squad, safety net for the most difficult stunts, like flying through a paper screen. And, second, I was geometry tutor for one of Miss Timmons's struggling students. These roles meant that during the next month I was with Patty three or four times a week. And both these activities moved me closer and closer to becoming this sweetheart's sweetheart.

Billy was sometimes put out with me, as we'd always done a lot of things together.

"You wanna go to the ball game Tuesday night?" he asked one afternoon while I was studying the cable system that would raise and lower my glider's wing flaps.

"I have to meet Patty there," I explain.

"How about shooting some pool afterwards?" Each of my cables has to ride on little pulleys and be free of the danger of snagging. Since there's no engine, keeping the plane in the correct relationship to the wind is vital.

"Well, she might want to review curves and shapes. She has a geometry test on Friday."

"Listen, are you guys going steady or what?" Each cable has to be securely anchored as well. When I manipulate the stick and foot pedals, stabilizers and rudder have to respond.

"We've only had one date, though we're going to the sockhop after the game Friday." This was an annual event: students stayed at the gym, took their shoes off, and danced to the latest tunes until midnight, their feet sliding on the polished floor. The removal of even so limited an article of clothing as shoes made all us horny teenage boys feel we had begun an inevitable process of stripping that would end with the objects of our desire completely naked. "Aren't you and Karen going?"

I continued to work at the pedals, imagining myself climbing the updrafts--up, up, and away. Once I'm airborne, I can go as high as I want, as far as there is to go.

Billy had probably seen my partner in Tipping the Scales as often as I'd been with Patty, but he seemed ambivalent about their status. He liked her enough, but he didn't seem interested in making her special in his life.

"I don't know. She's too serious for me, keeps talking about church and all."

I think about air pockets, those spaces of low pressure where the lift of a plane's wings mean nothing. You drop like a stone in there.

"Ah, I know what you mean. Still, she's got a great build."

"She doesn't let me enjoy it, though. How far did she let you go?"

"Me? Oh, we never did much."

"Come on. Let's go downtown."

Still thinking about whether I would need wire cables rather than the nylon cord I'd purchased, I got in Billy's car. Before I woke up to the fact, I realized that I was not going downtown, but on one of Billy's "robot runs."

At least once every day, Billy took the same ride in his Petting Machine, that '49 Ford always in the process of being rebuilt. While he also went places he needed to go--downtown on errands, to school each weekday, regularly to work--he traveled one particular path as a kind of daily ritual, a robot run.

It would be years before my prison library reading would give me some possible interpretations of this repeated, regular activity for an adolescent male. And years more would pass before I could see that something similar applied to me.

"What do you hear about Paterson and Roy?" Billy asked me as he eased off Black Street onto the highway.

"I don't know whether they're going steady again or not. I've seen them together."

"People say she stays home a lot more than she used to."

"So?"

"I don't know. Just seems strange. And Robert studies with her in the evenings."

These generally solitary drives by Billy were, I now think, essentially masturbatory in nature: 1) out, 2) turnaround, and 3) return was an analog of 1) rising pleasure, 2) peak, and 3) decline. Of course, none of us thought about such things then.

Teenage boys in those days were taught that self-abuse was sinful. The "sound of one hand clapping" led to hairy palms or blindness, if not eternal damnation. So we often channeled our desire into other substitute rituals--though, of course, masturbation itself is generally a substitute. Again, that's some of my jailbird wisdom.

Billy's hand rested on the end of the gear shift while he drove, as the Petting Machine tends to jump out of third gear.

At the time, all of his friends knew that Billy could often be seen driving out of town with an almost dazed, mindless expression, crossing the railroad tracks on highway 00, turning around at an old country church just past the fairgrounds, and returning by the same route to his house on Limestone Drive. He arrived with a curiously satisfied look on his face. He had exorcised some demon, at least temporarily.

Billy's friends generally tried to avoid getting carried along with him on one of these drives. If you were cruising Main Street together in his Ford, you always suggested a turn when he neared 00. However, if you (like me right now) weren't alert, he'd pass the starting point of his circuit and already be in the groove. Once he started on his route, the complete trip was inevitable.

Billy was right-handed, I should mention, so that hand on the knob is, I assume, the same one he uses in the privacy of his own bedroom. It rides on that gear shift that has a tendency to slip up to neutral as we cross the tracks on highway 00, turn around at the old country church past the fairgrounds, return by the same route to town.

At this time, I don't think my sexual frustration was being released in driving Black Beauty, but it might well have been in the imaginary flights I took in The Spirit of St. Louis. As I've said, Black Beauty was designed for right-handers. But the stick in Spirit was right in the middle, as easily used by southpaws like me as by the world's majority of right-handers. In fact, the stick's rising up between my legs when I sat in the pilot's seat makes its symbolic importance even more conspicuous now.

I can be seen in these winter months at least once each day in the cockpit of The Spirit of St. Louis II, flying (in my mind's eye, of course) high above Route 66 or even crossing the equator on my way to visit my tennis idol, Rod Laver, in the Southern Hemisphere. And sometimes Patty Simpson is in the seat behind me.

"Are you sure I'm going to be able to see from back here?" she asks me the day before the school dance.

I said she was behind me, but I might more accurately say she was around me. For, to save space, the passenger's seat in this glider is pushed up close to the pilot's, so close that the legs of the person in the rear go on each side of the person in front.

"Oh, sure. These things are perfectly designed. They would have checked that out."

We both lie back on a slant, conforming to the narrow body of the fuselage. So I am almost in Patty's lap. She reaches her left hand around my seat back and tickles me in the ribs.

"Come on. Let's trade places."

I squirm but say, "I'm the pilot. I go up front."

"I wanna be the pilot," she whines, imitating a child.

Patty has actually come by for a tutoring session, but we have gotten sidetracked, admiring Spirit.

"OK," I suddenly agree, climbing out of my seat. "You fly, I'll ride." It has occurred to me that she might reach more than my ribs right now, making me uncomfortable when we're this close to my mother in the kitchen.

We slide down into each other's places, the stick between her legs, my legs around her.

"Oooh, I can see everything!" she cries.

"Me, I'm going where you're going." I lean forward and put both hands on her waist. She moves the stick up, back, left, right, taking an imagined flight.

"This reminds me," she says. "We're flying tomorrow night."

"You mean bursting through the hoop?"

"Yes. Bluenose has given his approval, so long as we use the mats and you're there to make sure I land OK."

I squeeze my hands on her sides, as if already steadying her landing. Then I say, "Can I ask you something, Patty?"

"Sure, but hang on a minute, we're going to do a barrel roll." She leans to one side, pulling the stick. I lean too.

I want to ask her to go steady with me, but I worry that it's too soon. I'm still surprised that her father hasn't banished me, as he has all her previous dates.

"Um, what do you want me to wear tomorrow?" Of course, I'm thinking about what *she'll* wear: the short skirt pulled down when she jumps, the letter-sweater that lifts to show her middle.

"Here we go loop-de-loop," she sings out, pulling back hard on the stick. I think of her cartwheeling across the gym floor.

"Wear your letter jacket, khaki slacks. That will be OK with our outfits."

I could explain the loop-de-loop as a geometric formula for her, involving parabolas and the radii of circles. Centrifugal force and gravity pull the plane in their different directions just as I am torn at this moment between a noble enthusiasm for the principles of flight and a baser desire for contact with Patty's navel.

"Can I . . . can I . . . ?"

"Hold the stick a minute, Hugh," she laughs. "I want to fix my hair." She giggles, as if she has just done a series of aerial maneuvers. I reach around her with both hands, my head almost on her shoulder, to take the stick.

I think of the energy necessary to get something off the ground, plane or romance. There's all that preparation, the energy put into the scheme. At some point you cross a line, though, and realize that this enterprise is going to succeed.

"Can I . . . ?"

I try not to think about gravity pulling everything to earth, me in the Spirit, Patty coming off the little trampoline, through the hoop, down to the mat.

I wonder all of a sudden, was Lindbergh left-handed?

"Can I put my finger in your bellybutton?"

18

"What?" Patty looks back over her shoulder in surprise.

"Oh! I was . . . just kidding. I didn't mean anything." I struggle to pull myself up out of the seat. I realize I've made a tactical error.

Subconsciously, I had been thinking of an old joke Mark Landon told me:

Johnny takes Betty out on a date. On the front porch after the movies, he puts his arms around her and they enjoy a goodnight kiss. Then he asks her:

"Can I put my finger in your bellybutton?"

She hesitates but says, "Sure, OK. Why not?"

But in a minute, she jumps back: "That's not my bellybutton!"

Johnny responds, "That's not my finger either!"

I don't know why it's a favorite joke with me, unless it's the sense of inevitable sequence implied: petting begins half in fun but always jumps to more serious levels. I also like surprise, something unexpected happening.

But I had meant to go slow with Patty. Learning from Miss Timmons, I was supposed to take all the appropriate steps through each of the required stages: first time out, regular dating, going steady, and so forth. But my subconscious mind had leapt at least one major phase without warning.

Fortunately, Patty didn't seem to know the joke and was just puzzled at my odd request. Perhaps she thought it some response to her putting her hand on me at the Uptowne.

At any rate, we returned to the geometry tutoring we were supposed to be engaged in in the first place. Since we were going to the sock hop the next night, it was good we had avoided a fight. She may have remembered, too, that I was necessary to the Fairfield High cheerleaders' new stunt, their safety net.

She and the other girls stayed after school Friday for a last practice and went out together for hamburgers. I had decided to ride Black Beauty to the game after dinner at home. As usual, Mom and I ate while my step-father slept.

"Don't be out too late tonight, Hugh," Mom cautioned.

"I'm staying for the dance after the game, but it ends at 1:00." It ended at midnight, but I always wanted that extra hour. It's amazing that my mom never caught on to such stretching of the truth.

"Are you going with Billy?"

"I think he's taking a date."

"Well, don't be late. Your dad may have chores for you."

"OK, but don't forget, I work at Rexall's at 10:00."

All these reminders of deadlines turned out to be lifesavers for me. Without the familiar threat of my stepfather's anger and concern for my job on Saturday, I might have gone on that fateful ride with Billy, the one which changed Fairfield's history.

I arrived at the gym among the early comers. Miss Timmons was watching the entrance, and I was interested to see Gary Hamilton talking with her as I passed through. A former star at both basketball and football, he often came to games. Idly, I wondered what kind of couple they'd make.

I would have approached Hamilton about the progress of my glider--I had some questions on wing flaps--but I saw Patty and the others already getting their equipment together.

I don't think I had any inkling of the trouble my volunteering to be safety net would cause me until the moment I saw Robert Paterson and some of his buddies sitting up in the bleachers behind where the cheerleaders had stored their gear--pompoms, megaphones, their purses and coats. But I understood immediately that they were there to tease the girls. And the moment I stepped onto the gym floor I would become an inviting extra target for them for some time to come.

Remember that in these days all cheerleaders were girls. The boys were the athletes. So it took a few minutes for a disbelieving Robert and his buddies to interpret my standing beside the tumbling mats spread out on the gym floor. Once they concluded I was part of the team, however, the taunts began.

"Hey, No One, where's your skirt?" called Robert.

"I bet *she* can do the splits," announced Tommy Stoltz, pointing at me.

I reminded myself that I would be out there in front of the crowd for only a few minutes, at the beginning of the night's events. And then all eyes would be on Patty--running, bouncing, bursting, landing. My role would be quickly forgotten, the insults overshadowed by other memories. In this prediction, I was more right than I knew, but for reasons I couldn't imagine.

Patty's flight was, I must tell you, magnificent. I could see part of the takeoff even though I was on the other side of the paper-covered hoop. Barbara Record and Kathy Bell held it as high as their arms would reach, and I looked underneath to see Patty run full speed at the trampoline, take a high bounce up out of sight behind the fighting Fairfield Eagle painted on the paper, and explode into view, a gash in the paper opening to let her through.

While her flight was magnificent, her landing was not all that she'd intended, or what I'd planned for.

I had assumed that she'd come straight down after passing through the hoop, bending her knees to absorb the shock but staying in one place on the mat. If she had too much forward momentum, the plan was for her to take a single forward somersault and return to a standing position. I was supposed to step in only if she was off balance, leaning badly to the left or right, or if, completely out of control, she was coming down somehow headfirst.

What none of us anticipated was that she would come right down on top of the safety net! Even more embarrassing was the way in which she landed on me.

In practice, Patty, like a champion diver, had her legs together in her jump. And she went straight off the trampoline, up through the hoop, and down.

Tonight, however, under the pressure of performance, she was excited and jumped even more energetically than usual. Her flight path off the canvas trampoline was skewed to one side, the side on which I was standing down by the tumbling mats.

Her deviation from the anticipated trajectory was not so great at takeoff on the trampoline. But the path was fixed at that moment, and it was inevitable that she would miss the chosen landing spot. The farther she got from the point of the original jump, the more she flew toward me, standing at the ready on the gym floor.

I, meanwhile, was transfixed by the beauty of the form appearing within the frame of the hoop, Patty Simpson and her delightful navel.

Of course, that navel was visible as she burst into view above me, her cheerleading sweater pulled up above the tight skirt's waistband at her middle. So, I was frozen in wonder, not even realizing she was heading right toward me.

In retrospect, I understand that our scheme had had its flaws from the beginning. Our practices had been carefully controlled, just going through motions at a comfortable pace. And I wasn't familiar enough with vaulting maneuvers to anticipate problems or to avoid accidents.

So Patty came through the hoop headed right for me and with her legs slightly apart. I did manage to raise my arms waist high, intending perhaps to catch her, though it looked to the crowd as if I was reaching out to her. And then she came down on my shoulders, her feet just missing my ears on each side.

I went down on my back with her sitting on my upper chest. Her legs did take most of her weight, so I was stunned but not seriously injured. I had, however, a mouthful of cheerleader skirt. And now you can see how the jokes which followed embarrassed Patty and celebrated my achievement: I had eaten a cheerleader. Fortunately, neither of us was hurt.

To be truthful, I was of two minds about this unexpected event. I certainly didn't want Patty to become the butt of a famous school story--the horny cheerleader who straddled a boy in public. But, on the other hand, I liked standing out in the crowd, or, in this case, lying down in front of a crowd.

I had never had a public identity at school, even with my generally successful tennis career. I was still just one of those kids from Black Street, an average student who played a minor sport that few showed up to watch. This night catapulted me into the public eye as much as it saw Patty fly into the town's view.

My time in the spotlight inspired by this event would be brief, however. Even my friends would begin to forget what I had done at the game after Billy's accident in the early hours of the next morning. But I still trace a parabola of visibility for me going through this new role as the first male cheerleader in Fairfield history, perhaps in Missouri history.

One of the first who came up to acknowledge my part in what had happened was, of all people, Linda Roy, sweet mouthed dentist's daughter and subject of many boys' dreams.

Linda put an arm around my neck and pulled my ear close to her mouth to speak. The game had started and there was a lot of cheering, so it was hard to hear. Still, I was surprised. She hadn't spoken to me in weeks.

"You were great out there, Hugh," she said.

"Well, no one was hurt," I offered. As I spoke, she rotated her shoulder, lifted and lowered her fabulous breast.

"You're always there to help, aren't you Hugh?"

"Huh?"

This was strange. The way she got up close and spoke into my ear. It was almost as if we were a couple. Was she trying to make Patty jealous? Why wasn't she with Robert, if they were back together again? I decided not to think about it.

Long after the jeers from some and the cheers from others that night, I treasured my memory of Patty Simpson's wonderful form ripping through the paper-covered hula hoop: her hourglass figure at the center of a circle.

I think even now of her ideal shape, her waist the hourglass's narrow funnel for the sands of time. When I'd had my hands on it again this night, I thought I had control of history, at least my own personal history. How little did I understand that my course was through an entirely different intersection. What I'd sought, in fact--a position of esteem in my little community--was slipping through my hands. I know now that my arms had been around the form which was giving birth to my future some weeks earlier . . . in the back seat of a Lincoln Continental.

19

Still, it was Patty Simpson I danced with that night, not Linda Roy. The flying cheerleader had scrambled off the safety net quickly enough that everyone understood she had not been hurt in her awkward landing. And getting to my feet swiftly also, I asserted that the stunt had miscarried only slightly.

I knew I would take ribbings at the pool hall and in the locker room later, and there would be some giggling references to Patty's "sitting on my face" at future parties. But I also thought the mishap might help my effort to get Patty to go steady. We were now linked in the public mind. And I had at least been at my post when it counted.

On this night, in fact, Patty got exactly the fame she had hoped for, as most of her classmates remembered more the spectacular nature of her flight and the boldness of its conception than the awkwardness of the landing. She had accomplished the kind of athletic feat cheerleaders would take to amazing levels in later years. In fact, I have the feeling she was contemplating her next stunt that same night: going through the hoop and completing an aerial somersault before landing.

After the game (which we won, I'm happy to report), I was, then, ready to claim my date on the dance floor. With my arms around that fine middle, I hoped to sweep off her feet a girl who had risen yet another level in Fairfield High's social hierarchy.

Well, I wanted to sweep her off her feet, but my dance skills were only average, despite some serious effort on my part. Sometime in my early high school years my mother had diagrammed for me the old-fashioned box step: step forward, slide to the side, feet together; step back, slide to the other side, feet together again. But I soon learned that this repetitive motion wasn't going to be sufficient for the new dances everyone my age was learning.

Karen Murphy had taught me to jitterbug, though I had mastered only a few of the fancy moves that made the form so entertaining--the spins, dips, and passes through which a couple remained in contact while alternating from close hugs to fingertip extensions.

I looked forward to seeing Patty do the Twist, which had only recently arrived via television to America's heartland. It featured the dancer's middle, of course, Patty's most attractive feature.

But there were more dance crazes every week in those days, it seemed to me, and I wasn't in the right circle to keep up. The girls of the in crowd tried out the new moves at pajama parties or on weekend get-togethers. And the boyfriends (and some brothers) of those favored girls might be lucky enough to pick up the basics. But I had had no regular contact with such trend setters.

And then there was the problem of my left-handedness again.

I'm sure you think I should be happy that the man's left hand generally goes first in dancing. But it's the support arm around the waist--the man's right arm--that truly controls the flow of dance. It holds and positions the partner, a feature which girls in those days appreciated: they wanted to be led. So, once again, I was in the wrong relationship to the things of my world.

And, as I've also said before, handedness goes deeper than position. It determines your whole world view.

136

A left-handed boy trying to lead a girl instinctively moves counter to the way other partners she's had have gone (although not counter to the way her own right-handedness would guide her, if she could only give in to it, but she has been too well trained). Just as play moves in Tipping the Scales from left (bad) to right (good) around the garbage can lid, so couples traditionally slip and slide in the direction right-handed men find most comfortable. And I always found myself leaning the other way.

In addition, I had trouble with the whole concept of dancing because it does not seem to have any linear structure. It doesn't go anywhere.

Sure, you get to be close in the slow dances, work out your excitement to the fast tunes, and be provocative in the hip-swinging rhythmic pieces. But when does all that touching escalate into passionate embraces? If that wasn't our goal, why were we using up all this energy? During the process, I often found myself asking where I was in relationship to where I wanted to be. And I didn't know.

Still, doing my best to follow the correct form, I steered Patty around the dance floor for several hours that night. Since Miss Timmons stayed as chaperon (with Gary Hamilton still at her side), I was reminded that perhaps this was all part of the plan I was supposed to be following: slow but steady travel to intimacy.

During one of the breaks, when Patty excused herself to run off with her friends to the ladies room, I had a brief conversation with Gary Hamilton that gave me the first hint of what I was supposed to do to earn his help in launching my glider the next summer.

"Haven't seen you down at Ray's lately," Gary said as I took a tiny cup of Coke from the refreshment table. Miss Timmons was at the other end of the table talking to some students.

"Yeah. Well, I've been working on the glider. By the way, on those front wing flaps. . . ."

"There's going to be a contest there in two weekends."

"Contest?"

"Right. Nine ball."

Nine ball is a game for people with extreme confidence. You rack only nine of the usual fifteen balls in a diamond pattern and sink them in numerical sequence, one through nine. But only the five and nine balls win points. So the guy who can make shots when it counts usually ends up the winner.

"I might enter," I offered, thinking perhaps that more contestants would mean a larger prize for Gary to win.

"You need to come watch."

"Watch the contest? Why wouldn't I play?"

"If I'm going to help you test fly that plane, you'll want to show up at the pool hall Saturday, middle of the afternoon. In time for the finals."

With this pronouncement he turned to rejoin Miss Timmons. And I met Patty returning from the rest room.

"Dance with me," she said, as the band struck up "Moon River," one of our generation's great romantic songs.

"You're sure you don't hurt anywhere after the jump?" I asked, probably for about the third time that evening.

"I'm fine," she replied, pulling close. Her left hand slid from my shoulder and wrapped around my waist. The right, which had rested on my hip, reached around my back so that she had me in a comfortable hug.

Her obvious good mood inspired me to think that this might be the time to ask Patty to go steady. I didn't know why Mr. Simpson let me keep taking his daughter out after all her other dates had been told not to ask again. But, if he wasn't going to object to me, I wanted to make my position official with Patty.

"Great song," I said into her ear as I began my mother's box step: step, slide to the right, feet together.

"Ummm," she responded, her head on my shoulder.

It was clear Patty was basking in the glory generated by her vault, a gymnastic stunt new to the tradition of cheerleading. All her friends had been congratulating her, and her eyes sparkled with pleasure at each tribute. Now I needed to use the rhythm of the evening's events to advance our relationship.

"I think all our practice paid off tonight," I offered (step back, slide to the left, feet together).

"I want to do it again."

"Sure. I want to fly, too," I said, thinking of The Spirit of St. Louis II.

"I'll be your parachute," said Patty, pressing up against me. She had joined our two bodies so thoroughly, in fact, that I was approaching a state of significant arousal. She had to feel it, just about where her fabulous navel was.

"Parachute?" I wondered out loud.

"Maybe co-pilot. I'd take over the controls if you blacked out or something."

"Why would I black out?"

"Oh, I'm just imagining what might happen sometime, if you got really excited."

To tell the truth, I was having a little problem with my concentration right then on the dance floor, not blacking out but certainly losing my focus on the relentless box step: step, slide, back? or was it slide, feet together, back?

"I never lose control," I asserted.

"Not even when you're watching a movie?"

Patty's hips thrust against me, and I felt my erection pressed between us. I hoped no one was looking too closely, like, say, Miss Timmons. Where was she? I tried to pull back a bit from Patty, but her body followed--the perfect dance partner!

"Let's go steady," I blurted, completely out of control.

"OK. But we can't tell anyone for a while. My dad, you know."

"OK. Yeah." I whispered in her ear. "Kiss me."

"Not here, silly. At the real party."

"The 'real party'?"

"Yes, when we get out of here. You and me, Linda and Robert, Karen and Billy. We'll see who else can come."

"Where?"

"The fairgrounds. Billy can drive us. He has some beer, and Robert has rum."

"OK. I've got to take Black Beauty home first, though."

"Can't you leave it here? We want to go soon because everyone has to be in by 1:00."

"I need it tomorrow to get to work. Tell you what: I'll drive home right now, and you go with Billy. You can come by and get me at my house."

So that's the reason I wasn't in the Petting Machine when it made its unhappy run. Billy and his four passengers were on the way to pick me up.

Even worse, I was stuck back at the high school when Billy ran that train, because Black Beauty-- temperamental as usual--refused to start that night. If my motor scooter had cut on when I jumped on the starter, I might have heard the crash and even been able to help. But I was back in the parking lot cursing my left-handed destiny, which was linked to an ancient, right-handed motor scooter that wouldn't start.

20

There are times in your life when you feel as if you've fallen off the road of history. The linked cars of the world's events are moving steadily into the future down Route 66, but somehow the car that is you has gotten switched off on a detour. You're just sitting there on a stretch of abandoned roadway going nowhere, wondering how you'll ever get back to the main road.

That's the way I felt on the night of the sock hop that winter evening in early 1963. The Fairfield High elite were about to leave the chaperoned public event for their own private celebration. It would be one of those occasions later remembered as critical in this generation's growing up, a legendary night of adventure, romance, relationship. And this time I was supposed to be included--me, Hugh Noone from Black Street, arrived!

Robert Paterson (nephew of the mayor), Linda Roy (wealthy dentist's daughter), and Patty Simpson (her father an important town merchant) were already among the elect of Fairfield High School. If they were going out to the fairgrounds to drink and look at stars over the lake, anyone who was anyone in this town would be there, too.

True, Billy Rhodes and Karen Murphy were ordinarily at least one remove from that crowd, but Billy's always available car gave him a certain status. And Karen's regularly offering her parents' carport for barely supervised parties earned her inclusion on some occasions.

But this was a first time, really, for me. All I needed was a means of transportation to get me to the pick-up point.

So I walked out to the side of the gym where I'd parked and pulled Black Beauty upright off its kick stand. I opened the throttle wide to set the engine for choke. I checked the spark plug wire, which had a tendency to jiggle loose at the cap. I slammed my right foot down on the kick starter. "Kchung, pfft. Kchung, pfft." But no "Rrrooaar!" into life.

"Don't panic," I told myself. "Take a few minutes to consider the situation. After all, this is the new mode for me: steady, step-by-step progress rather than breakneck racing over all obstacles.

Remember, for instance, that you are now Patty Simpson's official boyfriend, going steady. And your new status came because you built the relationship in sequential phases, the same way you're constructing The Spirit of St. Louis II. You took lumber and glue and screws and canvas and wire--now there's a body and wings. You got a girl's attention, went on a first date, established ongoing lines of contact as tutor and safety net.

So, is there gas in the tank? (Yes.) Has the throttle cable come loose, making it impossible to choke the engine? (No.) Has something clogged the air filter or intake valve? (No.) Is the kick starter elevated to the highest notch so that its force will be enough to turn the engine over? (Yes.) OK, start the machine.

"Kchung, pfft. Kchung, pfft." But no "Rrrooaar!" into life.

They say your life flashes before you in moments of extreme fear, when death is near. Well, I was in no danger, but images of the past seemed to rise up in my mind's eye as I contemplated Black Beauty's inertia in the shadow of the high school gym.

I recalled, at a very young age, seeing my mother naked in the bathroom, her breasts before me--then Henry's angry face and the slap of his hand. It was my first real understanding of the degree to which a world ruled by convention opposes left-handedness. Was I now to be thwarted once again in my desire?

I saw myself in the little right-handed desks of Fairfield Elementary School, establishing an average to below-average academic ability in teachers' minds because of a weakness in writing script by the models they mandated.

At about the same time these images were rising before me, Billy and the others were moving across the parking lot behind the school toward the Petting Machine. Karen would sit with Billy up front, Robert, Linda, and Patty in the newly installed back seat. They would leave the parking lot and circle the building to 10th Street to go across town to Kingshighway. I would be stuck on the far side of the building, neither seen by nor seeing the others.

Suppose I'm not at home when they get there, I think, in a pause from kicking. I can still follow on Black Beauty once it finally starts. I consider again the mechanics of my machine.

The downward kick I give with my foot turns the crankshaft around, theoretically two and a half times. But the missing teeth on the drive gear cause some slippage, so there's a little bit less revolution than would be desirable. Still, the turned crankshaft pushes the piston up and down in the cylinder, drawing a mixture of air and gas through the carburetor. It also spins the magneto, which generates sufficient electric charge to make the spark plug fire--krrbamm!

There's an inevitability to this process: once sufficient gas, air, and spark come together in the single cylinder, an explosion occurs, the force of which propels the piston down, the crankshaft around, the exhaust out, the next burst of gas/air in, the magneto around, the next spark up--"Rrrooarr!"

You just have to reach that point where all the ingredients are present in sufficient degree, and then you've got a motor scooter in motion, you're a man on wheels, you're headed to the first in a series of parties that will track your escalation to social prominence. Ah, it's all happening!

It's all happening only in my imagination, unfortunately, as Black Beauty says again, "Kchung, pfft. Kchung, pfft." But no "Rrrooaar!" into life.

Still trying not to panic, I make sure I've done everything correctly, everything in the right order: choke, plug, kick. I review recent maintenance: oil change just a month ago; rebuilt carburetor one year earlier; ring job and bore by previous owner Jimmy Coughlin less than three years in the past.

At the same time that I review Black Beauty's history, I see my younger self taking free tennis lessons at the town courts in a summer program. I play right-handed there, as they instruct me. But later I practice left-handed alone against the backboard.

I surprise a lot of people by making the team in my freshman year. My mother, keeping house for my stepfather on Cedar Street and washing clothes for those more successful than a campus night watchman, is quietly thrilled at her son's modest success.

My romantic life is less noble: experimental kisses with neighborhood girls; hurried groping of older girls with questionable reputations in darkened garages or in backyard bushes; a series of wild encounters with Karen Murphy by which I begin to learn the mechanics of sex and the depth of lust.

Now, I've told you that Billy liked to take these robot runs out Highway 00: crossing the railroad tracks and heading south for about five miles, turning around at an old country church just past the fairgrounds, returning by the same route to his house on Limestone Drive. Well, you get from the high school to where I live on Cedar Street by turning off Kingshighway (Business Route 66) a block after you cross the Missouri-Pacific railroad tracks, which, like the Mother Road connecting St. Louis and Los Angeles, slice through Fairfield. On this crucial night Billy Rhodes never made it to that turn.

How did it happen that he, with Karen Murphy on the seat beside him and three others in the back, forgot what he was doing and slipped into his auto-pilot mode? I can only suspect that Karen's attention was directed elsewhere, probably to the others in the back seat. Were they reviewing the game, Patty's vault, the dance? Looking ahead to drinking that night, to graduation from high school, to a life of prosperity and achievement?

None of them, of course, could remember later, after the crash. That event and the immediate aftermath-- stunned witnesses trying to help, policemen arriving at the scene with admirable quickness, hospital personnel doing what they could to treat the injured--wiped out their memory of the moments leading up to what became known as "Cross Rhodes."

At the moment of the crash, I was struggling with mixed signals from my motor scooter and from the girls in my life. Black Beauty finally said more than the tentative "Kchung, pfft," though it hadn't come all the way to life: "Kchung, rrumble, rrumble. Kchung."

I also heard in memory Linda Roy call me "a little twerp" but then later choose me as her tennis champion. This was the girl with the perfect breasts I'd mock wrestled in the yard beside her house. It was also the girl who'd wrestled me in earnest in the back seat of her father's luxury automobile. What had she really been up to with me?

Patty Simpson had ridden on the back seat of my motor scooter and in the pilot's seat of The Spirit of St. Louis II. She'd chosen me to catch her as she erupted through an eagle screen, me to dance with on a formal date, me to go steady with on a regular basis. Was she truly my girlfriend?

My reconstruction of what happened in the Petting Machine as it moved out of the downtown area and began to accelerate to highway speed has Billy lost in some sort of daydream as the others are occupied in excited conversation. No one sees the train coming or hears the bells clanging until they're less than a hundred feet away.

One of the four passengers suddenly realizes that the hundred-car freight train and the '49 Ford are on a collision course. There's a cry, and Billy snaps back to consciousness of where he is. In the din of voices he decides he can beat the train. He can't.

This must happen almost at the same moment as Black Beauty at last coughs into life, "Rroarr!" In the exhilaration of the moment, I have a sudden vision of Richard Noone, my biological father, casualty of World

War II. Is it a reconstruction of some part of a picture my mother has shown me? Or a creation of my imagination, an image from my own beginnings nurtured and grown large in a lifetime's desire?

I see him then in cap and gown, at his own high school graduation twenty years ago. In twenty months he would be flying over the Philippines. Well, flying and then falling. The parachute never opened.

The train caught the back left fender of the 1949 Ford, spinning it and sailing it fifty feet into a telephone pole. Both of Billy's arms were broken. Patty and Linda suffered severe bruises and lacerations but, miraculously, could crawl out of the torn metal of Billy's former Petting Machine. Robert Paterson, however, was lying stone dead from a crushed skull thirty feet from the crash site.

Interlude: Breaking Points

My lawyer brought me a newspaper story today that has gotten me thinking. I'm midway through my account of the events that landed me in prison. And this story makes me think I might be midway in my entire life. Well, this story and my always optimistic lawyer. She thinks I'll get out of here soon and start that second half of a man's journey.

The newspaper article is about a guy who disappeared in the middle of what appeared to be a prosperous and full life. Forty years of age, he left home for work as usual on a Wednesday morning. But then he failed to return.

He was missing for twenty years. Eventually, he was discovered, and he did return home. But it seems clear he had had two lives, or perhaps two phases to one long and complicated life.

His wife thought the worst when the man she'd been married to for nearly two decades vanished from the face of the earth. She imagined murder, abduction, accident. It never occurred to her that he'd left voluntarily, that he'd reached the breaking point.

But apparently, the man, a mid-level corporate manager in a successful Kansas City financial company, had some sort of intellectual crisis about the way he was living his life. What was it for, he wondered, this moving of funds from one account to another, the investment of dollars in this mutual fund and not that, the closing of one office here in order to open another there? Where is it all heading? he asked.

Too, he questioned his family life. Was he really a good husband to his wife of eighteen years? Could he claim to be a loving father to three children? Was he satisfying his own needs for individual expression while laboring in the system in Middle America?

As he later admitted, he just caved in that day on the way to work, found he couldn't go on. With all his doubts, he had reached some kind of limit. It was either keep on the way he was going right to the grave, or make a break. He made a break.

"See," says my lawyer. "Lots of people make a mid-life change. When you're free, you can begin something new."

It's true that I've actually become somewhat nervous in recent weeks at the prospect of getting out. Not that it's certain, mind you. The judge has to consider all the new evidence and decide. But my lawyer insists I have to be optimistic and at least consider the options for what I might do if free.

"Yeah, well, this guy, this . . . this Bob Senter." I read his name from the paper. "He had plenty of practice in the real world. But me, I went from high school to prison and have been here ever since."

"Yes, but it's not as if you stopped learning about the world. You've gotten a college education pretty much on your own here, and some of the colleagues you've told me about have expanded your horizons, that's for sure!"

I have provided her with some horror stories involving famous inmates, as well as the few cases of redeeming social value I know. For a lot of years, after my mother's death, I didn't have anyone outside to talk to. So, I guess I was saving up.

"I'm still not sure what was driving Senter. When he got to the Falklands, he built up another life." There he had become a sheep rancher, married again with a daughter.

He'd drifted farther and farther south for several years after leaving his family in Missouri. Somehow he got new identification documents, driver's license and social security card. And he had skill with money, enough always to prosper.

"Well," she says. "Maybe once he crossed the equator, he changed, became what he'd always to be but had never realized it."

"But he'd had that chance from the very beginning. It's not like he was framed for something he didn't do and had to take on a role he knew wasn't right."

I can feel for this guy some, but I have just as much sympathy for his wife back in the middle of this country. She was left holding the bag--mortgage, children's education to pay for, aging parents on both sides of the family. And she had no idea where her husband was, if he was dead or alive. She was caught in a situation not of her own making.

"You know," my lawyer says, "the wife never gave up on her husband, never had him declared missing or dead. She could have cashed in on life insurance, started her own life over again."

"Yeah."

"Every day she got up, sent the kids off to school, went to work herself." She was offered a lot of help at first, as the story ran in the papers and she was interviewed on TV. But eventually, she had to find some way to pay the bills. She went back to school at a community college and became a nurse.

"His being discovered was a complete accident," I admitted. "It's not like he had regrets and contacted her."

After the Falklands War in 1982, British security was stepped up in a lot of little ways. People coming into the country were checked more closely. And authorities did much more detailed background reports on anyone on the islands applying for positions, licenses, or official documents. A routine review uncovered the truth about Bob Senter.

He realized that his life was to be changed again as he sat in a government office waiting to renew his agricultural lease. He wanted to extend for ninety-nine years his (and his descendants') right to raise sheep on a hundred acres of the Crown's land. And it should have been a routine transaction, the rubber stamp of bureaucracy. But the agent's computer stalled: the identification number had no match in the larger record; there would have to be an inquiry; where did he say he was born?

I felt that my life had changed forever at the moment of Cross Rhodes, the accident that cost Robert Paterson his life. And now as I talked with my lawyer about the appeal, reviewing papers I would soon submit to Judge Parker, I began to think that it might change once again. I'd been riding counter to Route 66, my generation's symbol of progress. Perhaps even a left-hander like me could take a turn to the right.

This surely was my last chance, though, to escape the life imprisonment I had been sentenced to. I had thought I'd exhausted all appeals years ago, until modern technology offered another way to look at the evidence. DNA testing was now assumed conclusive. I would stay in Missouri's penitentiary the rest of my days, or I'd be out on my own for the first time in nearly twenty years.

I had to be at another of those crucial moments of no return, then. After this decision of the courts, events would follow one fixed course to a determined outcome. Freedom or imprisonment. One or the other.

I believed I had already passed the breaking point of prison life, that time when you find yourself taking suicide seriously. If you survive that phase, you adjust, you learn to exist within the limits of your confinement.

"You can stay with me for the first few weeks," my lawyer said. She was divorced now, and she'd never had children.

"Let's don't count our chickens."

"I just don't want you to worry about the details of what you'll do the moment you walk away." She waved a hand toward the high barred window. We were in a conference room on the western edge of the complex. If I had been standing on a table, I might have seen trees, buildings, the countryside in the far distance.

"I can't let myself think about it too much. I'll start to want it."

"You should want it."

"But, when you're inside, you can't afford to, unless there's some real hope you'll have it--someday. It will break you if you let yourself want out."

Again, I think of Bob Senter, the sinking feeling in the pit of his stomach when the clerk began searching old data banks, looking for the past he had escaped. He couldn't stop what happened next, the question following question leading to answer. He would find himself tied to an old self he had buried.

He wasn't even sure how his application to farm had gone through the first time, since residency had been required back then. Things had been pretty casual at that time, and he'd gambled they would not check closely. He'd been living on the islands for ten years already, paying taxes, responsible citizen. Sure, since the war, everything had to be verified, but he'd assumed he'd slip by once again.

The rest of the story was pretty painful. They'd matched his record with that of the man who disappeared years ago in another country. The first wife was notified. He came back from the dead. Rather, he was dragged back from the dead.

He hadn't wanted to recover his old self, the Kansas City financier with wife and children. But that family rejoiced at his resurrection. They ached for his return even though they made no demands on him. No criminal or civil charges were being filed since the family had not collected on insurance or deliberately deceived anyone.

That's where the story ended: Bob Senter was scheduled to land in Kansas City this week. No one knew what he would do. The wife in the Falklands said she would let him make his own decisions. What generous women this man had found!

One thing about Bob Senter's story particularly intrigued me. The inquiry into his past had revealed a number of things he had done in the first months of his disappearance. The authorities found that he had changed his handwriting to avoid detection, just as, over time, he altered his looks by growing a trim beard, letting his hair go long, and avoiding the suits and ties he had worn as a corporate employee.

His new handwriting was slanted oddly, back away from each letter's base rather than forward, as most people's is and as his had been back in the States. Immediately I knew what this meant: he switched from right- to left-handed.

Did he do this to disguise his true identity? Or was this a real self come into view at long last? Had he, like so many of his generation (including myself), been straitjacketed into right-handedness when his natural inclination had always been to reach out for what he wanted with that left hand? Was the Southern-Hemisphere self the constructed one, made up to serve superficial ends? Or had the American citizen been the fiction, the social creation which came apart at the breaking point?

Obviously, these questions meant a lot to me, Hugh Noone, jailbird or free citizen, boy "on Black Street" or young man of promise, perpetrator of a crime of passion or innocent victim. I would find out the truth about myself very soon.

Robert Paterson, of course, was the nephew of the town's mayor. His father, director of Phipps County's most prosperous bank and a member of the town council, was perhaps as important in local affairs. So "Cross Rhodes" was immediately a community as well as a family tragedy for this small town on "America's Main Street," Route 66.

In the next few weeks there were a few letters to the *Mirror* about reckless teenage drivers, and some callers to the local radio station complained of unsupervised high school parties. But the status of those involved generally diverted public attention to such issues as busy traffic patterns and crowded road conditions. Within three months warning lights and crossing gates were installed throughout Fairfield. And an overpass was proposed for Kingshighway at the site of the accident.

The severity of Billy's injuries kept him from serious punishment, though he was not allowed to drive without one of his parents in the car for six months. That hardly mattered, what with his arms broken and the Petting Machine all but totaled.

Karen Murphy was the only one to come out of the wreck without serious injury, despite the fact that she was the most dangerous position, in front next to the driver. It was the seat in the back, of course, that did the greatest damage, as Billy had installed it inexpertly on his own. Patty and Linda luckily remained inside, though they were bounced about pretty badly. Robert was thrown to his death.

It doesn't seem possible to me now, so many years after the event, that I went to work the very next day. But that's what memory tells me. Technically, I had nothing to do with the accident, of course. And only family members were allowed to visit at the hospital.

When Black Beauty had finally started the night before, I had attempted a short cut home and come up against the stalled train at Fairfield Street. Retracing my route to the high school and eventually taking 10th Street like the others, I did come to the crash site, but that was after the ambulances had gone. By the time I found out what had happened, I had nowhere to go but home.

My main concern from the beginning was to find out if Patty had been injured. I knew she'd been taken to the hospital. On the next day I learned she suffered several cracked ribs and bad bruises, but she would be fine. Most people said she was lucky not to have any marks on the face. Sadly, with my continuing lust for her navel, I was just as worried about an injured midsection.

For some days I was haunted by alternating images of Patty's perfect form and the broken bodies of car crash victims seen in newspapers and cheap magazines. The hourglass shape of Patty's figure stayed with me from the basketball game, her vault through the hoop. Just as I'd imagined, her midriff had been exposed by the stretch of her leap, and her bellybutton anchored my daydreams at school and work.

But reports and rumors of what happened to the kids in Cross Rhodes generated nightmare shapes for the hours of sleep and the times of doubt. These pictures were made worse by my imagination, which deepened and darkened the worst features of the grainy photographs I saw routinely in the *Fairfield Mirror*.

I don't know why the Sweet family, which edited the local paper, printed such gruesome images of death, unless to scare us all to safer driving. Most people learned fairly quickly to ignore their impact, to see but not register what it all meant. I thought I'd passed that point myself, but now that it involved kids I knew, my response reverted to the shock of initial encounter. I feared some secret horror about Patty was being hidden from everyone in town.

Linda Roy had a bad cut on her forehead from shattered glass. And internal injuries would keep her in bed for more than a week. Patty went home the Monday after the accident.

I've often asked myself since that time if there was any way I could have known then the one thing about the accident that would come to shape my destiny. Only the family and their doctor were told on the night of the crash. And it would be months before town gossip suspected the one explanation for the event's unaccounted-for loose ends. Since many troublesome topics--especially the subject of sex--were deliberately avoided in public discussion in those days, I remained in the dark about Linda's condition until early spring.

One good thing about my life in those weeks in which Billy and Karen, Patty and Linda recovered was that I'd already learned some of the benefits of routine: the regular cycle of beginning, middle, and end. (Not that I like the routine I'm in now, of course: wake-up call; cell inspection; work duty; exercise; work duty; lock down. Now I look for any break in the daily regimen, any variation in the regular patterns.)

But I'd been punching the clock at Rexall's long enough to derive some comfort from the familiar that Saturday, even as I agonized about the unexpected of the night before.

My weekday work at Rexall's had always been routine: clearing dated items from the shelves, restocking, dusting, and mopping the floor. I came in as the store was closing and worked on my own until 9:00.

Occasionally Karen's father would stay to give additional instructions, or the owner (and pharmacist) Mr. Wicker would drop by to make sure things were done correctly. But, eager to earn the funds that would support my rise to high social status, I'd already shown I was reliable.

The only troubles I faced derived from my old complaint: a right-handed universe.

Mr. Murphy often demonstrated the "correct" way to sweep or mop a floor, the proper position of products on a shelf, the appropriate arrangement of cartons in the storeroom. And I was supposed to mimic every movement, every right-handed gesture.

"No, no, no," he would say. "Use your *left* foot to push the pedal on the scrub bucket; hold the mop handle *this* way!"

"I'm more comfortable doing it from this side."

"But look at the angle of the handle. It's backwards."

Eventually, of course, I adopted the same strategy I had in taking tennis lessons: I followed directions when someone was watching, then switched to a southpaw approach when backs were turned. If others had their secrets, I hid some truths about myself as well.

Mr. Murphy could have harbored unspoken reasons to be irritated with me. I felt he had some inkling I'd fooled around with his daughter but never declared myself a formal suitor. And in this religious household, few greater sins were known. But as far as I knew, Karen had kept her secrets from her family.

"The circular display racks need to turn the other way. Did you put them together backwards?"

"Um, I followed the directions. And they revolve nicely."

"Take them apart and reverse the construction."

Fortunately, such evenings were rare, and I marched through my chores with steady application. Weekends had been similarly standardized until about this same time. I generally unpacked shipments in the back and organized the supply room for the week ahead. But that all changed one day in the post-accident time when I received a new assignment.

Rexall's not only sold medicines, greeting cards, and small household items. It also included the traditional small-town soda fountain. We had perhaps a dozen stools at the counter and four booths. Serving hot and cold sandwiches, as well as ice cream desserts, we entertained a steady downtown lunch crowd from Monday through Friday.

On weekends, though, we ran popular specials to lure shoppers in the cold of winter or the heat of summer: sometimes twenty-five-cent hamburgers and fries; often hot dogs for a nickel; once in a while your choice of sundae for a dime.

Since I remained in the back most of the day, my routine had been unaffected by the midday traffic taking advantage of the soda fountain specials. But not many days after the accident, I received a promotion of sorts: I began to work the soda fountain cash register from 11:00 to 2:00, ringing up all sales during the most hectic period of the day so that the regular full-time waitresses could serve more customers.

Now that I think more about it, it was in this same period of tackling a new job that I recognized, almost to my surprise, that my romance with Patty Simpson was also developing. In fact, it was advancing to a new, more formal phase.

Patty's father often had lunch at Rexall's, as his clothing store was in the same block. I didn't realize how often he was there until I moved from the stock room to the cash register. But on Saturday he spoke to me as I was returning his change for an eighty-five-cent meal ("five makes ninety, and ten is a dollar").

Patty had been back in class just a few days, but she was being driven to and from school and I'd not had any real chance to talk with her.

"Hi there, Hugh," Mr. Simpson offered. "You're new up here, aren't you?"

"I've been at the store for over a year, sir, but, yes, I just began at the register."

"Ah. You like it?"

"Yes, sir. But it keeps me busy." I was a little bit nervous, as he was holding up the line of customers.

"I see." He glanced back at those behind him and stepped to the side of the register. "Are you coming to see Patty? She's asked about you."

"Oh, I didn't want to intrude. How is she doing, sir?" I had mailed her a get-well card, though I hadn't gone so far as to send flowers, fearing to anger Mr. Simpson.

"Oh, much better. There's not much you can do for cracked ribs. Just let them heal. Of course, she's not doing any cheerleading jumps right now."

"Right!"

"Say, you want to come over for dinner next weekend? Might cheer her up for us."

"Sure. If I'm not working. Which day?" This seemed to be better than anything I could have imagined, being invited by the father who in the past had opposed all second dates for his daughter. Of course, there was something underlying Mr. Simpson's offer that I would not understand for several more weeks.

And by then other complications had arisen in my life, making the enjoyment of Patty's hourglass shape that I finally gained far less satisfying than I had always thought it would be.

22

Just as Patty Simpson was not doing cheerleading vaults with her broken ribs, neither was she contemplating a ride high in the sky over Route 66 with Hugh Noone. Still, I felt it important to sustain progress on The Spirit of St. Louis II, my vehicle to impress a risk-taker, against that day when she would be fully recovered.

All the cables and linkages were complete by this time. And special varnish to seal the canvas covering was on order through a mail-order supplier. I had hopes of adding some design in paint as well--a shooting star, perhaps, or an eagle--once the fuselage and wings had cured.

I worked on the glider every evening I wasn't at Rexall's. With Billy laid up and Patty resting at home, I had plenty of time to put in on the project. Every once in a while I informed Gary Hamilton of my progress, as I often saw him down at Ray's. One Friday evening I was startled to see him there with my math teacher, Miss Timmons. They were playing together at a back table. I watched from a distance out of curiosity, as this was the second time I'd seen them together. I had thought they came separately to the high school game and the dance, but now I concluded they might well have been on a date.

Teaching a woman to shoot pool, of course, is a time-honored way of putting your hands on her in an acceptable but often intimate way. You can lean over her shoulder to show her how to line up shots. And your arm fits along her arm to guide the stroke. While

I'd not yet had the pleasure, I often imagined a hand on Patty's waist as I pointed out the appropriate angle.

Gary, much larger than Miss Timmons, was not glued to her the way I'd seen some men hang on their partners. In fact, his instruction was awkward for a reason that I suddenly took in: she was playing left-handed! This surprised me because she'd always written on the blackboard with her right hand. Still, both she and Gary seemed warmed by each other's presence.

I slipped out of the pool hall before very long. Whenever I talked with Gary about testing my glider, I didn't want to have to explain to others what I was up to. I was especially shy right then with Miss Timmons, who had begun to single me out in math class.

It seems that I'm pretty good at math. None of my previous teachers had realized this because, I believe, each was told by a predecessor that I had weak skills. Too, I made numbers poorly writing with my right hand (I used my left hand when no one was watching). So my columns for addition and subtraction were often slanted oddly, and I sometimes totaled the wrong units or misread what I was calculating.

In tenth grade with Mr. Mapp, I'd almost failed geometry, which insists on a precise perspective (remember all those "right" angles?). But I did fine in algebra the next year, and I was surprising even myself in Miss Timmons' college math class. (I'd signed up for this course more in order to be with the right group than to prepare for college.)

We'd been studying functions and graphs in recent weeks, and I seemed to have an instinctive grasp of curves and their related formulas. People now call what we were learning "pre-calculus." Whatever it's called, I liked working with those calculable trajectories of acceleration and decline.

This, of course, was how I'd come to be tutoring Patty in her lower-level class. Miss Timmons sometimes called on me along with other good students to work difficult problems for the rest of the class, and she thought I explained things clearly. I used my status as tutor to remind Patty's father that I had additional reasons to be calling at his house.

"Does your daughter need some help catching up on her math homework, sir?" I asked him the day before I was coming to dinner. I had stopped by Simpson's Clothing Store after school that Friday afternoon.

"Well now, Hugh, I'm not sure." We were standing in the formal wear section of the store. "She's been watching a lot of television while she rests, so she just might need to do more on the math. You plan to stay after dinner tomorrow, just in case."

Stay late? You bet! I was beginning to like this Mr. Pete Simpson, who'd been so discouraging to other boys. He was a large man, an intimidating figure even to fellow shop owners and local politicians. He'd played football in college, I'd heard, and that's probably where his daughter got her athletic skills. All the more flattering that he was welcoming me into his house.

All day Saturday I thought about what I might say when Patty and I were alone after dinner, how I'd try to console her for her suffering, how I was pledging myself to continuing support. We were still, so far as I knew, secret boyfriend and girlfriend.

That day moved slowly, as you can guess. Before I had been switched to the cash register duty, I had broken my work into two phases: unpacking and stocking. I knew once I'd laid out the products to be shelved and carried the flattened cardboard boxes to the dumpster in the alley, the worst of the day was over. I took my lunch break knowing I was closer to the end of my shift than its beginning.

Now that I was being caught up in the midday rush, however, I had trouble figuring out where the halfway point lay.

The long Saturday balanced on the hour of noon, of course, but the peak of the rush came somewhat later. And I was often so beleaguered by customers paying their bills and Mr. Wicker making extra requests that I wouldn't know when I'd passed the midpoint of the whole cycle.

This assignment of taking in the money, by the way, was less easy than you might think. Pre-computer cash registers didn't calculate totals or change for you. I had to add up individual items in an order to reach a final amount and then provide the correct change from whatever sum the customer gave me.

The keys on my machine represented fixed amounts: dollars up to twenty; cents in increments of ten and five. That is, a bill for $1.95 was rung up by pushing at the same time a one dollar key, a ninety-cent key, and a five-cent key. (There was, fortunately, no sales tax on restaurant food at the time!)

If a customer gave me a five dollar bill, I removed singles and coins from the register drawer and handed him his change of $3.05, counting out the amount added to what he owed that equaled $5.00: "$1.95 [what he owed] and five cents [I put a nickel in his palm] makes $2.00. Three [a dollar handed over], four [another dollar], and five [a third]. Thank you, sir."

While, as it turned out, I could run these totals in my head quite easily, the steady flow of customers drawn to our specials kept me moving at a near-frantic pace throughout the middle of my workday. And I've always been a person who wants to know where he stands in the course of any project. I had, then, to develop new strategies to order my day once it included my midday stint at the cash register.

Erotic fantasies were one of my favorite ways of blocking off time (sadly, that's still true today when I'm in prison!). I had several favorite scenarios I could run through in my mind. And I allocated portions of each tale to stages in the day's events. In this period of my bellybutton fascination, I daydreamed about a new version of the bunny hop.

You recall the bunny hop, I'm sure. Dancers formed a line with the one behind holding onto the waist of the one before. While dancers do some other steps along the way, the principal maneuver involves one hop forward, one hop back, and then three little forward hops. The whole line moves together--hop, hop, hop. We'd done this at the sock hop, of course.

Phase one of my Bunny Hop Fantasy involved me and Patty alone in her family's downstairs den (I didn't even know if they had a den!). We were hopping around a pool table. I stuck to this image through my morning hours--sometimes me in front, more often Patty.

"Let's see," I summarized. "That was two grilled cheese (forty cents), a hamburger (twenty-five), an order of French fries (twenty), two Cokes, and a lemonade (thirty cents)." I was reading the items, carefully printed by Ruth, one of our regular waitresses, from a green slip of paper. "That's a dollar fifteen cents, ma'am." Kchang! I rang it up and gave her the dime change. "And ten makes one twenty-five."

"Let's do it this way," says Patty in the second portion of my fantasy, which was indulged in throughout the lunch period. She turns around to face me, keeping my hands on her hips, her own hands on my waist. "Keep moving now." I have paused because I realize she is wearing only a bra and panties!

"We had two specials [ice cream sundaes at a dime each], a root beer float [fifteen], a cone of fudge ripple, single dip [five]." I can see this all written on the slip, but often customers think I can't read, let alone add.

"Forty cents ma'am." Kchang! "And ten makes fifty [I give her a dime], seventy-five [a quarter], and a dollar [another quarter]. Two, three, four, five [dollars]. Thank you."

After lunch, back in the storeroom, I imagine Patty and me still bunny hopping, but now we're pressed up against each other, belly to belly. Although my hands stay stubbornly on her hips, her arms are up around my neck. She pulls me close for kiss after kiss after kiss.

Another reason some customers read out the bill to me, I realize, is that they can't do the sums themselves. It reassures them to note each item, pretending they are checking my math. But the total I arrive at is a mystery to them. Producing change is even more perplexing to others, though they can follow the adding of money returned to money spent and arrive at the amount they handed me to begin with.

I learned, of course, to take and return all money right-handed, so that they can give and receive with their right hands. It's a form of hand-shaking, I guess, a social ritual that must follow prescribed rules. And I am eager to fit in.

My bare erection is pressed against Patty's bare stomach, the tip right at her navel. We bounce up and

168

down, but remain in one place. Hop, hop, hop. *Hop, hop, hop!*

People I know sometimes show up unexpectedly at the register, further confusing my sense of the workday's rhythm. I have to engage in casual conversation while continuing to take money and give change.

On the day of my dinner at the Simpsons', for instance, who should appear suddenly before me with some interesting news but my former "bunny hop" partner, Karen Murphy.

23

"Hi, Hugh."

"Oh, Karen. Hi. Um, a tuna sandwich (twenty), small coke (five), bag of Fritos (five). Nothing else? How are you?"

"I'm fine. Here you go. You?" She hands me the exact change, one quarter and a nickel."

"I'm OK." There is no one behind her at the register, so I can pause to talk. I have seen her around school, and she was at the memorial service for Robert Paterson, but we haven't spoken much. (The funeral had been private, immediate family only.)

"You should talk with me sometime." Karen has a dreamy sort of expression, kindly but a bit unfocused.

"About what happened? I wasn't there, you know."

I have assumed, by the way, that she has been visiting Billy. I'd been myself to the Rhodes' house almost every day, bringing books from school and filling Billy in on what was happening. But I'd not seen Karen on any of my visits.

"I know, I know," Karen said. "About *why* it happened. What's going on."

"Going on? What do you mean?"

"Come by our place. I'll explain. Tomorrow afternoon?"

"OK. Maybe. I will if I can." Now a customer, one of the two local barbers, has arrived at the register. "Let's see, what do we have here?" And Karen moves on, leaving me with a benevolent smile.

I can't imagine what she wants to talk about. I've heard nothing strange about something happening before the accident, just the sad facts of the collision and its aftermath. I have, though, been spending a lot of time thinking over the events leading up to the crash.

I recall that Billy and I had seen Paterson some weeks earlier with another girl down Old Farm Road. I still don't know who she was. All the gossip around school hasn't even produced a candidate.

I think about Paterson in another way, too. We were rivals, both in tennis and in pursuit of Linda, even if nobody else took me very seriously in those competitions. So his death weighs a bit on my conscience, even though rational thought doesn't implicate me in any part of the accident itself.

It's funny, though, how conscience works. Remember, I've been in prison for decades, so I've got some experience in guilt and punishment. Sometimes you feel bad for things others did that you couldn't have stopped from happening. But other unfortunate events, which you know you're responsible for, don't trouble you a bit.

There's a cycle to minor regrets, I think: an initial burst of sorrow, but after that a steady decline to zero. Other, bigger mistakes often move in the opposite direction: you ignore what you feel at first, but then guilt grows steadily to a crisis point. In the case of Cross Rhodes I wasn't sure where I was.

I decided it couldn't hurt to stop by the Murphys' trailer tomorrow. I'd try to avoid her dad, though. And tonight I had more important work to do: romancing my thin-waisted cheerleader who was recovering at home without the reassuring presence of the boy who had been granted the status of "steady."

Before I could resume that campaign, however, I had about three solid hours of work in the storeroom . And before the restocking even began, as it turned out, I encountered several more customers at Rexall's with special messages for me. Along came, for instance, Gary Hamilton.

"That pool tournament? One week," he informs me brusquely.

"Oh, yeah. You want me to watch." I glance at his bill, mentally arrive at eighty cents.

"I want you to talk with Doc Garnet."

"That's right. He's usually there for these tournaments." I give him two dimes in change.

"He usually *wins* these tournaments. But this time I'm going to come out on top."

"Ah. Well, you've got a good chance." I'm trying to be encouraging, though I don't think anyone's beaten old man Garnet in a long time. Sometimes he doesn't enter such contests, but when he plays, he wins.

"He likes you, you know." Gary gives me a firm look.

"He gave me some tennis lessons. He's a great tennis player, did you know that? Even at his age. . . ."

"I'm not interested in anything he does on the court," he interrupts. "I just want you to start up a conversation with him when he's playing me nine ball down at Ray's."

"Ah." Now it is all becoming clear to me: Hamilton is saying I should be a distraction at the tournament. This would be in exchange for his helping me with my glider.

Before I can agree or decline to be Hamilton's secret ally, he turns and walks away. I hope I can think of a way out of this predicament before the contest. In the meantime, it's back to work.

I do take this work rather seriously, by the way. And not just the new assignment at the cash register, but my place in the whole store, too. I no longer seem to have a professional tennis career opening out in front of me, even if Doc still talks about that possibility. And the life of a daredevil glider pilot is a little less attractive in the aftermath of the encounter of car and train. So I need to be thinking of how I'll take care of myself and a future family in a style more comfortable than that I've enjoyed on Black Street.

I've begun to think about myself as a businessman in a town along famous Route 66. My math skills have developed surprisingly this year, thanks to Miss Timmons. So perhaps I can calculate wisely and invest in growth. Patty's father seems to enjoy a pretty good life, a life I'm supposed to be sharing, for one evening at least, in just another few hours. And the Simpsons have prospered from Patty's uncle's position as civic leader.

So I begin to see my recent promotion as a key step in my professional development, a point I'll later look back on as pivotal in my ascent to prosperity. I'll still play tennis recreationally. And I am committed to launching The Spirit of St. Louis II, proving that I can fly. But there are other projects in my life picking up speed now as well.

As if to contradict this happy prospect, however, Big Henry Maas, my stepfather, is suddenly standing before me at the register.

"When you're done today, pick these things up at the grocery." He hands me a list and a five-dollar bill.

"I'm going out tonight, Pop. Can't it wait until tomorrow?"

The dark look he gives me is the answer. Now that I think about it, 2:00 is early for him to be up after a Friday night's work. Something has cut his sleep short and given him a more unpleasant look than usual.

"OK, OK," I tell him. And I try to be friendly. "You going bowling?"

"No, and I won't be home for dinner, either." With that he's gone, pushing his wide shoulders through the double glass doors to the street. This looks like one of those Saturday nights Henry spends at the Top Hat Lounge. (I find the name ironic, as this bar is under the barbershop on 9th Street. I've never known, however, if irony was intended.) I'd better keep this fact in mind after my dinner with Patty.

I wonder who else will show up to give me trouble before I can leave work today! But it's not another customer who throws me off schedule a final time, but our waitress, Ruth. She drops a gallon jug of Coke syrup.

Soda fountain soft drinks are "made" in a machine that blends syrup, water, and CO_2 (that is, carbon dioxide). A copper tube carries the water from the main line to the back of our drink machine. Gas from two cylinders underneath the counter turns the water into a carbonated liquid. And syrups from two-gallon reservoirs add the flavor (Coca-Cola, Hires root beer, Seven-up). The waitresses refill each reservoir periodically with syrup that's stored in gallon jugs in back. But Ruth lost control of one at 2:30 and made a mess for the stock boy.

Obviously, this system of making drinks saves shipping costs: rather than pay for large containers full of the drink itself, Rexall's has only to cover the cost of shipping the concentrated syrup and refilling the gas cylinders (which last for months).

Some days, of course, customers complain that the drinks are weak, watered down. And they're right. Mr. Wicker has to adjust the mixture for more flavor. On other days the drinks taste strong. And again Mr. Wicker has to check the flow of all three ingredients: gas, water, flavor. Getting the perfect balance is rather a juggling act.

Mr. Wicker had already confided the secret of this process to me one day in the stock room. The trick is to go back to nothing but water. Then add gas slowly until you get the right carbonation. Finally start putting in syrup a little at a time until it tastes right.

If you try to vary all three at the same time, you'll never know which of the three is too strong, which too faint. You'll be going back and forth across the intersection of even allocation. When you start with nothing but water, however, you can feel when the carbonation is just right. And then the moment when the flavor is where it ought to be. You know that if you go beyond each point, you're only making things worse.

Of course, adjusting the drink machine was not my job. I got the spills.

You would think the pool of dark brown syrup on the stock room floor was a finite problem: you mop the floor, flush away the mess, rinse your equipment. But it's a lot like the famous tar baby of Uncle Remus (the more you have to do with it, the stickier it all becomes) and a lot like the oil spot in our family garage (it never seemed to be completely gone).

Coke syrup has the consistency of molasses. And no matter how careful I was, I couldn't help getting a little on my hands. From there it showed up on my face or in my hair. And the cement floor of the stock room, already stained by previous spills, seemed to be producing Coke syrup even after I had mopped up Ruth's spill. Every time I rinsed, the water turned brown again.

Happily, by 5:30 I had finished all my chores and was on my way to, I hoped, a perfect balance of all desires: Mr. Simpson's for a recovering daughter; Patty's for a passing grade in math; and mine for going steady with the upper classes. (You can decide which of these is gas, water, flavor!)

24

"You don't play sports, do you, Hugh?" asks my host Mr. Simpson as we all sit around the living room before dinner. Patty rests on the sofa, propped by extra cushions. Her legs are tucked under her.

"Uh, yes, I do. I'm on the tennis team."

"He's their best player," adds Patty. Neither of us mentions who had been number one. Patty has wrapped her arms around her middle and occasionally rubs her sides gently. I assume she's testing the soreness from her injuries.

Mr. Simpson seems a bit surprised by my answer. "Tennis? That's interesting. The players used to wear long, white pants when I was young. Do they still do that?"

"Oh, no. We wear shorts and T-shirts. The school provides them for us. They have eagles on them." Now I think I see his interest, the clothes. Perhaps he thinks he can get the contract to supply the school. "I think they look pretty good, though."

"Yes," says Mr. Simpson with an odd chuckle. "Heh, heh! I can see that you would."

I know that my host played football and basketball in high school and college, but I don't know whether he ever tried tennis. It was generally thought in those days that large men did not make good tennis players. Speed and agility were primary assets, not strength.

"Daddy, Hugh looks great playing tennis. And he's really good." Patty shifts her position on the sofa. I see her face stiffen. It must hurt.

"Well," I say to Mr. Simpson, thankful for Patty's support, "I have worked hard on my game."

"I wouldn't think it takes much work," says Mr. Simpson. "There's not much to it." Of course, I want my good qualities to come out here, and I don't fully understand Mr. Simpson's remarks.

"We hit off the backboard a lot, trying to perfect our strokes. And a good serve takes practice."

Mrs. Simpson, an attractive, small woman, excuses herself to see about the dinner.

I try another tack. "I like sports, but I'm also trying to do well in my studies. Math is my best subject."

"Ah, that's right," says Patty's father. "You've been tutoring Patty. Girls aren't very good at math, you know."

"We do other things, Daddy. I received the highest score for kitchen design in home economics."

"Yes. And you're a big help at the store."

"Dinner's ready," says Mrs. Simpson quietly from the doorway. And she leads us to the dining room.

I am a bit anxious about this portion of the evening. I've learned to small talk pretty well on my way up the social ladder. So sitting together in the living room hasn't been that hard for me. But now trickier rules of behavior come into play. And someone from Black Street doesn't always have the right training for dining properly.

I'm also nervous about Patty's condition, as she does move cautiously. She doesn't seem like the same girl who vaulted through a hoop in front of a crowd of excited basketball fans. Or someone who will appreciate a boy who is building his own airplane.

Everything I think of Patty doing now seems to threaten her tender midsection. I imagine trying to straighten out her landing on the tumbling mat, but I certainly couldn't grab her by the waist. Climbing into The Spirit of St. Louis II, she might bump her side against the plane's fuselage, and the thought makes me shudder. Or, if we've parked in somebody's borrowed car after a movie and I lean across to kiss her, won't her rib cage crunch up against the armrest?

At dinner, though, Mr. Simpson provides me with a more comfortable image of his daughter.

"Hey, that reminds me. Have you talked to Hugh about working with us?"

"I haven't had the chance, Daddy. You've had me home resting since . . . since the accident. And at school I'm supposed to avoid any straining. Hugh and I aren't in the same classes."

"What do you want me do, Mr. Simpson?" I'm eager to help here, even though I don't know what he's talking about.

"What I want to do in a couple of weeks is give everyone in town a look at my summer line. It won't be exactly like a New York fashion show, but we'll try to be entertaining."

I have a vague idea of what is involved in a fashion show. In my mind's eye, I see a series of models in elegant dresses parade down a runway. Flashbulbs go off, and a sea of smiling faces studies the shapes and colors of the new season.

"I see. Would you like me to help set up?" Always the stock boy, I can't see any other contribution I might make to a fashion show.

"No, that's taken care of. You tell him, Patty."

"Well, Daddy's going to get me and some of my friends to wear some of the new clothes. Not model, really, just have them on so Daddy can point the outfits out to customers." I have an immediate mental picture of Patty in a two-piece summer outfit--her navel exposed. Since models stand alone, her precious middle is not threatened.

"OK." Of course, I still don't see how I would be involved. Perhaps I would be serving refreshments?"

"I have clothes for men, too, Hugh. You're slim, and clothes look nice on you. I could use you as a model."

Whoa! This really takes me for a loop. Men don't model; that's a woman's role. Even if it's not coming down a walkway under the gaze of several hundred observers, I don't see myself standing around as a living mannequin. In fact, I see a lot of unhappy similarities between my modeling and my being the safety net for the school's cheerleaders! Even though Robert Paterson's gone, I don't need to supply anyone from his set with more ammunition for ridicule.

"I don't think I'd be very good at this. In my family. . . ." I hesitate. I don't want to say that the Noones make their own clothes or that they get them through the Sears catalog.

"You'd be with me, Hugh," offers Patty. "After all, aren't you my . . . well, you're my math tutor and . . . friend." She smiles and raises her eyebrows in my direction.

Her father, who doesn't see the look she gives me, says, "You know, there's a key to a successful show like this. Careful preparation, of course. And having the right people for the show. But there's a shape to the event, if it's done correctly."

"Oh?"

180

"Sure. I'll have the show in our store. The models will be in the area where their outfits are available. Patty in women's formal wear. You, say, in men's casual."

"Ah." I like the idea that I'm among "men," not "boys."

"We make everyone comfortable with some refreshments," he continues. "Soft drinks, tea, that sort of thing. And then have cookies and little sandwiches all around. Let the guests just meander about, visit with each other, relax."

"Don't forget the music," offers Mrs. Simpson. This is one of the few things she says all evening.

"Right. It's there, but in the background. Not distracting."

"'Moon River''s a nice song," offers Patty. I recall our dancing together to that tune at the sock hop.

"And then, just at the right moment, I announce that from this time on, everything is, say, 25 percent off. Only for those in the store right then, of course. If we've set everything up right, most of the people who've come end up buying at least one item. They've been in the store enjoying our hospitality long enough that they feel they owe us something. They've gone too far to just walk away. I usually make enough money to pay for the show on the same day."

I like all this store-running advice, especially now that I'm thinking of myself as a future businessman. "I guess I can do it," I find myself proclaiming.

"Great," says Mr. Simpson. "You'll get a chance to show yourself to a lot of important people in town. Who knows where things might lead from such an encounter?"

I hadn't thought about it that way, but perhaps he was right. I could be nearing a crucial moment in my relationship to the entire town, a point of transformation from laborer (stock boy) to something more (model, advertiser, promotions expert). Will this dinner be remembered for the resumption not only of my relentless climb up the social ladder but also my equally impressive ascent to commercial respectability?

Perhaps my willingness to go along with Daddy's scheme makes it easier for Patty to take me away to their den after dinner. (There is, by the way, no pool table for me to bunny hop around. But the pine-paneled room does have a game table, a TV, and a stereo.) On the surface, we're studying triangulation.

"You must be sore," I offer.

"It's not bad. Sometimes it's hard to get comfortable." She adjusts herself on a sofa, again her feet drawn up under and cushions beside her. I'm standing beside her with her math book.

"You know, at the dance that night, before . . . ," I say.

"Yes?" She looks up at me.

"We were talking . . . about . . . about, well, that we've been seeing a lot of each other."

She helps me out nicely here. "Our going steady?"

"Yes. I still want to. Do . . . do you? Are we?"

She pats the sofa for me to sit at arm's length.

"Yes," she says and reaches out her left hand to touch my right resting on the back of the sofa. "But Daddy is so protective. We can't *say* we're going steady. And, besides, at school, everyone makes such a big deal about these things. We just won't go out with anyone else."

"All right."

"But to be fair, I have something for you to wear. So you'll know." She reaches into a pocket of her dress.

"To wear?" I'm surprised, but pleased.

"It has our initials on it." She drapes a silver identification bracelet around my wrist. It's a heavy silver chain with a rectangular name plate about an inch long in one section. The top of the plate lifts up, and I see engraved there the letters "H.N.P.S."

"Wow!"

"Now," she says with another smile. "Now you can kiss me."

25

For someone with cracked ribs, Patty was quite a kisser.

She stayed curled up in her corner, but, once I leaned across to kiss her, she wrapped her arms around my neck and held me to the task. As for me, well, this wasn't an unpleasant task.

After a while, though, one of Patty's arms slipped from around my neck, and she began to rub my shoulder, my side, my hip, my leg. It occurred to me that, if I wasn't careful, she might repeat her little maneuver from the movie theater.

"Should we look at your math?"

"Maybe in a minute."

I wanted to caress her the way she was massaging me, but I was afraid to touch anywhere that might be bruised.

"Your mother's some good cook." We had had country-fried steak, mashed potatoes, a vegetable casserole, homemade rolls.

"I haven't been very hungry."

I risked my hand on her thigh. After all, there had been no mention of injury to her legs. Through the fabric of jeans I could feel the muscles that propelled her off the trampoline. On the other hand, so to speak, her parents were just upstairs.

"I'm not hurting you?"

"I'm OK."

Eventually I became more aggressive. She really had little mobility. And I'd begun to heat up. I was about to put aside completely the strategy of slow courtship inspired by Miss Timmons when I ran into a snag. Literally. My new bracelet caught on the edge of her pocket.

"Whoops!" Making it into a joke, I tug gently. "Let me go."

"It's just a loose thread. Break it."

"You kids want a Coke or something?" Yikes! It's Mrs. Simpson at the top of the stairs.

We say we're fine, but this interruption is not good for the mood we'd been trying to maintain. My focus is beginning to blur, though, not just because of Mrs. Simpson, or Patty's restricted movement, or my tentativeness because of her injuries. I've also run into handedness again.

Patty had snapped the bracelet onto my left hand (like most lefties, I wear my wristwatch on the right). But that was the hand I was leading with in this petting session, and, from the moment she snapped the clasp shut, my new piece of jewelry was distracting. I had felt it hanging, heard it jingling, seen it glittering in the path of my advance. This silver bauble made my hand conspicuous to me. Its catching on her clothes made me feel even more that it was in the way.

There may have been other associations playing around in the back of my mind, times when my left-handedness had caused me to feel awkward. I was always embarrassed when someone caught me turning the crank of an elementary school's pencil sharpener with left hand crossed over to the right. And I was also laughed at in shop class for rotating the old brace and bit counterclockwise, taking it out of the wood, not in.

I don't believe I was thinking all the way back to my young childhood, when I'd reached out to my mother's breasts with that my instinctive hand only to have it struck down by my stepfather. But who knows?

In the end, the difficulties caused by the bracelet, as well as the recurring appearances of Mrs. Simpson, put an end to our making out on that night.

Still, with some qualifications, I had advanced my cause quite a bit overall, I thought. I'd solidified our arrangement of going steady, though I wasn't sure I liked the idea of keeping it secret. What I wanted was public recognition that I no longer was tied to Black Street.

I had agreed to help out the family business by modeling in the fashion show, and that seemed to put me on good terms with Patty's parents. But I wasn't completely happy about displaying Mr. Simpson's clothes at a public gathering.

I also came home at a reasonable hour, pleasing my mother. Henry was still out. In fact, he didn't come in until early morning, quite drunk. Fortunately, he was so drunk he got as far as his bed and fell into a deep sleep. He was still there when I left to see Karen Murphy in mid-afternoon.

Karen had probably been looking for me. When, riding Black Beauty, I pulled under the Murphys' carport, she stepped out the kitchen door to meet me.

Perhaps sensing that I would be nervous if her father was around, she quickly explained that her parents had gone for a Sunday drive. I was nervous in general with Karen, given our former times of sexual experimentation. Now that she'd become a born-again Christian, I hoped she would see we had no potential for a lasting relationship. She was now, I felt, Billy's girl.

She was baking oatmeal cookies and invited me to sit at the table and sample as they came from the oven. While I watched, she moved a batch of partially cooled cookies from a baking sheet to a strip of wax paper on the table.

"What do you see out there?" asked Karen, gesturing through the window by my side. It looked over a backyard and to countryside beyond. After another block, St. James Street turned into a gravel lane, and you were outside the town limits.

"See? Oh, I don't know. Fields, fences, a barn. What am I supposed to see?" I looked at her taking spoonfuls of cookie dough and placing them onto a second baking pan.

"I see the straight way and the crooked path."

"Where St. James Street is straight and the cow tracks are crooked?" She opened the oven door, slipped in the sheet, spun the dial on a little timer. Her skirt was tight across her bottom as she bent down to open and close the oven door.

"I see where God wants you to go, and where Satan lays his traps." This was sounding a lot like my own idea of Route 66 for the good guys and detours down Black Street for people like me.

"Ah, Karen, you know I don't think that way. There's no such thing as the devil. That's superstition." She sat at the table.

"Do you believe in sin and evil?"

"Yes, there's doing wrong, hurting people. But you're not going to tell me evil caused the crash, are you?" She took a cookie from the wax paper and offered it to me.

"No. But it did lead to the crash."

"Didn't Billy just try to beat the train? And the Petting Mach--. . . and the car didn't accelerate?"

"Billy was being tempted."

"Tempted to drive recklessly?"

"Tempted to want me."

"Oh, well, I don't know. . . ." As she leaned earnestly toward me, her ample breasts pressed on the table. I *did* know how Billy could be tempted.

"Robert and Linda were being tempted too."

"Robert and Linda?"

"And I'm worried about you, Hugh. Do you know why you *weren't* in that car?"

"I had to take my scooter home. What do you mean, Robert and Linda?" The timer dinged, and she jumped up to take the cookies out.

"Do you know why I wasn't hurt? Hugh, God was looking out for me. God has another plan for me. And for you." She was spooning cookie dough to the first baking pan. She handed me the spatula and told me to start moving cookies from the second pan to another sheet of wax paper she'd put on the table in front of me.

"Listen, I'm glad you weren't hurt. But others were, and they were churchgoers too."

"Look at this." She reached under her blouse and pulled out the thin gold chain with a tiny cross I had seen the night we played Tip the Scales. "I always have this on, you know. I had it on that night."

I was beginning to tire of this little Sunday school meeting we were having. Karen was a nice girl, nicer probably than Patty or Linda. But I had no interest in her religious theories. If there was a God looking out for folks, he wouldn't let Satan kill some people just for the

188

sport of it. He'd take Satan out of the game from the very beginning.

"Karen, I know this was a terrible experience for you. But I think some bad luck, and some bad timing, are what's responsible. I'm glad you're OK."

"Hugh, I want you to wear this." She took her chain off and pushed it at me.

"I can't. That's yours. From your preacher, right?"

"I have others. Please, take it."

"Really, I wouldn't wear it. You should give it to Billy."

"He doesn't need it now. You do. You don't have to tell anyone."

"It would be awkward. I can't wear something like that."

"You don't have to wear it. Just keep it on you. Take it."

To my surprise, I did take it. I wasn't sure then why I did, though I could identify some of the reasons. For one thing, I figured I could take the silly necklace, pretend to wear it, leave it at home. Karen would never know the difference.

Too, maybe I did have a tiny little superstitious fear deep inside me, not that God was out to punish me, but, hey! why risk insulting whatever forces ruled the universe?

Karen was also an attractive persuader. She seemed somehow more mature there in her parents' kitchen than she'd been before. Perhaps just knowing how close she had come to death had changed her. Or changed my perception of her. I didn't know.

But there was one other thing. I'm not sure how long it was after this Sunday that I figured it out, but Karen had gotten to me when she handed me the spatula. You see, replaying that scene in my memory, I realized something very important: she had put it in my left hand. And it wasn't accidental, her right hand just going straight out to meet my left as I faced her. She had taken my left hand with her left hand and placed the spatula in it with her right.

Was this instinctive? Deliberate? Random? Well, now I think I know. It *was* part of a plan. Maybe not exactly the plan as Karen saw it, but it was part of my destiny, the course my life was doomed to take.

Oh, yes; when that secret left-handed young man, who was hidden deep inside my right-handed public self, took a cookie-scraping spatula from the hands of an earnest young churchgoer, it was a landmark in my life's course.

One other thing: there's no handedness to necklaces. They hang there right in the middle.

26

Although I had been somewhat uncomfortable at Karen Murphy's house, it turns out I was just about equally uncomfortable at home. Henry was up, and Henry was mad.

He'd been caught asleep on the job by his boss. This, of course, was not the first time. And now he'd been given what Sergeant Pritchard called his "final warning."

I could hear my parents as I came in through the kitchen.

"That son of a bitch is out to get me." Slouched in the easy chair in the living room, Henry was trying to ease his hangover with Alka Seltzer and whining. A baseball game was on the television, with the sound turned down.

"We can't afford to lose that job, Henry." Mom was ironing in the kitchen, but they could hear each from where they were.

"Hi," I offered, trying to just pass by to my room. I hoped to study the book on flying a sailplane I'd received through the mail. I felt I was getting close enough to finishing the construction to make plans for actual flight.

"Hey! You get those groceries?" Henry called to me.

"Yes, Pop. Mom and I put them all away last night."

"That's right, Henry. I'm cooking a meatloaf for your dinner right now."

"Yeah, well, we got to make every dollar count around here. We don't know how much longer the old man is going to be able to bring in the dough. That damn Pritchard!"

Here my mom became more assertive than usual. "You have to keep that job, Henry. Hugh wants to go to college."

I wished Mom hadn't brought this up now, as Henry didn't like to think of me going beyond his own high school education. And the idea of additional expenses was sure to anger him. To his mind, I should be out on my own after graduation. He thought I was too small for the military, but he figured I could get work in construction, especially if I could build my own plane.

"The kid can go to college. He just needs to keep working at Rexall's and get him some of those student loans."

"We don't have to think about that now, Pop. I've got four more months of high school." Actually, with Mom's help, I had already sent in my application to the University of Missouri, but we'd agreed there was no need to tell Henry until later. She'd saved the application fee from her washing money, though we had no clear notion of how to pay for tuition. The whole idea of going to college, of course, was part of my scheme to rise up the social ladder, to leave Black Street.

Henry turned the sound up on the ball game, and I moved on to my room. It seemed that we could avoid a family battle for now, though this was one we'd have to fight eventually.

My book on gliding was a wonderful escape from such painful matters. It also gave me relief from Karen Murphy's concern for my salvation. (I tucked the necklace into an old cigar box, where I kept things I couldn't throw away but didn't use often). Even my romance with recovering Patty faded into the background of my fantasies for a time as I imagined myself soaring over Ozark hills in The Spirit of St. Louis II.

Of course, after a while one more nagging worry made its way into my daydreaming: Gary Hamilton and the nine ball tournament. I needed this pilot's help with my glider, but I didn't want to turn against my old tennis coach, Doc Garnet. I was, remember, supposed to provide sufficient distraction at the tournament that Doc Garnet would lose to Hamilton. I had some time to study my options, but no clear path appeared before the end of that Sunday night.

In fact, no clear path appeared before me all week. I worked my nights at Rexall's (no cash register duty then), and went to school each day (unremarkable except for Miss Timmons's class). Because Patty was still dropped off right before school and then driven home at the end of the day, I only saw her one evening, Wednesday. I stopped by around 4:00 for a quick tutoring session.

She told me the fashion show her dad was planning would be the following Friday. I was still ready to please, but I can't say I looked forward to this event.

The nine-ball tournament was usually an all-day affair at Ray's. The preliminary rounds went slowly Saturday morning because of the limited number of tables. Some matches, where the most deliberate players took time to study every shot, often held up subsequent rounds. Once the field had been narrowed, however, by the elimination of three-fourths of the players, the competition moved speedily toward its conclusion late that afternoon.

Ray cut down the number of tables to two for the quarterfinals. And the crowd of spectators was swelled by the band of defeated players. So, by afternoon, the hall had been transformed from a sea of little competitions with only a handful of spectators to a central stage on which a few players battled before a host of onlookers. In the end probably forty to fifty people circled the challenge table for the semifinals and the finals.

I timed it about right, arriving just after lunch. I had come to work early that day and promised to return to Rexall's from 6:00 to 8:00 to make up for my time away. I got to Ray's just before the quarterfinals began.

Nine ball, by the way, is a game I have never liked. While it appears to have order--you shoot the balls in numerical sequence, one through nine--the order is almost always violated. You see, the game is won by the player who sinks the nine ball. And this usually happens on a combination. That is, you're shooting the six ball, say, and you knock it into the nine ball, which goes into the pocket--you win. In this case, then, the six through eight balls never go down.

I believe in sequence myself, in going step by step to the end. And I like to know where I stand in the process, the point from which--given the most recent act--all other events must proceed. But nine ball is chaotic, unpredictable, incalculable. The nine might go down at the break (though that's rare), or after the three, or at the end. You just never can tell.

You can also think you're in control of a game by sinking all the balls in order up through the eight. But if you miss on the nine, and your opponent sinks just that one ball, you lose the whole thing. It's a game that can be won by eccentrics, people who do things on a whim, gamblers who go against the odds.

It made sense to me that Gary Hamilton would like nine-ball. Since high school he had ignored most of the rules. He should have pursued a career in professional sports. While he might not have had the skill to play at the highest levels himself, he had the contacts and the knowledge of the game. He also could have stayed in the Air Force. A decorated fighter pilot, he seemed to be wasting his abilities running a charter passenger and cargo service out of this small town.

But why Miss Timmons would like Gary or nine ball made less sense to me. Here was the perfect believer in order, in numerical sequence, in logical progression--a math teacher. Even her advice to me, one of her many students, to "go slow," seemed to be contradicted by an appreciation of the erratic, unpredictable game of nine ball, or the erratic, unpredictable life of Gary Hamilton. But there she was by his side again when he met Doc Garnet for the championship match.

Now the moment of truth was coming for me: would I cooperate with Hamilton by distracting Doc Garnet? Or would I return my tennis mentor's kindness by remaining a quiet and respectful spectator?

I tried to work my way up to the front row of onlookers as the match was beginning. I had hoped, I guess, to size up the situation and go with my instincts.

When I finally slipped around a former football teammate of Hamilton's--not as tall, but even more wide--I found myself directly behind Doc Garnet. On the other side of the table stood both his opponent and, once gain, my math teacher, Miss Timmons. There were far too many people here who knew me and expected things of me!

Hamilton, bending over to make the break, saw me and nodded his head deliberately in my direction.

Without even looking around, Doc Garnet said, "Hello there, Hugh." I didn't see how he could have known I was there!

Then he turned toward me as Hamilton broke up the pack, sending balls careening off the cushions. The six went down. It was still Hamilton's turn.

"I heard about Paterson, the tennis player. Terrible thing. I know you're taking it hard."

"I . . . it . . . he didn't have a chance." I didn't know what to say. Hamilton had sunk the one and the two. Then he made the nine on a combination off the three.

Garnet had stepped into the row of observers, looking occasionally to the side to record Hamilton's scoring. (The first to win fifteen games would win the match.)

"You're still playing tennis, I hope?"

"Well, the spring season doesn't start for another month, but I am going to get out soon, you know, start hitting."

"Let me hear. I'll come watch, maybe hit some with you."

"Great. I'd like that." Hamilton won two more games as Garnet chatted with me. He questioned me about my serve, if I was still tossing straight overhead. He recalled a rival of his youth, who'd had to retire early because of a leg injury. He wondered whether America was going to produce any real rivals to the great Australians dominating the game.

Then Hamilton had to play safe. The cue ball was positioned so that he had no chance to hit the five ball after he'd sunk the four. He left it similarly blocked for Garnet.

Doc continued to speak to me as he moved around the table, looking at the lie his opponent had left him. Then he struck the ball in what looked to me exactly the wrong direction: into the corner farthest from the five ball he was supposed to sink.

But the old billiards player knew what he was doing: the ball banked out of the corner, reversed directions, bounced off the side cushion, and collided with the five, knocking it into the corner pocket at the far end of the table.

He began to talk to me about rivals he had played in billiards and in call shot. When he passed in front of me to take another stroke, he patted me on the shoulder. He gestured in my direction as he studied the arrangement of balls. From a crouched position over his cue, cigar firmly clamped in his mouth, he winked at me. He won fifteen straight games and the match.

27

Let me assure you that Gary Hamilton was an excellent pool player. I would learn later that he had not been seriously challenged by anyone before he reached the finals. Doc Garnet was simply playing at another level.

There was, then, no chance to "distract" this long-time medical man and veteran pool player. He was like the grand master at chess who defeats a roomful of people simultaneously. Walking confidently from one player to the next, he quickly looks over each board, makes the single move among all the possibilities that will eventually defeat his opponent, then moves on. Once Hamilton missed that one time, Doc Garnet swept through rack after rack.

I came off rather luckily, then. It seemed to Hamilton that I had cooperated with him, though I had really only responded to Doc Garnet's questions, comments, and observations. He had no reason to renege later on his promise of help with my glider. To top it all off, Doc Garnet agreed to give me some more informal tennis lessons before the season opened.

In the weeks which followed I did occasionally have some twinges of guilt about my role in the nine ball tournament, as if I had, after all, tried to undermine Doc Garnet's concentration. I couldn't always identify the source of that bad feeling, the sense that I had done something wrong.

It may have had something to do with Miss Timmons. I had realized that she was not at Gary's side by accident. There had been a dreamy look in her eye at Ray's Racks while she watched this former star athlete and war hero compete. Before much longer it became fairly well known throughout Fairfield that the two were dating. Some even speculated that marriage was probable.

But I didn't know if marriage would be good for this intense young educator, who had pulled even me out of obscurity to become a student of some promise. Would a hard-working, idealistic teacher suddenly begin to lose her energy in a romance with a man who seemed to have very little ambition? Would her steady rise in popularity with students, parents, and administrators halt when it was learned she was spending time in the pool hall rather than at concerts and dinner theaters?

These possibilities made me wonder if my presence had been somehow a catalyst in her attraction to the local fly boy. Was there a connection between her interest in a poor student and her attraction to the underachieving aviator? Committed to strict convention in her own behavior, she was also drawn to the rebel, to the one who didn't always fit in.

I gave these modest feelings of guilt about Miss Timmons's fate some play in the following week, but not too much. I had a fashion show to get ready for. And my wooing of the slim waisted Patty Simpson and her social position was a more significant item for my attention than the life of my high school math teacher.

I spent more time that week, however, with my old friend Billy Rhodes than with my girlfriend. He was ecstatic to have had the casts on both arms significantly reduced, freeing up two fingers and a thumb for wiggle room and unlocking an elbow to flexibility. Up to this point, he'd been helpless at the most routine activities of eating, dressing, and--painful for an adolescent boy--personal hygiene.

I was glad to talk with a happier Billy, even about "Cross Rhodes." I wanted him to help erase the concern Karen had inspired. Her references to what everyone had been doing before the accident were, I assumed, products of her own religious enthusiasm. She had the typical convert's obsession with the idea that anything fun or pleasurable is a "sin." But my friend did not completely ease my mind on that score.

"I was trying to score with Karen," he said simply.

"OK. Well, who wouldn't be?" We were in his room at the back of the house. I had stopped by on my way home from school. Billy's major goal right then was relieving the itching under his casts. The skin gets really dry in there, and the lack of use makes the muscles restless.

"She seemed to like necking," Billy admitted. "But stopped me cold, anything below the waist."

"You like her?"

"Sure. You know. She's got one tight rump." He was poking a pencil between plaster and skin, the strain of not quite reaching the offending spot visible on his face. "But that Linda has the knockers."

"You're right about that. Hey, what was with her and Paterson? Were they together?"

"You mean, going steady? Or doing it?"

"Well, remember that time we saw him out Old Farm Road? Who was he with?"

"Hey, that's right! It couldn't have been Linda. She went with the other girls." He was swinging the arm most covered in plaster gingerly back and forth, trying to get the cast to rub against areas that were bothering him.

"Yeah. So was he two-timing her?"

200

"I don't think so. They were pretty close back there in the back of the Petting Machine. Karen said something to them about keeping their hands off each other. And something else."

"What?"

"She said their 'little scheme' wasn't going to work. And it was immoral. Hey, can you blow in here?" He held up the arm he couldn't bend and that he couldn't have reached with his mouth.

"I'm not blowing in there, you homo! What scheme was Karen talking about?"

"I have no idea. But she said that whatever they had done already, they would have to own up to."

"You heard that?"

"Yeah. Well, you know, I wasn't saying much, just listening. I was cruising. The mind in neutral." He stood up from the bed and starting hopping up and down. He couldn't stand the itching.

Suddenly, I realized I was supposed to be at work in ten minutes. I left Billy trying to unbend a coat hanger so that he could fashion an effective tool to scratch the inside of his elbow.

I had a lot of sympathy for my friend. Not only was there the accident itself. And the fact that he couldn't drive now. But the whole process of recovery was full of these minor but irritating little problems like itching, things that might seem to stand for your larger sins, but don't have any solutions either.

I hate itches myself. Some insect bites can drive me crazy, but poison ivy's the worst.

In those days, it was like a blow to the stomach when I saw the first poison ivy blister rising on my skin where I'd been mindlessly scratching just the moment before. I would not even be thinking about what I was doing one minute, the next I knew it would be weeks before I could be free of torment. I would rack my brain to recall how I'd gotten into the stuff, the point my suffering could be traced back to. But most of the time I had no idea where or when the contact had occurred.

One of the few positive features of my present environment--jail, that is--is that I never encounter poison ivy. Although this is a low-security establishment, most everything is paved in concrete, surrounded by cement block walls topped with barbed wire. There are plenty of other irritations here, of course, but I don't worry about finding myself in contact with that distinctive pattern of three green leaves.

Pulling away from Billy's to go tell Mom I would eat something after work, I thought about all he'd told me. Something had been going on with Linda and Robert--that was sure--but what? Was it ended with his death? Would whatever they were doing get in the way of my possible life as a businessman in Fairfield? Or of my courtship of Patty?

Unfortunately, I had to abandon my contemplation of possibilities once I arrived at Rexall's: right at closing, Ruth had spilled a second bottle of Coke syrup.

What made this accident even worse than the last was its location. The storeroom's concrete floor could survive stains, and all our supplies were kept up on wooden frames to avoid water or other spills. But this time Ruth had lost control of the gallon jug directly behind the counter where the drink machines were. This three-foot-wide strip running behind the counters and the booths where customers sat was now covered with sticky syrup. And there wasn't much room to operate in there.

Ruth and her co-worker, Margot, had abandoned their posts when the bottle hit the floor. So, before I could get the mop and bucket out, the syrup had spread into many a crack and corner.

I realized my entire night of work would probably be taken up trying to get the mess cleaned up. The tile floor had been cleaned and recently waxed (by me, of course), so Coke syrup spread easily over the smooth surface. I knew I would mop and mop, but still find sudsy water turning brown as it splashed on and around the cabinets, under the counter and against the wall.

In the first hour, I got up the standing puddles of half-dried syrup. But brown liquid continued to ooze out from along the base of the cabinets. I let the mop sit under a faucet in the back with the water running to get it clean. And I wiped off the cabinet doors, checking to see into which sections the syrup had dripped or spread. Then I resumed mopping.

Of course, I often recalled, as I worked, the garage floor at home, where the family Buick's oil stain resisted all my efforts to bring it up. In the racket the bucket made as I shoved it from place to place, I almost heard my stepfather's angry instructions to put some weight into my scrubbing, elbow grease!

Then, in the varying areas of water, bubble, stain, and floor I began to see shapes. It was like finding sheep in clouds. At one time I thought I saw the face of Karen Murphy. Was she entreating me to consider my own salvation? Then I imagined her offering one of her fine oatmeal cookies.

Did those two puddles resemble the hourglass shape of my girlfriend, navel marked by an island of drier floor? Or was I seeing Linda Roy's superb breast standing out in an expensive silk blouse as she rotated her shoulder?

When water sloshed along the floor and splashed into the base of a cabinet, did I see Cross Rhodes, a '49 Ford sent flying across the landscape by a roaring freight train? Surely those weren't passengers bumping around inside the twisted automobile! Patty's crushed ribs, Linda's lacerated face and hands, Billy's broken arms. Robert Paterson, dead, dead, dead.

Was it possible, I suddenly wondered that, in these last days and weeks, I had been all along mourning Robert Paterson?

28

When I went to bed that night, the images of people I knew and recent events continued to haunt my consciousness. I strained to concentrate on The Spirit of St. Louis II flying high over Fairfield, maybe away toward an entirely new place.

I also thought of myself with Patty at the fashion show her father was planning. What would she wear? Surely, nothing with a bare midriff yet. Though she was healing with the speed and soundness of youth, her father would hardly want to display the belly of an accident victim before the town's important citizens when he was trying to sell them clothes. Still, I fantasized about the current center of my universe-- contemplating her navel.

Billy Rhodes slid in and out of my wakefulness too. I imagined myself caught in the Petting Machine while he headed on his route out highway 00. In my semi-conscious state I knew this was bad. Not just because I preferred to be with girls, Patty especially. And not merely because I would have to endure a pointless out-and-back drive. But also because there was an ominous feeling that he wasn't paying any attention to crossing traffic!

The next afternoon I stopped by Patty's house for a tutoring session. She was becoming more active every day now, though her mother especially insisted that she wasn't ready for the rigorous activity of cheerleading.

As usual, I pulled up to the Simpson house on Black Beauty, announcing to the whole neighborhood that I was there.

This motor scooter had had a muffler at one time, but when it disintegrated from corrosion, former owner Jimmy Coughlin simply put a metal sleeve in its place. From then on the engine's roar ran directly from the point of origin (the cylinder) down a straight exhaust pipe to announce to the world Black Beauty's arrivals and departures.

Patty and I spent some more time on the downstairs den sofa, though we remained wary of interruptions. We also made plans for the night of the fashion show. She was beginning to want to be out of the house more. And she thought in that crowd of people her father wouldn't be able to keep so close an eye on her.

"You know, there are six changing rooms in my father's store," she noted. We were sitting next to each other at a work table, math book and notebook open before us. "One of them is bound to be empty, and we can sneak in there for a little pilot and co-pilot activity."

"Come on! The store'll be full of people."

"We could slip out the back, then, and go over to Rexall's. You have a key to the storeroom, don't you?" She was supposed to be calculating the volumes of cylinders with radius x and height y.

"I do not." Actually, I did. Mr. Wicker sometimes wanted to be able to send me down there on errands without leaving home himself. He said he trusted me, but he kept a very accurate inventory too. "But maybe I can walk you home afterward. And your parents will still be downtown."

"I'm going crazy staying in so much. If I don't get out soon, I'll reach a bursting point!" She reached down and grabbed my thigh with a firm grip.

I had to get out of the house myself! Not out with Patty, but away from her for right now. We were just

206

going to get in trouble with her parents here, and my mother expected me for dinner.

Miss Timmons's advice had generally kept me under control with Patty. And her injuries had insured against too much contact for the past several weeks. But I was only human, and the daredevil reappearing in her was going to break down the last of my defenses pretty soon!

Also, with Henry's sour mood and more frequent drinking these days, I felt I should be checking on my mom more often. So I had to get a move on.

That doesn't mean that Patty and I weren't able to heat up the downstairs den with some heavy petting before I left. But both of us were looking to do this in other circumstances. I got her back to geometry a final time, then staggered out to Black Beauty. Some cold wind in the face on the way home helped cool the flames of passion. Ah, the old scooter served well in some ways!

"Where's Pop?" I asked Mom when I came through the kitchen of our little house on Cedar Street.

"Henry's gone."

"Bowling on a Wednesday night?"

Her silence suggested he was at the Top Hat again. She was working at the sink.

"How is your airplane coming? It looks almost finished back there." She gestured out the kitchen window.

"There are some instruments to install." In fact, I hadn't earned enough money for the altimeter yet. And I felt several more coats of shellac would insure against wear.

"I went flying once," said Mom. Now she was putting food on plates for us, the warmed over mashed potatoes, ham, and green beans Henry had had when he came home from work that morning.

"You did?" This was a surprise, although I actually knew fairly little about my mother's past. She had been orphaned in childhood, raised by a spinster aunt who passed away when she was in high school. But she seldom talked of her life. When she spoke, it was to remind me of chores or to tell Henry about the bills that were due (or overdue). Her life was generally concentrated on clothing and feeding her men.

"It was at the county fair. Years ago, with . . . with your father."

"My father?"

"Richard wanted to fly, you know, just like you."

"Really?" I think I did know he'd tried to get in the Army Air Corps but ended up in the infantry. "Pass me that bread there." Store bought white bread was always a part of our evening meal, three to five pieces stacked on a saucer.

"There was a guy selling rides at the fair. Took off in the field right behind all the booths. Your father paid for us to go up, half an hour, right down Route 66."

"When was that?"

"Oh, we were, maybe, fifteen and sixteen. I didn't know that much about him then. And my aunt was still alive."

"What kind of plane?"

"It had one wing on top of the other. A crop duster. What do you call that?"

"A biplane. Open cockpit?"

"Open . . . ? No, the, uh, roof pulled over once you got in. Richard and I were squeezed together in the back seat."

"Ah, sliding cockpit cover. Did you like flying?"

"We could see all of Fairfield, the countryside, Route 66. I liked that. It was summer, fourth of July. Everything was so green down the highway. We live in a beautiful country, Hugh."

"Is there any dessert?"

"You can have some cookies." She took a package of Oreos down from the cabinet.

"You want to go up in my plane?" I asked.

"Oh, no." She laughed softly. "Richard showed me all I want to know. He even had the pilot do a stunt."

"Yeah? What stunt?"

"Loop-de-loop. I got dizzy."

"That's not an easy trick." Even kids knew about this aerial maneuver: the pilot climbs straight up, then pulls the plane over on its back, then down again to level flight, making a giant circle. "If she stalls going up, you're in big trouble. Once you commit to it, you have to go all the way."

"It didn't stall. But we were upside down."

"Well, that's the way it's supposed to be. You see," I swung my arm in a giant arc, "centrifugal force keeps you in your seat at the top of the loop. I think it's neat. Of course, you can't do that in a glider--no engine."

"You're not taking a girl up there with you, are you?"

"No, Mom. And it's still going to be a while before I'm ready just for the trial run. I need to finish the work, then wait for warmer weather and better updrafts."

"I want you to be careful, Hugh. It is safe, isn't it?"

"Oh, sure. I'm getting Hamilton, the charter pilot, to test it for me. He won't let me do anything without his OK." I was stretching Gary's role there, but mothers deserve peace of mind.

I thought for a moment about all that was still before me. I wasn't sure exactly what Gary Hamilton meant by "testing" the plane before actual flight. Perhaps this was just pulling the plane behind a car at modest speeds, not even freeing it from the tow rope. You would make sure all the parts are secure and that they function in the air.

"Your father did something when we were upside down."

"He did?"

She didn't respond.

"What did he do up there?"

"It was something he said."

"OK. What did he say?"

"He asked me to marry him."

"He proposed while you were looping the loop?"

"He said he'd make the pilot do it again if I didn't say 'yes.'"

"So what did you say?"

"I said 'yes.' I said I'd marry him, and I did. I never looked back from that moment until the day he . . . the day they told me . . . that he was gone."

She got up from the table and began clearing, stacking the dishes for later washing. I had to leave soon for work. But I added a new item to my concerns: was my mother worrying about losing her son after having lost a husband?

What a whirlwind romance her first marriage must have been, from county fair to bearing a son to widowhood in the span of months. That plane ride had been a pivotal moment in her young life, beginning a family but foreshadowing its breaking apart, loss of the father.

At that moment the black telephone on the kitchen wall sounded the two rings that meant it was for us. (We were on a party line.) Mom picked up the receiver.

"Hello. Yes, it is. He's where? OK. I'll come for him."

In answer to my inquiring look, she said, "It's Henry. He's at the Top Hat."

29

"I'll go," I volunteered. "I'm headed for work anyway. I'll get him home first and then go back downtown."

"You shouldn't. They say he's . . . he's been . . . difficult."

"He's been violent before. I know that. But I don't want you having to deal with it."

"No, it's OK. I've always. . . ."

This time I interrupted her. "I'm going." And I was out the back door.

This was one of those times I was glad I had my own means of transportation. Black Beauty roared up to the Top Hat within minutes.

I pulled into the alley beside the barbershop, spotting our Buick parked awkwardly at the end of the block, one tire up on the curb. I leaned my scooter against the building, then went down the stairs into a world I had never actually seen. This world was off-limits--but powerfully appealing--to teenagers.

Before I bought my motor scooter, I had walked everywhere I wanted to go. Fairfield was very much a small town of those innocent, post-war decades, so I traveled without fear. I knew just about every street and every block on that street, especially in the downtown area. I'd gone past the Top Hat, a bar beneath one of the town's two barbershops, hundreds of times. A neon sign, the top half of its letters darkened for as long as I could remember, pulsed at one corner of the white brick building. A dark alley ran along the west side.

The Top Hat was on 9th Street, which crossed Main in the southern end of downtown. The bar's entrance was at the bottom of a set of stairs in the sidewalk. A heavy wooden door with darkened panes of glass in the top half opened inward at the foot of the stairwell.

More times than I could count in my junior high and high school years, I had heard the juke box through the doorway as blue jeans-clad construction workers pushed into the establishment at quitting time. Young women who worked in the shoe factory east of town came in small groups on Friday and Saturday nights to unwind and perhaps speak with off-duty soldiers from nearby Fort Leonard Wood. And I'd seen the forms of shadowy waitresses, hair piled on top of their heads in the style of country-and-western singers, carrying trays of drinks through the smoky darkness of the ground level windows.

But actually to descend into those depths was to take a journey I don't think I had ever seriously contemplated.

True, it was my stepfather's regular drinking establishment. And I had pictured him many times before quite at home with his bowling buddies watching a television set up over the bar. Or I saw him generating a gruff chorus of laughter from a circle of other men (and their girlfriends?) with an off-color joke or a sarcastic comment about his boss. My mom had been to the Top Hat only a handful of times, always to drive him home in the family Buick when he'd had one too many.

At the top of the stairs I hesitated just a moment, listening to the steady rumble of bar talk, the brash competition of dart games, the occasional treble note of laughter from the booths along the side wall.

"Watch that first step--it's a doozy," I remembered one of the Three Stooges saying as another walked off a ledge many stories above street level (he landed safely in the back of a truck full of garbage). Would I be so lucky with this step down to the basement level of the Top Hat? I hoped I'd only get a bit dirtied in corralling Henry. I certainly knew, however, that, once into the Top Hat, there would be no turning back from a confrontation with my stepfather.

Pushing open the door, I drew looks from a bartender stacking mugs under the bar and a number of customers at the nearer tables. But I didn't wait for them to stop me, a minor, from coming in.

"I'm Hugh Noone," I told the bartender. "I've come to take Henry Maas home." The bartender nodded toward a booth in the front corner. I turned and saw my stepfather slumped back against the vinyl-covered seat, probably too drunk to stand. He might even have passed out. I knew from watching my mother deal with him in this state that he would be dead weight now, hard to get to his feet and harder still to move.

I saw something else as I turned from the bar to the booth where Henry sat. I saw it for only a second, an image that lodged in my memory and that I studied more carefully only later that night, after Henry was home and after I had stocked the shelves at Rexall's.

Henry called out, "Wha's he doin' here? He can't come 'n here."

I went quickly to stand in front of him. "Pop, it's time to come home." I was happy to see no barked knuckles on his large hands or a blackening eye, which would have indicated more trouble than I wanted to deal with. I assumed he'd been calmed down by other patrons and had never gotten completely out of control.

214

"I got . . . go work."

"That's hours from now. You need to get home, get some coffee."

He had not moved from his slouched position, and I began to wonder how, in fact, I was going to be able to transport someone so large up those steep front steps and out to the car. I needed emotional as well as physical leverage here.

"Where's Betty?" he asked, still not moving.

"She's not coming. I'll get you home."

I calculated again Henry's typical explosions. He always went quickly to a point of loud accusation-- someone had angered him, disappointed him, cheated him. Most often his temper then receded, and the worst would be behind us. Every once in a while, however, he went from that pause up a rapid ascent of rage. Had his self-pity slipped back to simmer? Or was his resentment about to escalate toward some new danger?

"I'm . . . uh . . . stay here. Not go home."

"Upsa-daisy!"

I had decided that discussion would not help my cause. I had to start Henry moving and keep him moving. So I took one arm by the wrist and pulled his upper body forward toward the end of the booth. Then I ducked under that arm so that I could hoist him on my shoulder.

Perhaps I just took him by surprise, I don't know. But he made an effort to stand, and my rising from a crouched position got him upright.

Well, not exactly standing. But at least to a 15-degree angle off the vertical, leaning on me, one heavy arm across my shoulder. And we started to walk.

I have sometimes been struck by the kindness of strangers. And this was one of those cases. Someone I didn't know, another Top Hat customer wearing work clothes and a crushed St. Louis Cardinals hat, slid off his barstool and stepped over to open the door for my staggering stepfather and me.

I maintained the momentum gained from rising and leaning in the right direction to pass by this Good Samaritan. I grunted my thanks but tried also to focus on the true challenge of this operation: getting a man twice my size up a baker's dozen steps to street level. From there on it would be downhill--literally and figuratively--to the Buick, to Cedar Street, to bed.

That's when the surprise occurred. Big Henry Maas woke up, if only for a matter of fifteen seconds. Just when I felt the extra energy I had generated from the sense of crisis being overcome by gravity as I tried to lift my left foot up to the third step of the Top Hat stairs, my stepfather sang out: "Whhuupp! Whhuupp!"

It was what he had called as a boy on the family farm at the end of the day, when the milk cow and her calf were being brought to the barn. And with that call he dropped his giant hand from my shoulder down to around my waist and together we raced up the rest of the stairs.

Whhuupp!! There we were at street level. We leaned to the left, where the Buick rested half a block away, just at the moment Henry's momentary transformation from bulk matter to animated human ended. But we were going in the right direction, and I got under his arm again to steady him past the parking meters, away from the storefronts, up against the passenger side front fender, where he leaned while I got the door open.

While I needed my mother's help at our house, I had Big Henry Maas stretched out on his own bed and was on my way to Rexall's before 7:00 that evening. I was an hour late for work, but I would just stay to make it up.

What had I seen when I first came into the Top Hat, as I turned from the bartender to the front booth filled with Henry? It was another woman's middle.

My obsession with bellies and navels had begun, remember, when I'd seen Gary Hamilton lifting a young woman by the waist in Ray's Racks to give himself room for a winning shot at the challenge table. And I'd known at that moment that I wanted my hands around the waist of high jumping cheerleader Patty Simpson, a dream date for someone of my social standing. I had later seen that hourglass figure outlined in flight above a trampoline set up on the gymnasium floor. Now one more erotic vision was launching my desire on to a greater goal.

One of the Top Hat's waitresses was stepping from behind the bar as I entered. With a trayful of beer mugs balanced deftly on her right palm, her left hand at the rim steadying the load, she was negotiating her way between two tables. Out of the corner of my eye I saw her raise the tray higher to avoid bumping the heads or shoulders of the customers in her path. That stretch pulled her short sweater up her rib cage. Large breasts above a flat tummy were outlined in the light from the far wall, and the tight waist of her full skirt followed the roundness of hips below.

Now, lest you misunderstand, let me say immediately that I did not desire this Top Hat waitress at the time I saw her, or later, after I had delivered Henry to Cedar Street and myself to Rexall's. No, when I saw her very attractive female form I was hit by another rush of desire for Patty, my similarly shapely girlfriend.

And I think that, at some level, I knew right then that I was about to throw to the winds Miss Timmons's go-slow policy. I wanted Patty Simpson, daredevil with healed ribs and a body hot to trot. Even more: I knew I would have her on the night of her father's fashion show.

30

Weeks after this incident, I asked myself why my mother had not resisted more forcefully my going to the Top Hat. She'd always been the one to take charge before.

Was it because she thought I was now old enough and strong enough to take on the difficult responsibility of bringing Henry home? Perhaps she hesitated to go herself because it had finally occurred to her that her husband had no right to make her walk downtown, help him into the family car, let him sleep it off in a comfortable bed. Or had she suddenly reached a point herself in a long and tiring marriage where she no longer had the energy or the will to forgive, forget, and keep on living?

The question would come back to me with even more force later that same year. But I would not learn the answer even then.

I tried similarly to figure out what sort of luck inspired my stepfather's sudden spurt of energy on the stairs leading up to 9th Street. Had his alcohol-befuddled brain short-circuited to the past, making him think he was the sixteen-year-old boy with a problem? (His problem would have been getting the cows in for milking.) Or had he all at once seen those thirteen steps as a difficulty of the present, a challenge he was determined to overcome? Or, somewhere deep in a troubled man's thinking, did he come to see the boy trying to help him as someone deserving assistance in his own right?

I never got a satisfactory answer in this case either because, from this point onward, events in my life began to move at a faster pace and in a direction I had not been predicting.

Of course, the fashion show was only two days later. And there, more than new clothes was revealed to me. I uncovered a major town secret.

Before that revelation, however, Patty had already, during one of our tutoring sessions, fired my imagination about what might occur. And she kept feeding fuel to my burning with several titillating phone calls.

"I like what Daddy has you wearing."

"Um, what's that?"

"It's a white sports jacket, with heavenly peach slacks."

Peach slacks?

"The shirt is a kind of red, and the tie is even brighter. But you'll also be wearing your bracelet, won't you?"

"Well, I guess so. What are you wearing?"

"For the show? Or for you later?"

"For me . . . ?"

"Whoops! Gotta go, Mom wants the phone."

An hour later, Patty called back. By then my imagination had made me a more aggressive conversationalist.

"I'm wearing a revealing top with tight black pants."

"Revealing?"

"Well, the neckline has a tendency to buckle out. . . ."

"I'll always be at your side."

"And my pants ride low on my hips . . . "

"I'll keep my arm around your waist."

"But I know you won't take advantage of me."

"Only if *you* won't take advantage of me!"

I had hoped to borrow the family car and drive Patty from home to the store (and from the store to somewhere else, like Old Farm Road). But my plans were rejected by both sets of parents.

Because I'd helped Henry home the other night, I thought I might have earned the use of the family car for one night. But Pop growled at me that he needed it for bowling.

"I'm still the guy paying for gas around here," he added, ignoring the fact that on those rare occasions when I had the car I filled it up at my own expense.

Of course, I later learned that Henry was really angry at Sergeant Pritchard and the world. The boss had threatened to fire my stepfather if he was caught sleeping on the job again.

I wouldn't have been able to take Patty downtown even if I'd had the Buick, though, as it turned out. Mr. Simpson insisted that his daughter needed to be at the store early to try out her outfit. Still, I worked on other plans about how we could be together before the night was over. I was counting on our desire to be alone and on the crowd to give us cover.

The forecast of numbers proved accurate, as probably one hundred townspeople came in the course of that Saturday evening. Among them, by the way, was Miss Timmons, this time appearing without her current flame, my aviation engineer.

Only one person surprised me by appearing at the "New Line Evening"--Linda Roy. I had heard that the cut on her forehead would leave a conspicuous scar, but on this occasion she covered it with a bold sweep of hair in a new style. My attention was drawn anyway, as of old, to her magnificent breasts, especially whenever she rotated that shoulder, lifting and settling one of God's finest creations.

Her outfit was as provocative as Patty's, which seemed odd, given the fact that she'd recently undergone fairly severe physical trauma. She wore an unusually tight skirt, which seemed to draw attention to her flat tummy, and a silk blouse that outlined her best features.

I will say, however, that I resisted the temptation to go to Linda as soon as I saw her. For my objective was still the glorious middle of the store owner's daughter. And how surprisingly conspicuous that middle was!

Patty had not exaggerated the gap between loose-fitting top and low-slung pants. Any reaching up or out she did generated a flash of flesh. The high heels she wore also accentuated the long line of her legs, the athletic build of an Eagle cheerleader. My overriding question of the night was when and where I could be alone with this superb specimen of young womanhood.

Of course, I had to put in my time as model myself-- pink slacks, bright tie, white jacket. Patty insisted that I show the bracelet also, especially to her father. So I put myself on display in the "casual dress" area, where Mr. Simpson pointed me out to a number of fellow businessmen.

Several times he brought to my area young men who struck me as--well--a bit effeminate. They touched me on the arm to say how much they liked the jacket. Or put a hand to their cheek to exclaim that they simply "loved" the shirt and tie.

I was not the center of attention for the whole crowd, though, as both Patty and Linda found themselves surrounded by men and women, old and young. People especially seemed to comment on Linda, although it was often in whispers, subdued and even a bit sorrowful. Of course, she had been in a fatal car crash. But she had also recovered and looked absolutely fabulous. What were they saying about her?

I put Linda out of my mind, however, when Mr. Simpson finally announced the surprise sale. He was offering all the outfits everyone had seen at 25 percent off, and the rest of his stock at 10 percent off. There was, as he had predicted, a flurry of activity from that moment until the end of the night.

When even he had to help handle sales, Patty took my hand and led me to her father's office.

"Not here!" I exclaimed.

"Here," she insisted and opened the door to a small rest room in one corner. It was just a toilet and a sink, with barely room for the two of us to stand. But Patty was as eager as I was, and we were instantly wrapped in each other's arms. All that ogling I'd been doing since 6:00 had evidently been matched by an escalation of desire on her part!

In the first break for breath in our almost violent kissing, I gasped a question. "Why was your dad, whew!, bringing, um, strange men, whew!, to see my outfit?"

"Strange?"

"Well, kind of. . . . They were pansies, really."

"Oh," she giggled. "I guess I might as well tell you."

"Tell me?"

"You know, my dad doesn't really want me to date in high school. He thinks I should wait until I go to college to find the man to marry."

"So?"

"So, I told him you were . . . you know, a homosexual."

"What!" I jumped back and almost fell over the toilet. "A queer! Are you crazy?"

"No, wait, Hugh. That way, he doesn't worry about us. See, he doesn't think we'll do what we're about to do." She pulled me to her again.

Of course, I was furious. I didn't want to be known all over town as a homo, a homo in pink pants who wears jewelry! Fairfield in 1963 was not the time or the place for any but the straight. I had to explain the truth to Mr. Simpson.

And I wanted to knock my secret girlfriend into next week for this. But, then again, that could wait until she finished doing what she was doing.

I had fantasized too long about this moment, especially over the last week, to be able to stop now. Perhaps her revelation of this bizarre strategy with her father made me even more a slave to passion: I was going to prove I was all man by banging this cheerleader's brains out!

Patty was willing to help however she could, as she had resumed our kissing at the same time she was tugging on the zipper to my peach colored pants. I slipped my hands under the waistband of her black slacks and panties and ran them both down to her knees. Garter belt and stockings could stay where they were.

Patty stepped out of her pants and pulled off her top. Holding onto my neck, she hopped up (one more cheerleader stunt!) and wrapped her legs around my waist. I had never thought about having sex standing up, but here I was doing it!

And in a few seconds more, there I was *having* done it. In the words of the men of that time, "Wham, bam, thank you ma'am!"

I collapsed onto the toilet seat, out of breath. Patty leaned back on the sink, also breathing heavily, a wry smile on her face. She had certainly escaped her parents' control!

I marveled again at her marvelous belly, now at eye level. The strong legs, the fine breasts. Looking at those breasts, I rediscovered a question that had come to me during the fashion show.

"Hey, why was everyone talking about Linda Roy tonight?"

I think the look on her face was genuine surprise, but I can't be sure even now. There may also have been a touch of pity.

"You don't know? Linda was pregnant. She had a miscarriage at the hospital on the night of the crash."

Part Four:
Revelations

31

You can be sure Patty's revelation brought me up short: Linda Roy had been pregnant at the time of Cross Rhodes?

Now, I know you'll think me stupid, but I didn't see myself as the possible father right at that moment. I assumed--as, in fact, everyone else who knew about her condition did at first--that Robert Paterson had impregnated his long-time girlfriend.

In some other compartment of my mind, of course, I knew that Linda had ridden me to satisfaction in the back seat of her father's Lincoln Continental. And so little prepared had I been for such a thrill on our first date that I had not used a rubber. But it never occurred to me that in that moment we might have started a baby together.

Perhaps I unconsciously assumed that Linda, knowing her own cycle, had measured the risk ahead of time and decided it was OK. Too, she had, right after that event, so firmly drawn a line in the history of our relationship that our one date separated itself from the rest of my life, as if it had happened in a dream. Hugh Noone from Black Street had laid a dentist's daughter, a senior class beauty, Linda Roy? No, no; not possible.

Linda's miscarriage was, I concluded, yet another level of tragedy for the Paterson family, even if it were something not universally known. Please remember that getting a girl pregnant in these days was a crushing blow to all involved: the girl would have to leave high school; the boy would have to marry her before she began to show; the parents would pretend that their children had decided to get married and then--whoops-- earlier than planned, those kids had gotten pregnant! The boy was always at fault in such cases, as no girl of Linda's status would want sex before marriage. So Robert would be remembered not as a star high school athlete with great promise, but as a boy who had gotten a good girl in trouble.

Let me assure you that, innocently, I also foresaw no legal action deriving from this event. Paterson was dead; there was no baby. Except for a whispered shame that would hover around Linda Roy for months, or even years, there would be no additional price to pay by any concerned. The Roys' wealth would sustain respectability for their daughter until graduation. Then she would go away to college and a fresh start.

Apparently, that's what Linda Roy and her parents had assumed as well, letting her appear in public (the Simpsons' fashion show) after a suitable time of healing. (She was healing from injuries suffered in the car wreck, of course, not from any miscarriage.)

When I learned of Linda's condition, I was still reeling from what Patty had done to me. She had told her father I was a homosexual! And from the attention I had received at the fashion show, I concluded that he had shared this information with a number of others around town. I had to take care of my own reputation in Fairfield before worrying about what people might be saying or thinking about Linda Roy.

I thought back to my one appearance as the safety net for the high school cheerleaders, when I had been called a sissy by other boys. If Mr. Simpson's generation

227

was passing its rumors down to their children, my contemporaries, my cheerleading role could be linked in the town's mind with my role in the style show, confirming everything.

I woke up the morning after the fashion show eager to restore my identity. Rather than be thought queer, I would much prefer to remain a boy from Black Street forever! I planned to go to Simpson's Clothing Store on my morning break.

"Mr. Simpson, sir," I would say to him first thing. "There's been a bit of a misunderstanding."

"Oh?" he would say, perhaps rising from behind the desk in his office, where I would have found him. When he stood, I would be reminded of how tall he was, and wide. A big man.

Hmm, a big man in his office. With its little bathroom in the corner. Where I'd been "dancing" with his daughter only the night before. I suddenly imagined myself being shoved headfirst into the toilet.

Time for a new plan, a more deliberate, thoughtful plan.

I would get Karen Murphy to spread the word that I had proven my manhood to her. "Karen," I would say. "I need you to do something for me."

"Sure, Hugh." She would be eager to help. It would almost be missionary work. "You *are* wearing the chain I gave you?"

Whoops. The chain with its tiny gold cross was stuffed in its box in my sock drawer. It was hidden away because I didn't want to continue any special relationship with Karen. And yet, I had enjoyed her favors. And I worked with her father at Rexall's.

Clearly, a still better plan was necessary.

Once again, I was grateful for the routines that gave me time to think: work at Rexall's, classes at school, a hobby of glider construction, the beginning of the spring tennis season. The steady march of these activities gave me time to adjust to the shock of what I had learned and chart a course for the days ahead.

Of course, I little knew of another plan for my future growing out of Cross Rhodes, out of the Paterson-Roy romance, out of the crazy thinking Patty had done to deceive her father about our sex lives. All that was grinding down its own path--the path that would land me in prison--while I marched along as stepson of troubled Henry Maas, average student at Fairfield High School, would-be boyfriend, entrepreneur, high flyer.

One new activity helped distract me from the rumors that, I would later learn, were already swirling around me and Linda Roy. I finally earned a part in a school play.

Fairfield High's drama coach was ambitious that spring, deciding to stage, of all things, *Oedipus Rex*. Re-reading Sophocles's classic tragedy years later in prison, I realized how ambitious Mr. Ferguson's project for the senior class really had been. This is not an easy play to put on, especially for boys whose voices still crack when they get excited and girls more ready for babysitting than motherhood.

Still, even high school teachers should think big now and then, I guess. And occasionally that regular string of musicals and set pieces like *Our Town* should be broken with something more grand, even a try at high Greek drama.

I didn't get any of the big parts in the play, of course. I played the shepherd who had saved Oedipus as a baby. I was brought on stage late in the action and questioned by Oedipus about a long-ago act of charity.

Years earlier, Jocasta, warned by prophecies, had given her child to me, the shepherd. Instead of putting the baby to death, as he had been instructed, the shepherd passed him on to a stranger from Corinth, where he (Oedipus) grew to manhood. Unknowingly, Oedipus later killed his father and married Jocasta, his own mother. I was the one who explained how this terrible curse on the house of Oedipus had been fulfilled.

I recall liking the shape of tragedy more than the details of this particular play: the hero's tragic flaw, reversal and recognition, the inevitable shape of past, present, and future embodied in the prophecy. Once Oedipus's life is saved by the shepherd (me), the entire sequence of events goes forward to its tragic end. And I felt this was true for many in real life, especially left-handers. I can trace my destiny, remember, back to an elemental conflict between me and a right-handed stepfather, if not to the womb.

There were more factors besides aesthetic appreciation that landed me among the company of seventeen-year-olds attempting to resurrect Greek drama in small-town America. Patty was playing the part of Antigone, one of Oedipus's daughters. Linda Roy was Jocasta, and others members of their circle, including Karen Murphy, were scattered throughout the chorus. So I was still trying to travel with the in-crowd. And, for however long the shield of my rumored sexual preference disguised my relationship with Patty, I concluded that I might as well be enjoying what she was willing to give.

Here we are, in fact, at one of the earliest rehearsals slipping in and out of the backstage curtains while the

230

principals in the cast read their parts. We're supposed to be listening for our cues, but there's a lot more sneak kissing and quick squeezing going on just out of Mr. Ferguson's sight.

"Are you coming over tonight?" asks Patty. I am still officially her math tutor.

"Can we go for a walk down the block?" With spring coming on, we do go for walks. Not down the street so much as out on the college golf course a block and half to the north.

"Sure. Daddy thinks you're great."

"Yeah, well, he needs to know. . . ."

"Know what?" she teases me. "Know that you're not, uh, this way?" She holds one hand out palm down and then rocks it back and forth. "Or know what we're doing out on the golf course?"

She's got me here. All I can do is return to a topic which presents me in a better light--The Spirit of St. Louis II. Patty has become as excited as I am about this project.

"Maybe he should see what we're doing in my back yard. Hey, you know, the sealant is dry, the weather is turning warm, I'm thinking it's about time for those tests."

"You mean really fly it?"

"Well, Gary Hamilton has some ideas about what I need to do first, things to show it's aerodynamically sound. He says we can test it on the trailer first, then in controlled flight."

I have modified a boat trailer to transport Spirit, though, of course, I don't have a car to pull the trailer. I had counted on Billy's Petting Machine, but it is still out of commission, as is Billy himself, though his casts are due to come off in the next week. My second option is Henry's Buick.

Things had been slightly better between me and my stepfather ever since I had gotten him home from the Top Hat. He felt the whole world was against him now, against him and his family. In circling his wagons, he sometimes included Mom and me among the potential victims of unprincipled slaughter.

"I'm going to be there, aren't I?" asks Patty of the test flights. "I could even take the stick occasionally."

Completely healed from her injuries, Patty is more daring than ever. She wants not just to try more difficult stunts as a cheerleader, but to pilot my glider. I'm drawn to this enthusiasm, but I'm also a bit wary. I often feel that she's going one step farther than I have planned. A few weeks from now, in a field down by Devil's Elbow, I will learn to my regret how right I am about Patty's character.

32

I enjoyed play practice not only because Patty and I were tickling each other backstage, but also because it added a new, pleasurable element to my school day.

Practice was after class, from 4:00 to 6:00. So I was able to continue my evening and weekend job at Rexall's. And I generally stopped by to tutor Patty on the nights I didn't work. Thus, my day now had a new phase in its larger cycle.

My life that spring, in fact, was very full, and that may account for my inattention to certain signs in the world around me, signs that suggested people were taking perhaps unusual notice of me. If I was aware of anything, I assumed the attention I was receiving had to do with my rising status as member of the senior class play, as boyfriend of a major cheerleader, as stock boy of promise, as future aviator.

Actually, little more needed to be done on my glider at this point. I was painting some required identification numbers on the wings and fuselage. The landing gear I had ordered from Texas had finally arrived and been installed.

I hadn't thought much about landing initially, only flying. Getting up into the clouds and surveying the land crossed by famous Route 66 had been the goal of this entire effort, and how I would come to earth hadn't really entered my head. This was foolish, of course, as every flight has equal parts of rising and falling. The zenith is equidistant from beginning and end, unless of course you don't return to your starting point.

I had bolted the two covered wheel assemblies to the underside of the wings. A smaller bare wheel kept the tail of the plane from scraping at takeoff and landing. In my view, of course, these features would receive little stress because of my natural skill in flying.

An initial flight plan had been laid out on a recent drive into the country with Billy, Karen, and Patty, who had the use of her mother's Chevrolet Bel Air. Since her recovery, Patty's parents were giving her more and more freedom. (Or she was taking it!)

Billy was down to a small cast on one wrist, happy to be returning to circulation. He and Karen were officially going steady now. I wondered if that meant he had agreed marriage was in their future, but I didn't feel comfortable asking. I knew what he was after from her (sex). And I thought I knew what she desired from him (commitment). But I didn't want these things spelled out by either of them.

Anyway, the four of us drove out Route 66 to Devil's Elbow, then took a back road down to some wide fields along a big stretch of the Gasconade River, high limestone cliffs marking the other side. Behind those bluffs a small range of Ozark mountains spread to the west. It looked like an acceptable site.

The idea was that warm air rising off the flatlands would give me the updrafts I needed to get airborne. This section of bottom land was perfectly flat and open for miles.

"Where will you take off from, Hugh?" asked Patty, surveying the broad expanse of winter wheat and hayfields.

"There's an old cropduster's runway in the straightaway where the river spreads out." I pointed to the middle distance. "They took it for hay last fall, so it should be clear enough for another few weeks for me to use." I would be pulled by a car on a tow rope until I caught the updraft.

"Where will you land?" asked Karen, as if I might be planning to glide to Kansas City.

"Well, the first few times, I plan to circle back to the same place. You land and take off in the same direction, into the wind. But after that, who knows?"

"What does Hamilton say about when he can check it out?" asked Billy.

"He says he's ready when I am. But I do have to fit into his work schedule. And his love life."

"He's going with Miss Timmons, isn't he?" asks Karen.

"She'd better be careful," offered Patty. "My daddy says he drinks too much."

"He can hold it, though," claimed Billy. "He says he was tanked on half the missions he flew in Korea."

"Hugh, you watch out, dealing with him," said Karen, with an earnest look.

I ignored her worry and got us all back in the car to complete our survey of the terrain. The old runway had to be smooth enough that it wouldn't tear up my wheels when I was being towed. But I'd calculated that I wouldn't need more than a hundred yards to rise off the road, so the whole area didn't have to be perfect. The car might pull me a bit farther to get up to speed, but I'd be airborne fairly quickly.

You see, the entire plane didn't weigh 100 pounds. And I was 130 tops, even after one of my mother's fried chicken and mashed potato dinners. It wouldn't take a very large automobile to launch the Spirit of St. Louis II. I could already see myself soaring up over the river.

The picture of myself airborne was the subject of my daydreams at play practice when I was more a hired hand than an actor. Since my role was a minor one--and my time on stage came late in the play--I was often not involved in rehearsal proper but stayed with the chorus working on related projects. The girls were going through all the old costumes in wardrobe to see what might be adaptable for *Oedipus*. And the boys had to build platforms for use on stage, as well as backdrops to the different scenes. The advantage was that Patty was sometimes here as well.

"Building a set is a lot like building an airplane," she observed at one point. "I mean, it's using wood, sawing, hammering."

"Well, these don't have to get off the ground," I responded. She was helping draw pillars on a sheet of plywood. When she'd finished, I'll cut them out with a jigsaw.

"Oh, yes, they do. Some of them at least. Remember, Mr. Ferguson wants the scene changes to be done by hoisting one backdrop out of the way to reveal another."

"You're right. I forgot that. But that's just ropes and pulleys. Spirit has to go up on the wind."

"What are you going to wear when you fly?"

"Wear?" I hadn't given that a thought. Patty's working in her dad's store made her fashion conscious, I suppose, always wondering what people should have on, what effect that would have.

"Well, you don't want to appear on the football field in regular school clothes, do you?" This was a fantasy I'd shared with Patty, surprising all of Fairfield by gliding over downtown and then landing in some public place, like the school's athletic field.

"I guess you have a point. But what should I wear?"

"I'll show you tonight," she said, rising from her crouched position. Then she whispered, "When we're on the golf course."

Being on the golf course at night in the springtime was my idea of romantic bliss, so this hint sufficed to keep my level of anticipation high the rest of the afternoon.

There was little relaxation at rehearsal, however. Despite having a full day of teaching English behind him, our director, Mr. Ferguson, allowed only one break each afternoon near the end of the first hour ("Take five, people!"). I had recognized that moment, however, as central to another emerging project.

I had decided that, if, as Miss Timmons had discovered, I was better in math than I had always thought, I might be better in English too. So I listened and watched carefully through the first hour of practice, looking for something helpful to say or do in the second hour. At the break was when I reviewed in my mind what had happened, decided on a course of action, and prepared to follow through with a plan.

Right after our taking five, I might say something like, "You know, Mr. Ferguson, I was wondering if Linda [Jocasta] shouldn't be more forward in that scene? So her facial expressions are clear to the audience."

"Hugh, that's an interesting thought. When they try it after the break, I'll go to the back rows and see how it looks."

"Of course, she'll have stage make-up on at the performance. That makes a difference."

Well, these weren't ground-breaking innovations in the history of theater, but I was involved. And I know my making comments and suggestions gave me a visibility I hadn't had before.

It may be that this idea of self-promotion had begun at tryouts, when I'd surprised my classmates by auditioning for lead roles. In the past I'd been more modest, reading for and hoping to get any small part. The regular stars, who assumed they'd monopolize the production as usual, were obviously taken aback by Mr. Ferguson's casting me in any role.

No one ever mentioned, by the way, that Robert Paterson would have been Oedipus. We all knew it, but acted as if Charles Riddick, senior class president and quarterback of the football team, was destined to take the lead. I read for Oedipus too, though I assumed that was well beyond my reach.

A lot was going on for me in these late afternoon rehearsals, then. I was daydreaming about flying, building a set, playing the shepherd, asserting myself as a student of the theater, and flirting with Patty. It's a wonder I had energy left for the rest of the evening. But, ah, youth!

Having worked an extra shift in the morning, Henry was still in bed when I ate dinner that day after practice. He had avoided conflict with the boss in the last few weeks, so we were all a little bit more comfortable on Cedar Street.

I went out back to view my pet project after dinner and before I headed over to the Simpsons'. The days were getting longer now as spring came on, and I had enough daylight to work for an hour or so on Spirit before mounting Black Beauty and scootering across town. We would want it to be completely dark when we sauntered off to the golf course after an hour of apparent math tutoring.

"Here's your scarf," Patty said that night when we took a break from necking behind the clubhouse.

"Scarf?" It was bright red, with long fringes at the ends.

"Haven't you ever paid attention to the movies? Pilots always wear a scarf that trails behind you in the wind."

"Oh, right. Thanks." I wrapped it around my neck, then moved to resume our necking.

She pulled back and smiled that mischievous grin of hers. "And here's *my* scarf."

33

Now, wait a minute! Patty, even with blue silk scarf and gorgeous middle, was not going to be in that plane with me on these first trial runs. I was the pilot, even if she often had the controls when we were in the shadows behind the clubhouse.

She really liked, by the way, to make out standing up, though we didn't repeat on the golf course our vertical performance from her father's washroom. We agreed that we needed more privacy. And, I learned, she had more stringent requirements for birth control than had Linda Roy. She had been the one with the rubber on the night of the fashion show.

"You need a bigger plane," she gasps in my ear. She is breathless from long, deep kissing.

"For longer flights?" As she leans back against the side of the building, I try to lift her athlete's leg up behind me.

"For riding higher." She lets that leg rest on my rump and presses a hip against me. "I mean so we can ride together."

We can't keep *this* riding up for long, as she does have to go back to her house. And there's physical discomfort for the adolescent male remaining in so long a state of arousal, especially standing. I would be at her house again in two nights, anyway, and we have a date for the weekend.

In the meantime I have other tasks to perform, including the one that, for me, pays the bills of dates with Patty and shellac for The Spirit of St. Louis II. I must report for my regular hours at Rexall's Drugs.

My primary assignment continues to involve unpacking shipments of supplies and arranging them on storeroom shelves. Generally, the clerks replenish empty stands out front, although occasionally I, too, carry boxes of deodorant, hair spray, and liquid cleaners for display along aisles and under glass countertops.

The store is open for the first hour of my evening shift, so on those occasions when I'm stocking out front I will often run into friends getting a soda or dessert at the counter. On the night after my walk on the golf course with Patty I found Karen Murphy studying items on aisle 3.

"Can I help you, miss?" I have decided to be cute.

"Oh, no. I just . . . oh, Hugh! How are you?"

"Fine, fine. What are you looking for, shampoo?" I was holding a crate of various items, including probably five different brands of shampoo.

"Shampoo? Yeah, fine. Let me see what you have there."

This seems to be a casual approach to shopping. I always want to be orderly in such matters, though I sometimes go by advertising jingles and slogan more than product quality. "Lather, rinse, repeat," for instance is my favorite. It's such a solid structure that I follow it at home when I wash my hair, getting special satisfaction from the rinse action in the middle.

"I hear you have a part in the play."

"Yeah, *Oedipus*."

"You're the king?"

"Oh, no. I'm the shepherd. In the play, *Oedipus*."

"Right. Charles is the king."

"Robert would have gotten that part, of course." With Karen it seemed comfortable to just say what everyone knew. "Mr. Ferguson liked Paterson."

Karen gave me a funny look. "Liked Robert . . . ?"

"You know, always gave him good parts. Remember *Our Town*. He was the narrator, ran the show."

"Listen, Hugh. . . ."

Just then Karen's father came around the corner of that aisle and interrupted our conversation.

"Karen? I didn't know you were here."

"Just came by to get Mom's prescription."

"I could have done that for you. Why didn't you call?"

"Well, I was out anyway."

"Hugh, you can go on back. I'll finish this." He took the crate of supplies from me.

At first I thought Mr. Murphy was trying to get rid of me, keep me away from Karen. But, looking out from the back a few minutes later, I saw he was still talking intently with her. In fact, I had found my fellow employee to be a lot more friendly lately. With Billy now Karen's steady, I guessed he had concluded that I was no longer a danger.

Mr. Murphy had even pitched in to help on the most recent disaster--rancid grease backed up in the drain behind the grill. The heat of the system is supposed to keep the overflow in a liquid state as it moves to a ten-gallon waste tub. But something had blocked the passage, allowing the grease to harden around it.

The drain slowly overflowed with new grease, but no one noticed because it was oozing down behind the grill itself. Slowly grease had seeped down the back of the grill and along the bottoms of the cabinets. Only when the smell caught the attention of the girls working the counter did we realize we had a problem.

Mr. Murphy got right with me hauling carbon dioxide cylinders and cases of canned sundae syrups out of the way so we could study the problem. And when I had opened up the drain again, he helped me move several booths to get at hidden grease pools.

It did occur to me, as I recalled now my scraping up hardened grease with a spatula (it had taken hours), that I seemed to be using a lot of my energy cleaning up grease from grill fixtures, Coke syrup from the backs of cabinets, oil from garage floors. Most of the time I had not even caused the problem, so I was cleaning up other people's messes.

Somehow the places I was spending my time at were characterized by accidents, failed systems, irreparable flaws. Was this again the product of left-handedness, a dark destiny fixed by my earliest preferences? Or did it come from living in a poor part of town, a detour from Route 66 onto Black Street?

As I grabbed the mop to do the store's floor, a scene from the more distant past came back to me, a time when Henry tried to play the father with me. I was eight or nine, and my stepfather was going to teach me how to hit a baseball. Although Henry was slow, he was also, as I've said, very strong. And when he connected baseball bat to ball, it went for a long, long ride.

"Take a big step with your front foot," he explained, planting a giant right-footed work boot in the uncut grass of our backyard, kicking out the left. He threw the ball up with one hand, holding the bat in the other.

"Crack!" The ball sailed out of our yard, over the house of the Martins, who lived behind us.

"Ha, ha," he laughed. "Go get that and I'll give you a try."

I hated this. I could hit a ball quite well even at this age. After all, it's the same skill that would make me number two on the high school tennis team: strike a round object with a long, straight one. (Hell, I would have been number one that spring, if I hadn't been arrested. But I'm coming to that unhappy end to my athletic career, to the end of my life "outside.")

Henry, of course, insisted that I hit right-handed. And I couldn't do that. I mean, I just don't come at the world from that angle. When I'm at the plate, I plant the left foot, step with the right. My right arm pulls, but the left guides the bat. It makes the contact, drives the contactee.

When I got back from digging the ball out of the Lindseys' potato patch, Henry set me up to hit.

"Firm grip. Straight swing. You do it." His directions were restrained, embedded, he assumed, in example. But for me everything I saw was backwards.

I swung and missed. I tried again.

"Keep your eye on the ball, kid."

Two more tries, two more misses.

"Ah, you're never gonna get it. Go chase this."

He took bat and ball, swung again, and sent the ball this time even farther, beyond the Lindseys' garden. When I got back from this expedition, Henry had gone inside, probably for a beer.

I switched the bat to my left hand, tossed the ball with the right. I stepped, swung, connected. And drove the ball through our kitchen window.

244

I didn't get a terrible thrashing that day, but I was assigned extra mopping and scrubbing chores. Even worse, Henry claimed that, since I couldn't have hit the ball with a bat, I'd thrown it. This wasn't true, though I later wished it had been. Or that I'd hit him with the bat! I winced at the memory.

When I came out front from the storeroom at Rexall's, Karen was gone, though I got a friendly nod from Mr. Murphy. Whatever had been the subject of their conversation earlier seemed to have faded from his mind. It was just about closing time, and I started on the floor in the vacated areas.

As I passed by the prescription counter, I overheard Mr. Wicker talking to the day's last customer. My boss was ringing up a charge in the cash register and returning a card to his files.

"This will help her sleep," he said. "But make sure you keep them away from her in the bad times." Did I recognize the man waiting in front of the counter?

"Of course," said the customer. He wore an expensive suit, and I noticed clean, neat hands as he reached up to take the bottle of pills from Mr. Wicker.

"You just can't tell with girls at that age," said Mr. Wicker. ". . . girls who've had troubles."

"Thanks, Fred." The man slipped the bottle of pills into his pocket and turned to leave. That's when I recognized him.

I had not met Dr. Roy on my one memorable date with the high school princess, though I knew who he was. As you remember, Linda picked me up in her dad's Lincoln. I'm not even sure her family knew she'd gone out with me, though I had been calling that house on the phone often enough for a period of some weeks.

Since my cover was tennis practice, Linda's parents may never have known I was also trying to take her out.

Were these pills for her? Was she more troubled by her miscarriage than appeared to be the case at the fashion show? She'd seemed quite comfortable, drawing admiring looks from men and women alike. A picture of her breast visible from three angles in one of the store's triple mirrors rose up from memory.

Another memory from that night came to me and led to a discovery: Mr. Murphy was relaxed about me now because, like Mr. Simpson, he assumed I was queer. His suspicion that I had laid his daughter probably disappeared that same night when Patty's father imitated for him and half the town's men the limp wrist he associated with my playing tennis.

34

Two nights later I found another familiar face among the customers at Rexall's: my unofficial tennis coach, Doc Garnet.

"I have something for you, Hugh," he said. I was hauling the mop and bucket up to the front. As soon as the store emptied, I would mop myself back to the storeroom.

"A book about tennis?" I saw that he was holding out toward me a small, tattered volume.

"No, it's about gliders. Gliders in the war."

"How did you know . . . ?"

"Oh, your friend, Mr. Hamilton, was talking about it down at Ray's. He said that you're building--what do you call it?"

"The Spirit of St. Louis II."

"Ah, good. Well, this might keep you inspired."

I looked down at the worn paperback, *Above the Line*. "Thanks. Thanks very much."

"Well, don't let it take up too much of your time. You and I need to get out on the tennis courts soon. When is it, next week?"

"Yes. I'm ready to work on my serve again, hitting it right at the peak of the toss, straight overhead."

"Good. You're going to be a star this year."

How well this old guy seemed to know me! I wanted desperately to have a great season, and not just because it was my senior year, my last for competition.

Now that my chief rival was no longer there to outsmart and outplay me, I would be number one on the team. But the confused sense of guilt I felt about Robert Paterson's death also made me want to win any match that he would have won. I was playing for his memory, I guess.

There was even more, though, to Doc Garnet's wisdom. Somewhere along the line of building Spirit, I had linked in my mind my own imagined flying with my father's doomed career in the war. I would soar where he had crashed. I would redeem some loss in my family history. I would recover one portion of my mother's youthful dreams.

And the book Doc Garnet gave me, *Above the Line*, seemed to provide just the model for success I needed. I translated its plot into an imagined story about my dead father. Scanning the first few pages, I learned that the book was about a secret military operation. I ended up reading the whole thing the same day.

When Doc Garnet spoke to me about tennis and sailplanes, by the way, I wondered if this man of many talents wasn't also going to give me some tips on acting. He probably knew everything about Greek tragedy. For all I knew, he had written *Oedipus*!

Getting back to the book: There had been in World War II a seldom acknowledged program to use gliders in combat. Allied forces had learned early on in the war that silent sailplanes could parachute spies behind enemy lines, study troop placement without detection, and even deceive forces on the ground about the size and depth of aerial support.

American sailplane pilots were involved in reconnaissance and surveillance before D-Day and in the continued push into German-held territory in

Europe. Even in the Pacific, gliders sometimes figured in local operations as Allied forces pursued the Japanese army through island archipelagoes. Most often built of wood, they did not show up on radar.

The Pacific theater hosted the most dangerous flights of sailplanes in the war, probably in history. The distances that had to be traveled and the variable winds along island chains made missions extremely hazardous. Gliders were towed aloft by small fighters and released at high altitudes. Flying at night above enemy positions, pilots had to use extraordinary skill to return to friendly bases. Sometimes they had to ditch in the ocean and hope to be picked up by Navy boats.

Dr. Garnet's book contained an account, long classified, of one extraordinary pilot whose exploits had been crucial to the American effort. As I read about this man, I saw myself at the controls of a wartime sailplane. I floated above the line. Or was it my biological father I sometimes imagined, spotting the enemy troops about to make an unexpected attack?

Philip Reuter had been a simple Kansas farm boy in the 1930s, but he'd flown gliders with his father on the hot plains around Salinas. Mr. Reuter senior had been something of a pioneer in early aviation.

The day after Pearl Harbor Philip volunteered and spent the war years as an aircraft maintenance worker in the Navy. In a two-year stint on an aircraft carrier in the Pacific, he built his own glider out of discarded material from military packing crates and excess sailcloth stowed on the ship's lifeboats. As later events showed, he had a gift for construction and great drive to succeed.

A small man whose poor vision barred him from military flying, he never gave up the dream of becoming a pilot. He learned from the airmen whose planes he serviced, and he read all the books about navigation, aerodynamics, and instrumentation he could get his hands on. All his study made him the unexpected hero in one operation in the island-hopping Pacific campaign.

A battalion of Marines had gone ashore on one of the smaller Solomon islands, initially meeting no resistance. But 200 yards from their landing point they came under heavy artillery and sniper fire. Japanese troops had dug in along the volcanic slopes of the island's mile-high central mountain, but they held their fire until our men were out of the landing craft and moving cautiously inland. The cliffs were so steep and their guns so well camouflaged, it was hard for Navy ships or aircraft to determine their position and thus provide cover.

The Marines who survived the initial barrage took cover among high dunes in back of the beach. Supporting fire gave them some relief, but if they tried to advance farther, they would present easy targets in the open grassland which lay at the mountain's base. Retreat would have to cross a sure killing zone of open sand, as several days of full moon and cloudless sky would light even night movement.

The invasion was stalled, then, between success and failure. If the Marines didn't move from their present position, enemy fire would eventually wipe them out. But if they could identify the precise location of the Japanese artillery, fighter bombers from support carriers should be able to clear the way.

Reuter provided the solution to the Americans' dilemma.

Without his superiors' knowledge, Reuter decided to fly his homemade sailplane by the island at night and pinpoint the deployment of enemy guns. He convinced the pilot of the usual spotter plane, a single-engine light aircraft, to tow him aloft while the rest of the ship's crew were awaiting a decision from the commander on how to rescue the Marines.

Although he knew that he would be visible in the night sky despite the glider's black coat, Reuter felt the small and silent glider had a good chance of making several sweeps before detection. Then fighter planes could provide the pinpoint bombing that would free the Marines. He explained to his co-conspirator, the spotter pilot, that, in the past, the Japanese had been alerted to attack from the air by the sound of droning engines. Without that alarm, they would never even look up.

Because of the steep wall of mountain above the coast, western winds were shunted away from the very path Reuter would have liked to follow to spot the guns. If he rode the currents and went too high, he would be unable to see clearly. But going low, he might lose the updraft necessary to swing out of range and return to the ship. So he had to cruise precisely between these two extremes.

Reuter had himself towed to 10,000 feet on the far side of the island, then took several passes high above his intended course.

"I found the current right away," he wrote in his journal. "I could have gone up another 10,000 feet. With the moon above me, the vast sea glittering beneath, I was suspended between two sources of light. Everything was quiet and peaceful."

"The island looked like a paradise under moonlight. The waves could have been Kansas wheat rippling in a warm summer breeze."

"I had some strange thoughts up there, about what I'd do with the rest of my life if I survived this flight, the rest of the war. I knew this was the turning point in my life." Reuter had taken a small radio aboard his plane, and thirty minutes into his operation, he began to call in everything he saw.

"The guns were all on ledges along the mountainside," Reuter wrote, "hidden from ocean view by netting filled with brush. Checking my altimeter, I could radio in the exact elevation of the three major batteries. And the moonlit land below gave me easily visible coordinates."

Several explanations were offered for Reuter's unexpected success. Some believed he swept by Japanese gunners so closely that they couldn't trust their senses. Rubbing their eyes in disbelief at a dark flying object, they would have seen nothing in the next second.

Perhaps they thought they'd seen a giant tropical bird. The only sound would have been the whir of wings cutting wind.

Others who learned of his flight argued that Reuter's small glider up close to Japanese positions would have looked like a larger plane far away, thus nothing to worry about yet. The most convincing theory offered for his escaping detection, though, was Reuter's own: hearing no engine, the hidden gunners never looked to the sky. He was invisible so long as he made no sound. Reuter and his flight remained invisible after the war as well, for the use of gliders received little publicity.

Veteran military pilots had taken up all the flying jobs back in the States, but Reuter found a fresh field for his imagination and effort on another continent. He emigrated to Australia and started a business flying doctors to the far-flung population of the Outback. Perhaps at some point he even flew my idol, Rod Laver, the left-handed tennis star from Down Under.

There was only one hitch in Reuter's silent glider operation of World War II: directly in front of the middle battery, his handcrafted plane hit an air pocket. The cliffs blocked all wind, and his glider dropped like a stone.

The fate of this Kansas farm boy's jerry-rigged glider was grim, far worse than the end of my Spirit of St. Louis II. But at least we both came away from our wreckage alive.

35

Reuter's glider was ruined, and my sailplane survived. What was lost in my case was the ability to ever fly again--unless, of course, I finally get out of the Missouri State Penitentiary.

Philip Reuter's glider nose dived directly onto an anti-aircraft gun, its tail striking the barrel protruding through a camouflaged screen. While the gilder hung together after the impact, the collision made it impossible for Reuter to climb, even though he passed out of the air pocket and back into the night breeze.

He was able to swerve away from the battery he'd struck, which was fortunate because the troops there leapt into action following the ripping sound of plane on gun. The Japanese began firing small arms and a machine gun at the falling glider.

Those bursts of fire were echoed quickly by the other big guns, which proceeded to shell the Marines dug in below. It was assumed in *Above the Line* that the Japanese, panicked by the appearance of Reuter's plane, thought the Americans were finally making some sort of move, either coming forward in attack or retreating toward the shore.

Reuter, meanwhile, realized he was in trouble. He'd already risked coming so low with his final effort to pinpoint the enemy that climbing again would have been difficult. Now he could barely control his damaged plane, which was losing altitude precipitously.

"Try for the sand," was all he could tell himself as he fought to avoid the mountainside.

To make things worse, ironically, his last radio calls had provided just what the ship off shore needed to target the enemy. Realizing that a fresh bombardment was raining down on the Marines, they opened fire with their big guns too. So now Reuter was in danger not only from Japanese but from friendly fire as well.

He crashed in a stand of trees at the mountain's base, actually hanging what was left of his glider in the branches. The already damaged tail assembly broke loose, and the wings were shredded. But, miraculously, Reuter himself sat in his cockpit with only minor cuts and bruises, a broken middle finger on his left hand. He could not free himself from his mangled machine, however, and his fate hung in the balance of the larger battle.

Although he was relatively well hidden in the tree at that hour of the night, daylight would have revealed him to the enemy as an easy sniper target. When American firepower at sea and in the air finally knocked out the Japanese big guns, however, and the Marines swept up from the beach, he was rescued.

An effort to decorate this self-taught pilot in a homemade plane was lost in paperwork at the end of the war. And the reluctance to reveal the effectiveness of our glider campaigns kept his mission classified for a decade. But his story, given to me by Doc Garnet, inspired me in my first trial flight down by Devil's Elbow on a warm spring day of my senior year.

Gary Hamilton had agreed to meet Billy, Karen, Patty, and me at the site of the old cropduster's runway, if the weather was right. The bright sun of early spring was just what we needed, Route 66 out of Fairfield was the perfect path for this ambitious effort, and The Spirit of St. Louis II looked grand resting at the side of the dirt road along the Gasconade River.

Billy, now free of casts and pronounced fit for all activities, helped me get Spirit off its trailer and attach the wings and wing supports. I was ready to fly.

I hadn't gotten away from my house on Cedar Street without some anxious questions from my mother, however.

"Are you sure it's safe?" she had said, wiping her hands on her apron as I passed through the kitchen.

"That's what we're checking today. We won't cut it loose from the tow line today. Just pull it behind the car for a mile or so." This was Hamilton's plan, testing the stability of the machine, the functioning of elevator, aileron, rudder.

"Who's driving the car?"

"Patty is. The V-8 in her mom's Bel Air gives us plenty of power. But we'll take it slow. Don't worry, Mom."

Actually, I wasn't as comfortable as I let on with Patty at the wheel. She couldn't always be counted on to do what I asked, so I hoped I could talk Karen into riding with her. Billy's girlfriend was always willing to help me. And, for the first trials at least, Hamilton would have the stick.

Patty didn't ease my anxiety about her cooperativeness as we rode out to the site. While Karen and Billy were talking, she whispered to me, did I have my red scarf on?

"I have it in the plane," I said. "I'm not sure this is the time, you know. It's just a test."

Both couples in the car, by the way, were smashed up against each other in these days before seat belts. Patty energetically squeezed my thigh as we rode.

"I've got my scarf. You want to know where it is?"

256

"Uh, sure." I had no idea what she was getting at here.

"Look." She turned to face me and slid back on the car seat. She glanced back toward Billy and Karen, who were totally absorbed in each other, then pulled open her coat. Lifting the bottom of her sweatshirt above her hip-hugging jeans, she exposed a naked middle, the fabled navel.

I gasped as if I'd been struck. Cutting across her tummy two inches below the bellybutton was a swath of navy blue--her aviator's scarf. It was tied in front, and the ends fell down out of sight. She pulled six inches of tassel out with her right hand and waggled it at me.

Later, of course, I realized I should have read this sign more carefully, not as an invitation to later pleasure but as an indication of character. Patty's swashbuckling outfit did not belong with a person who would take orders. Here was a rebel, a rule breaker, someone under no one's control. Yet I let her take the wheel of her mother's Chevrolet, with my prized homemade glider in tow behind her!

Hamilton had examined one more time all the hinges, cables, and pulleys in my plane's movable parts. And he'd made me show him the way I had anchored the wings to the body, the nuts and bolts at joints as well as interior braces. We were ready for the first attempt.

I was so excited at the first run down the field, Spirit rising gracefully to an elevation of perhaps forty feet at the end of the tow line. Hamilton maneuvered the plane carefully: up a little, down a little; swing left, swing right. Everything seemed to be working perfectly.

Karen acted as a spotter from the Chevy's back seat, keeping Patty posted on what was happening behind them. Billy and I were stationed along the route, he near the launch point and me about midway down the runway where I could get the best view of everything that happened. Spirit came at me first at ground level, then rose before me, then floated gracefully above.

We had agreed on some signals for the pilot to communicate with the driver of the car, if necessary. Right arm straight up meant more speed; left arm bent down was slow; either hand waving indicated stop immediately. But no signal was needed; we executed the flight exactly as planned.

Patty accelerated steadily to a fixed speed, went one half mile, slowed gradually to a stop. And Hamilton set the glider down gently at a little under a mile. After a successful second run it was my turn.

"Let me fly next," Patty said while we reviewed the procedure. She had gotten out of the car as I was settling myself in the cockpit. Hamilton had walked down to my old position. After checking the tow line at both ends, Billy joined Karen in the back seat of the car.

"I can't let you do that yet," I said, hoping to put her off with the promise of a later opportunity. She reached her hand out to the stick.

"I'll take it easy, just a short ride."

"Let me check it out first. You're the tow driver today." I tried to flatter her. "I need someone I can trust behind the wheel."

"Oh, OK. But next time. . . ." She pushed the stick forward, then asked, "Where's your scarf?"

"It's here." I showed her where I'd stowed it under my seat. "I'll put it on."

She twisted it around so that the ends fell back over my shoulder and smiled. "Let's fly!"

And for perhaps three minutes I became the man of my dreams, the glider pilot, war hero, potent lover, beloved son. And all in a sailplane I had built from scratch.

I suppose I should admit that such enthusiasm far exceeded the circumstances. That is, I hadn't really broken free of the earth yet, as the tow line still bound me to Patty's Mom's Bel Air. And gravity had a hold on that.

I wondered if I should have brought my mother to watch. Would she have thrilled to think of her ride at the fair with Richard Noone twenty years ago? Or would it have brought back memories of the day she received that terrible telegram: downed in the Pacific?

I indulged in some fleeting "what if's." What if my father had survived that flight, the war? What if he'd come home the honored veteran? Wouldn't my childhood have been different with my real father there to support me, no defeated Henry Maas a heavy weight on my every ambition?

Then there was some confusion in communication. I was ready to come gently to earth, so I lowered my left hand along the side of the plane, the sign to slow down. But Patty sped up.

Whether this was playful exuberance from someone who routinely challenged limits, resentful retaliation because she was not in the cockpit, or a genuine mixup, I don't know. Whatever the cause, the effect was immediate: I dove to the ground.

I had just pushed up on the stick and changed pedal position, so that naturally brought the nose down. But the Bel Air's acceleration made Spirit's swoop to earth even more rapid.

I give myself some credit for quick reaction, yanking the stick back quickly and beginning to reverse my descent. But it wasn't in time to avoid the nose dipping into the soft earth of a Missouri spring. The car pulled the plane like a plow for a good fifty feet before Karen and Billy's screams finally registered with Patty and she stopped the car. By then, however, I was unconscious.

36

Long after the airplane crash, I wondered if, once again, I had been doomed by my left-handedness, my recurring habit of going counter to the grain, across Route 66.

That is, I had chosen *left hand down* as the signal to slow, but the right-handers watching may naturally have focused on my other side. That's where important things happen in the view of everyone, everyone except Karen perhaps. She, remember, seemed to understand me as a left-handed person.

Of course, there's also the reversal problem. Karen was looking directly at me, but Patty saw me inverted in the car's rearview mirror. There, left is right, and vice versa. So she could have interpreted my "slow down" as "speed up."

When I considered this possibility, I also wondered about my imagined mentor in this flight--Philip Reuter. Had the unsung war hero been left-handed? His career in the right-handed world had been uninspired, Middle-American farm boy and a steady maintenance worker except for his single adventure. Down Under, however, the place where I, at least, thought left-handers might get equal recognition, his was a genuine success story. He ran his own company, and he probably hired left-handed pilots whenever he could.

Whatever caused the end of my own aviation enterprise, I was at least grateful that not only had I survived--with a nasty concussion--but so had my glider. A lot of the canvas covering on the fuselage was torn, and there were a half dozen cracked or broken supports. But they could be replaced, the plane restored.

It said something for the overall solidness of my construction.

Before I had fully recovered from a knock on the head, however, an unofficial, quiet inquiry into my past had begun. And that inquiry eventually prevented me from resuming my aerial career. I was soon, in fact, grounded.

Gary Hamilton got me to the hospital quickly on the day of the test flight, taking over automobile driving duties without objection from Patty. And I began to come to not long after I was admitted and headed for X-ray. But apparently I did some talking when I first got there that aroused curiosity.

Fairfield was, remember, a small town in those days, with limited medical staff and facilities. There were really only a handful of doctors, most practicing general medicine. And they shared emergency room duty on a rotating basis.

On the day I came in, Dr. Younger had his hands full with an elderly couple who had turned their truck over on the way back to their farm. They eventually recovered, but their case left no one to deal with me except Dr. Roy, who happened to be in the building.

A dentist is not the best person, perhaps, to see about head injuries, but not the worst either. Dentists do know a fair amount about that part of the body. And, judging from the results--I recovered completely--I can't complain. This particular dentist was not, however, the person I might have selected to hear what I babbled about as I was struggling back from darkness.

I received the blow to the head when Spirit first slammed into the ground. In order to reduce the wind resistance as much as possible, a glider pilot slides down and forward in the cockpit until he's almost lying on his back. The eyes are barely over the top of the fuselage. But he's also so far forward that your forehead is only inches away from the front lip of the cockpit. That's what I banged my head on. And, of course, I used no helmet in piloting.

The first thing I remember afterwards occurs as a kind of dream sequence. I am lying in the back seat of a car, and I feel a terrible pain in my head. I conclude that there's been an accident, that I'm a victim.

I hear someone say something like, "He's opening his eyes." But at the same time I realize (or dream) that someone is on top of me. Someone--the same person?--is holding my hands, rubbing them.

Billy is close, I somehow know. Have I been in Cross Rhodes after all? Did I decide to abandon Black Beauty and ride with Karen and Robert, Linda and Patty? And then were we all hit by the fast-moving westbound train?

"Don't rush him. He'll come to now. It's OK."

It is probably about now that I begin to speak myself, although this fact is something I come to much later, picking it up from others who were there, chiefly Karen Murphy. "Linda, we shouldn't be doing this. Let me up."

I must think I'm in the back-seat of the Roys' Lincoln. Linda is screwing my brains out on our one and only date.

"What's he saying?"

"Wait a minute. Let him talk. Listen."

I can feel the leather upholstery sticking to my bare skin, the weight of Linda, her regular, powerful movement.

"Ooo, does your dad know what you're doing in his car? Well, let's not tell him, shall we? Aiiee!"

Suddenly I see a circle of faces taking shape above me, and I am terrified. They've been watching me have sex? How did they all get inside the car?

"Hugh. Hugh! Wake up." I see Karen's face, deeply concerned. She always seems to be there in the important moments of my life.

"Shh. Let him talk." There's Dr. Roy, waving Karen back with one hand, leaning closer to me. Oh hell, Linda's father!

"Hugh, I'm sorry. It wasn't my fault." This is Patty. Now I recognize Gary Hamilton beside her, Billy in the background. I have no idea what I'm doing with all these people!

Dr. Younger later told me that I had temporary amnesia. And my old buddy, Dr. Garnet, explained exactly what happens to the brain in a concussion, the bruising and the little broken blood vessels. He even considered the effects of a blow like the one I received on left-handers versus right-handers.

Right now, I at least recognize that I'm not in the car with Linda Roy. And, instinctively, I clam up. I'd better see what these people tell me has happened before I find myself admitting to things better left secret.

The next thing I remember clearly is my mother pushing her way through the others.

"Is he OK? Is he OK?"

I learned later that Karen had gotten her down to the hospital. She'd called her dad at Rexall's and convinced him to pick the panicked mother up and drive her over.

I was conscious if a bit confused by the time Mom arrived, and I had quite a lump in the middle of my forehead. She'd left Henry in bed even though he was due to get up in about an hour.

"I had to find out," she said, the drained look in her face not yet replaced by the full sense of relief. "I didn't want . . . I couldn't think. . . ."

When I did get all my senses about me, I realized the extent of her anxiety. When I'd left the house earlier, I had assured her that everything would be fine, that we'd taken all the safety precautions. I can only assume my father had made similar promises twenty years ago.

Another person to show up at the hospital, though this was a few hours later, was Miss Timmons. Of course, I'm not sure she was there because of me.

We learned then that she was engaged to Gary Hamilton. And later that spring they announced plans to leave Fairfield, start a new life together in St. Louis after the end of the school year.

He sold his charter airline and signed on at McDonald Douglas as an engineer. They wanted him to pioneer a new kind of containerized cargo shipping. It turned out to be quite a break for Hamilton, as his career took off with the move.

Miss Timmons taught for one more year in a metropolitan Catholic school, then began having babies. She switched from overseeing the maturation of others' children to the raising of her own. From all I've heard of them since, the Hamiltons did nothing but prosper.

Anyway, I stayed the night at the hospital and was released at noon the next day, cleared to go to school and even to play practice, so long as I took regular breaks and didn't overdo. This was good because we were in the last week of rehearsals before production of *Oedipus the King*.

Although I sported a black-and-blue forehead for some days and suffered some headaches, in general I came away from "Cross Winds" with no lasting injury. One nice result of the general disaster was Patty's behavior toward me. She seemed genuinely repentant, though she never would admit that she had sped up on purpose out by Devil's Elbow. At play practice all that week, she seemed to go out of her way to demonstrate her feelings for me.

Mr. Ferguson had me (the shepherd) working that week with Linda Roy (Jocasta) and Charles Riddick (Oedipus) on some of the final moments of the play. In those late scenes a terrible sense of foreboding grows in the mind of Oedipus's wife, and in the audience. A grim truth is about to be revealed.

As the innocent shepherd, who'd actually done a good deed years ago in saving the infant boy, I should have felt sorry for Jocasta. She'd condemned her own child to death and then unwittingly married him a lifetime later, a horrific destiny.

Somehow, though, Linda seemed to look at me with pity as we rehearsed this part of the play.

Of course, we were not on stage at the same time, as Jocasta races off when she sees Oedipus determined to question the shepherd about events at the time of his birth. I arrive shortly after she departs.

The king innocently seeks out the shepherd, not realizing that the secret of his birth will reveal that he has slain his father, married his own mother

"Does anyone know that shepherd," asks Oedipus, "the one this herdsman received me from? Anyone seen him in the countryside or in the city? Speak, someone! The time has come to reveal the truth once and for all."

Jocasta begs her husband to abandon this inquiry into his own past. "Stop--in the name of the gods, if you value yourself, stop asking these questions!"

When the shepherd is found, Oedipus threatens him with torture if he doesn't reveal all he knows. But revelation is just as terrible:

"Oh no, don't make me say it. I'm right at the edge of telling what you least want to hear, the horrible truth."

37

With Mr. Ferguson's encouragement, I took to the challenge of acting. Being on stage is taking everyday life and amplifying it, making it larger. Each actor has to take this process one step further, making himself larger than the rest of the cast in order to stand out for the audience. He has to take the foreground from the background.

This was something I'd been trying to do all my life, certainly in my senior year. I wanted to emerge from the blur of many faces ("on Black Street") to be someone of distinction, Hugh Noone, number one on the tennis team, BMOC, lead in the senior play.

Wrestling Linda Roy in her side yard and battling Robert Paterson on the tennis courts had been part of this same project. So had taking Patty to the movies and being the safety net for her cheerleading stunt. Riding Black Beauty and piloting The Spirit of St. Louis II, all this was my effort to become someone, to have an identity.

I got Mr. Ferguson's backing in this project, though he had never seemed to consider me material to work with until now. At tryouts in the past he would look right through me to the well known stars. Now he was at my side at rehearsal, pulling me into just the right position, taking my hand to show me how to make the gesture of the moment, so close to my ear demonstrating my lines that I was almost embarrassed for those who didn't get so much attention. Patty, in particular, was unhappy with the director's style.

I thought Mr. Ferguson took less time with Patty because she was naturally so good in her part as

Antigone. She didn't hesitate to project herself on the stage any more than she feared to propel herself off the trampoline. I realize now, however, that Ferguson saw her as a distraction for me.

Feeling guilty because of the crash, she was taking every opportunity we had to draw me away from the others for demonstrations of her feelings. We were together at times behind the curtains, in wardrobe, in the set construction room. Eager though I was to excel under the lights, Patty's wiles lured me into the darkness as well. Once again, her slender middle was irresistible.

One of her favorite maneuvers in that last week of practice was to back up to me while we watched something going on in front of us--the principals rehearsing, the stage crew fixing the scenery, the costume people adjusting dress. She'd lean her head back on my shoulder, pull my arms around her waist, cross my hands right over her navel. And she'd move beneath my fingers.

Her athlete's build and years of exercise gave her remarkable control over all her muscles, including the stomach muscles. She was like a belly dancer in my arms, but stationary. The firm, tight flesh flexed and tensed as I held her. The others couldn't tell what we were doing, but her abdominal pulsing was generating an almost painful erection right behind her.

"Stand that column up," says Mr. Ferguson to Timmy Horton of the stage crew while we watch in the shadows. *My* column is up.

"Jocasta's dress must drape down from that shoulder," he tells Beth Revard, one of the costumers. Splendid as that breast is (and I see it sharply outlined in the robe as she rotates her shoulder), I merely note it in an academic manner as Patty's hips do a rhythmic little sway and her tummy presses against my palms.

I oscillate, then, between these titillating encounters with Patty and serious attempts to learn the elements of classical drama. Hot and cold for art and love, I am leading the life of intensity I have long desired.

Occasionally, I have moments of rest, when Patty is on stage as Antigone. I'm grateful for time to recover.

As much fun as all this is, an undercurrent of worry rises up during some of these breaks. Henry's been difficult ever since Mom left him sleeping to see about me at the hospital. He missed work to stay at the Top Hat that night, which she spent in the hospital with me. And now Sergeant Pritchard says he has to make up that time or he will be out of a job.

At least Henry sobered up after that one night, making it only a minor binge for him. And he returned to work the following evening. So he was still on the payroll, but he told us he would never work the extra hours.

"Dammit, I've done my time for the college. They got to give me some time off when my boy is in the hospital." He didn't seem to recognize that his drinking wasn't caused by concern for me. He was mad that his wife wasn't there to feed him and take his abuse.

Mom tried to sweet-talk him. "Well now, Henry, it would just be one night. And you say not much happens. You get to listen to the radio."

"The hell!" His huge fist thumped the kitchen table. "I've got to make the rounds. And you don't know what I run into out there."

I tried to catch Mom's eye, to signal that he was approaching the crisis moment in this fit of anger. If we backed off now and agreed with him, he would probably calm down. But if we pushed him, his rage could escalate suddenly, peak at violence.

"You're right, Henry. You're right." She decided to play it my way. Henry finished his dinner and went to work at the regular time. But later Mom told me what she had wanted to say--that we couldn't afford to lose that job right now. I'd just been accepted at the university, and they had to find a way to pay my fees for next year.

Miss Timmons had helped me with the application. And she must have written a strong letter of recommendation, because my grades, except for her classes, had never been better than average. I surprised many of my teachers just by taking the College Boards. And then my scores were good enough to get me in most of the state schools. So, I'd made an impression at my high school at last, if only by surpassing expectations.

Of course, I'm sure many there felt my acceptance was a fluke and that I wouldn't make it at Columbia. I never had the chance to prove them right or wrong, though. My arrest and trial gave them all the evidence they needed to conclude that I was what they had always thought.

Right now, however, I was on stage with important seniors in the last major event of the year, except for graduation itself. And I was achieving a measure of success there that continued to surprise even me.

One aspect of my newly achieved stature was evident in the last days of preparation. The stage crew was ready to test the raising and lowering of set pieces, the movement of backdrops that would occur between acts.

One particular situation stumped the crew: hoisting the backdrop of the palace to show behind it the skyline outside the city of Thebes. Ropes and pulleys all worked, so the structure did rise into the rafters. But there was a hitch in the ascent, a disturbing pause that Mr. Ferguson was determined to remove.

The scene change came at a crucial moment in the play, the arrival of the messenger from Corinth. His presence will begin the unraveling of Oedipus's past, the revelation of the terrible secret of his identity. So the director insisted that the scene change go swiftly, smoothly.

"Timmy, do you see the problem?"

"No. We pull the ropes, the backdrop rises."

"Yes, but it has this bump in it, when the bottom is just here." He holds a hand about one foot higher than his head. "It can't stop there, then go the rest of the way up. We need it to rise smoothly all the way."

Patty and I are watching with the other members of the cast. At this point, we're generally released from our duties in production to concentrate on our roles. So I'm only half listening to Mr. Ferguson here. Well, maybe one tenth listening. Patty has backed up against me, and my hands are on her hips.

"Get Noone to look at it," offers Timmy. "He's the mechanical expert."

"That's right," says Mr. Ferguson. "Hugh, use your airplane-building skills to fix the set here while I work with Antigone."

"Hm? Oh, yeah. Sure." I try to look studious and move forward slowly as Patty heads for center stage. There's a stiffness to my walk I don't want to have to explain.

"The ropes are clear, "says Timmy. "I don't see any problem with the winches or the pulleys." He is peering up into the rafters, the ropes disappearing in darkness.

"Maybe it's not the equipment," I suggest. "Maybe it's how you're doing it."

"What do you mean?"

"Just bring it down again. Then hoist it. I'll watch."

The answer becomes obvious as Timmy cranks the wench handle. He begins with a fury, turning the handle in a blur. But he tires at about 15 seconds and does the rest at a significantly slower pace. At the end of his first effort there's a clear hesitation, catching his breath, so to speak. And that's what the director has seen in the backdrop's pause midway in its ascent.

I explain this to Timmy, get him to try again, slowly but steadily from start to finish. The set rises without a hitch.

But there's a slight hitch in my view of the past now caused by Mr. Ferguson and Timmy's recognition of my building skills. Did I get a part in the play because I could do a great job in construction and not because I actually had acting ability? I think back to how much I've done over the last few weeks. I've built frames on which scenery is hung, constructed risers for the chorus to stand on, put together steps for palace and throne.

But, wait. It's true that Mr. Ferguson put me in charge of the more difficult set-building tasks. And others deferred to me regularly, understanding that I had expertise here. But I was still the shepherd, the guy who reveals the truth to Oedipus. That important role wouldn't be assigned to me just because I could use a hammer and saw!

"That's perfect, Hugh, just perfect," says Mr. Ferguson when Timmy repeats the hoist as I've instructed him. Mr. Ferguson, the director, squeezes my arm above the elbow in appreciation. He squeezes it, and he keeps his hand there.

In fact, he keeps his hand on my arm and gently massages the muscle longer than seems appropriate.

I think about this for a minute, then turn and see a look in his eye that I recognize, though I've never seen it in a man's eye. And I know all of a sudden that I am in some trouble here.

38

Oh, man! Another person who's heard that I'm a queer. Ferguson's a homosexual and has learned from Mr. Simpson or one of his circle that he'd have a chance with me. And that's why I've gotten a role in the play, not because I'm a budding actor.

This rumor has gone far enough. But how do I convince the citizens of Fairfield (who, I now assume, all think me queer) that it's false?

Maybe I'll have to find the real queers in this town. If I can point them out, it will be clear that I'm not one of them. But who is a homosexual in my school? Young boys don't talk about these things in these years, at least not in the conservative middle of the country.

These suspicions, by the way, are the first glimmerings I had of what was going on behind the scenes at this time. Most people remained ignorant of the varied sexual preferences of others even after I was accused and found guilty. When I learned the truth, I was in no position to get others to accept it. My only ally, though I didn't realize it for years, was Karen Murphy.

Karen, in fact, gave me one of the key pieces of the puzzle on the night before I was arrested. But even that wasn't enough to save me.

Up until that time I was busy trying to put some distance between myself and Mr. Ferguson. I kept him at arm's length, literally, that night after he massaged my triceps. And I got out of the building as quickly as I could, riding Patty home on the back of Black Beauty and staying to neck in her front porch swing.

She was frustrated at having been kept busy by Mr. Ferguson and was not interested in my problem. She had me in her arms before we had even settled on the swing.

"Did you see the way Mr. Ferguson looked at me tonight?" I asked when she finally gave me a break.

"He's the director. He's supposed to look at you. Now you look at me." She took her blue aviator's scarf, which she again had tied around her middle, unwound it, and hooked me by my neck.

"You, you're cute," I say. " I like you. But you're a girl."

"Ooo, how observant! You're supposed to like girls."

"According to your father, I'm supposed to like boys. I think Mr. Ferguson really likes boys."

"Maybe so. Who cares?" She comes forward for a kiss, for several kisses.

"I care. Ferguson was fondling me tonight."

"Fondling you? Like this." She giggles. Holding both ends of the scarf with one hand, she runs the other up my thigh.

"Stop that! We've got to do something. You've got to tell your father the truth." I try to slip out of her scarf noose, but she holds on.

"We can't do that. He'll make me stop seeing you. He might even beat the crap out of you."

She's got a point there. "Why don't you. . . . Hey, I've got it. You tell him I've changed. I changed with you."

"You mean I converted you? With this?" She drops the scarf and lifts her blouse. I see all the way from the bottom of her bra to the top of her bikini underwear. If I hadn't been interested before, I believe this would do it now. And I like this way out of my dilemma--conversion.

"I'm serious. You tell him that you've nearly converted me, but I'm still shy about it all. He'll think it's good to rescue a boy from being queer."

"He'll still beat the crap out of you, poor boy." She puts her arm around me, tries to rest my head on her shoulder.

"Not if we do it right." I pull back. "See, you say I'm almost OK. You've been helping me resist those nasty impulses. But you're worried I might slip back to my old ways, especially if I start keeping company with certain guys. So you need to keep going out with me, keep talking to me and keep me away from the homos. I'm teetering on the verge of becoming normal. But if you let me go, I'll fall back . . . back into the grasp of Ferguson, or whoever."

"It might take all summer to get you straight," she says with a laugh. "But I'll work on you." She puts my hand under her blouse, presses it flat against her stomach. I accept another therapy session.

Later I stagger out to Black Beauty and ride home. I actually believe this plan might work, if Patty takes her part seriously. I'll try to find a way to let others know that I was never queer, that it was an ugly rumor started by my enemies. Maybe by Robert Paterson. No, that's not right. The dead can't defend themselves.

Right now, though, I need to be home before it gets too late, and not just because it's a school night. I need to help Mom keep Henry in line. More and more often these days he threatens not to go to work. Pritchard is still waiting for him to make up those missed hours, and Henry's about out of excuses.

I sense trouble as soon as I come in through the kitchen. Henry is slumped in his favorite easy chair in the living room, drinking a beer. Drinking many beers, I realize, as I see a row of empties on the coffee table in front of him. I know things are bad because my mom hasn't carried the bottles away. When he's fuming, Henry won't let her clean up.

Where is Mom, I wonder? She's not in the kitchen ironing. And I don't hear her sewing machine at work in the bedroom.

"Hugh," Henry calls. "That you, boy?"

"Yeah, Pop. Where's Mom?"

"She went over to the Martins'. I wanted to have a talk with you."

"Sure, Pop." I'm trying to be casual, but this is grim. Mom did visit sometimes with her close neighbors, but never at night. He had gotten her out of the way.

"I was down at the Top Hat earlier, watchin' the fights on TV."

"Uh-huh."

"There was a couple of lightheavies going at it, a real slugfest. I used to box some, you know."

I'd heard the stories before, how he'd whipped all the other farm boys around in a makeshift ring set up in a neighbor's hayloft. "Yeah," I say, cautiously sitting on the sofa. I also pretend to watch the television, more boxing.

"Well, anyway. Boxing and football, those are real sports, know what I mean? Not like that sissy tennis you play." He takes a long drink of Falstaff.

"I'm going to be number one on the team, Pop. And it's a hard game. You have to be in shape to win."

"Naw, not like football and stuff, where you take a pounding. I've always worried about you with your sports, but usually I just thought it's 'cause you're small, a little fella'."

All of a sudden I feel a connection in his rambling. A long-buried fear wells up in my mind.

"Now, Hugh, I was talking with Mr. Simpson today. He come in the Hat for a minute. And he tells me you're dating his daughter. That right?"

"Patty and I are sort of going steady."

"Your Mom told me that, but I didn't much see it. She's high class. Her family lives over there by the hospital, don't they?"

"Yes, but she likes me. We do things together."

"According to her dad, it's what you *don't* do together that pleases him. He says you're a queer. That right?"

He's gotten angry now, his face flushed as he drains the most recent beer. He cranks off the cap of another, flips the opener back onto the table.

"Listen, Pop, Mr. Simpson *thinks* I'm a homo, but it's not so."

I'm between a rock and a hard place here. I don't want to admit to being queer, but I also shouldn't confess what Patty and I do in places like the bathroom of her dad's store.

"Why are you in that play with Ferguson, the little homo? And you used to hang around with that other homo, what's his name?"

"Patty and I have been going together for a couple of months, Pop. And before that I was dating Linda Roy and Karen Murphy, other girls."

"Yeah? What do you do with this Patty Simpson?"

"We just neck and all, Pop. We're not going to get in any trouble."

"You neck and all!" Now he's up and moving. He gestures in the direction of town, as if Patty and I are out there wrapped around each other. "If you do, why does Simpson think you like boys?"

I stand up too. If he goes too far, I want to be on my feet, ready to run. But I lose control in what I say. "He probably's been listening to you."

He glowers and says, "You've always been a little sissy, just like your dad was."

"Don't you say anything about him."

"Richard Noone, he thought he was goin' be a war hero. Went off and got his ass shot down, didn't he?"

"You're drunk. And I'm leaving." I should have gone out the front door, away from Henry. But I was thinking of getting on Black Beauty, riding somewhere. So I tried to step quickly behind the couch, on into the kitchen. I'd stop at the Martins' and tell Mom not to go home.

Henry spun and beat me to the doorway, however. "You're not going anywhere until I get some answers. If you're not queer, you've been trying to get some off that Simpson girl, right? You do know what to do with girls, don't you?"

Now he's coming at me, shoving me in the chest with his big fist. I push his hand off with a swing of my arm. "Get out of my way."

"I'm not getting out of your way." We've come head to head in the middle of the room. "You're gettin' the hell out of my house."

"I'll be happy to go, but I'm going to tell you something. You lay a hand on my mother, and I'll come back here and. . . . "

"And what?" he thunders, grabbing my shirt with both fists. I grab his shirt in return, even though he's jerking me up on my toes. We're eye to eye now, close enough to kiss. But that's not what we're going to do.

"I'll. . . ." Before I can say what I'll do, I see his face change expression. From red it starts to turn to blue. His eyes glaze, his hands relax, and he crashes to the floor.

39

"What have you done?" screamed my mother. I looked up to see her stepping from the kitchen into the dining room.

"I . . . ? He. . . ." I saw Henry's huge form lying on the carpet, but I couldn't explain what had happened. My mind had gone numb.

Anxiety about the rumors that I'm queer, worry about Mr. Simpson's finding out I'm banging his daughter, anger at insults to my real father, troubled memories of being with Linda Roy, questions about why Karen Murphy is present at all the crises of my life, concern about my mother's safety--all these feelings made my brain a den of confusion.

Seeing her husband fall, Betty Morgan Noone Maas froze. She thought her son had somehow brought this big man down. I don't think she went so far as to imagine the event--a subtle poison, an unseen blow, electric shock. All she saw was me standing and him flat on his back.

He was turning blue, though, and we both came to our senses in another minute. We knew we had to get him to the hospital.

We would discover that, in this confrontation with his stepson, Henry had suffered a heart attack. Of course, years of bad diet, hard drinking, and little exercise made him a likely candidate for such an event. The high tension created by Pritchard's ultimatum coupled with rumors about me had pushed his system to the point of collapse.

I also found out that Mom hadn't been able to stay away from the house that night, nervous for both Henry and me. She came in right at the end of our shouting match.

Together we dragged Henry to the kitchen door, pushed him into the Buick, and raced to Phipps County Memorial. Dr. Younger got him on oxygen and medication right away. There was nothing for Mom and me to do but wait.

We were both in an excited state, the adrenaline flowing from emotional and physical exertion. When our systems calmed down enough for us to talk sensibly, I tried to make her believe that this had been a minor altercation.

"What did you say to him?" She was accusatory at first.

"Oh, he got onto the sports thing again. How I should play football."

"He wants you to do like he did."

"Then he got all worked up about the college thing." This wasn't true, but I didn't want her to know what he was really mad about.

"I told you not to bring that up. You let me handle it."

"Well, I was worried about his not being ready to go to work, too. He was drinking, so I knew he wasn't planning to go."

"He told me earlier he had heard things about you. He was going to have it out about what you were doing. What did he mean?"

"Oh, he was . . . he's not sure I should be dating Patty."

"Why not?"

"Well, he thinks her family wouldn't like us, wouldn't have anything to do with a boy on Bla- . . . with a boy who lives in this part of town."

"Doesn't she work in the store downtown?"

"Yeah, but her father *owns* the store. They're country club people, Mom. But Patty and I are OK. You don't need to worry about this. Really."

Then the doctor appeared.

The smile on Dr. Younger's face when he came into the waiting room immediately relaxed us. And the report was basically positive. Henry was a strong man for all the abuse he had given his body. The doctor indicated he had an excellent chance for full recovery. He was conscious right now and stable. We could go in to see him in a few minutes.

I thought it best for Mom to go alone. After ten minutes with him, she told me to go on home. He would need the rest. But I stayed the night with her.

We didn't talk much after that first exchange. We were both drained. I'm not sure how much of her life she was replaying in her mind, but during the hours we dozed on the waiting room sofas I kept coming back to several things Henry had said.

Was I the last person in Fairfield to realize Ferguson was a homosexual? If Henry knew this, he probably knew who, if anyone, was Ferguson's "special friend."

Of course, in those days we didn't think of homosexuals as having partners or long-term lovers. The stereotype was always of meetings in public rest rooms, usually for money. We heard of young boys "queered" by their piano teacher, their eccentric scoutmaster, the single uncle from San Francisco. But there was no such things as an enduring homosexual relationship.

We were terrified of getting tricked by such a character. The theory then had it that, once screwed, you would be queer for life. So don't get caught by "one of them."

I remembered a strange incident one time with a barber. I was the only customer in the shop above the Top Hat. The regular barber was trying out a new guy so he could take a vacation.

Mr. Forbes went back to the storeroom when the new guy was finishing up. As I turned to get my coat off the rack, he told me I had a nice back. "Back?" I thought and got out of there. The new guy wasn't hired.

What "other homo" had Henry thought I was running around with? Of course, Billy was my best friend, so at first I thought he probably meant him. But since Cross Rhodes, Billy had been pretty much out of circulation. And once he got back in circulation, it was all with Karen Murphy. I suspect my stepfather knew her reputation as well. She had dated quite a few guys before this year. Word had been that she would go all the way, but I wasn't sure that was the case anymore.

Anyway, Henry continued his improvement the next day. And Dr. Younger still believed he would recover, though not perhaps his former strength. He was going to have to take up a different lifestyle after a substantial stay in the hospital.

Mom insisted I go back to school after missing that one day, even return to rehearsals of *Oedipus*. She could stay with Henry as much as was necessary. The performance was the coming weekend, so I had to be there or be replaced.

Henry improved steadily and was soon sitting up in bed, pretending to be grouchy about hospital restrictions. What he wanted, of course, was a drink. I knew he also liked having a good reason not to be at work.

Ferguson was happy to have me back at rehearsal, but I was uneasy around him. I needed to find some way to show him that I wasn't interested. Still, I didn't want to make him angry right in the middle of production. This was, to put it delicately, a ticklish situation.

My plan was to get Patty's help. We talked on the night of dress rehearsal, sitting in some back row seats half an hour before we were to begin the final run through.

"Just, you know, give me some little pecks on the cheek or something," I said. "I'll show where my interests are."

"Oh, I can *do* that." She gave me one of those little grins of hers, and I worried she'd do more than I'd asked. I wished I had found some way to suggest moderation. But I liked her next suggestion.

"How about I help you with your make-up tomorrow night?"

"OK. That could work. Your hands on me."

"And after the performance you can put your hands on me."

She took my hand off the arm between the seats and placed it in her lap. The lights were down as the stage was bright. She lifted her sweater and slipped my hand under the waistband of her skirt.

"Hey!" I said. "Tomorrow, where Mr. Ferguson can see. But maybe not quite so much." Still, I didn't move my hand.

She flexed the muscles of her abdomen, rolled her hips on the seat. I thought about some way I could get one of her hands in my lap.

Ah me, as much as I was enjoying our hands on each other, you'd think the message would be clear to the whole world: I liked girls! I especially liked Patty Simpson, her navel right then probably at the center of my universe.

Then we saw Karen Murphy come out on stage, shade her eyes to look out into the auditorium. Patty was being called to the girls' dressing room.

I stayed where I was, letting the effects of that tummy rub subside. Karen plumped down in the seat on the other side of me.

"How's your father?" she asked.

"Stepfather. He's improving."

"Ah, good. You ready?"

"I guess so, how about you?"

"Oh, you know, I'm just a member of the chorus, someone in the background."

"Hey, the chorus is important. It's the whole community."

"You're right, I suppose. What everyone around thinks is important."

"I know. In fact, right now, people are saying things about me that aren't true."

"What?"

"Well, that I'm, that I, uh, I like boys not girls."

"Oh that's silly. It's because you were with the cheerleaders. You know how people talk. I know what you like."

That was certainly true, and it occurred to me right then that Karen, along with Patty, might be able to help me.

"Do you know what I heard?"

"Hm?"

I looked around to make sure no one had come close. "I heard that Mr. Ferguson, um. . . ."

"Yeah, now, that's true."

"How do you know?"

"Well, my dad is downtown all the time. He hears things. He told me a couple of weeks ago that he doesn't know why the school board hasn't fired Ferguson."

"Has he done something?"

"Well, my dad thinks so. But there's no reason to let everyone know now."

"What do you mean?"

"Well." This time *she* looked around to see that we were still alone. "They say Robert Paterson was his . . . his guy."

At that moment, Mr. Ferguson himself appeared on the stage and shouted, "Curtain call. Everyone in place."

40

Dress rehearsal went smoothly, but the actual performance of *Oedipus* the next night proved a totally unrehearsed event for the entire town of Fairfield. The police came at the intermission, and you might say that "a play within the play" stole the show. I was the reluctant star, and the director of "the play outside the play" found himself in a role he hadn't anticipated, either.

Thank God my mother wasn't there for all of this. I insisted that she stay with Henry, who had had a bit of a relapse. He had been asserting vehemently that he was completely well in order to get out of the hospital, but exertion produced chest pains and shortness of breath. Dr. Younger teamed with my mother to insist that he stay in the hospital through the weekend. I told my mother she could come on the second night of the performance, once Henry had stabilized again. Of course, there was no second performance.

And Henry didn't leave the hospital alive.

Originally, I thought things were going my way at the premier. Patty did a great job of flirting with me, and I responded enthusiastically whenever Mr. Ferguson was around.

Examining the blush she'd applied, she caressed my cheek. She tousled my hair when she was spraying gray over it. And she tapped my lips with the eyebrow pencil she was using to give me the wrinkles of age.

I put an arm around her waist and pulled her onto my lap.

Catching her hand, I suggested I keep her calm for her role by holding tight. I made repeated remarks about Antigone's attractive figure. While Mr. Ferguson scowled at us through all this, I never knew whether it had achieved the desired effect. Once the play began, he paced backstage in total absorption. That night he was the director, and we were his cast, not potential lovers of either sex.

I prepared, then, to realize a long thwarted ambition, to take the stage. Appearing before the citizens of Fairfield in a major production like this was a significant step up from playing tennis for the high school, even as number one. We seldom had spectators at our matches who weren't family and close friends.

My theatrical debut was, however, never to occur. I was arrested before I even came on stage as the shepherd who reveals the king's past. The chief of police marched down the center aisle right as the lights went up for intermission. What a reversal! Lights, camera, action, and they took me out in handcuffs. I had been accused of raping Linda Roy.

Eventually, I learned how it all happened. And, finally, I have the chance to set the record straight right here. If my lawyer is right--and the lab tests confirm my story--I'll erase from the books a conviction that's stood for nearly twenty years.

You see, Linda Roy's father became convinced that Robert Paterson could not have gotten his daughter pregnant, as everyone in the know (everyone who *thought* they were in the know, that is) had concluded after Cross Rhodes. Dr. Roy had found out that Ferguson had discovered the boy's true sexual identity, and that there were witnesses.

Ferguson--that's probably who Paterson was with that night out on Old Farm Road, by the way, when Billy and I had gone driving after playing Tip the Scales at Karen's house. Naturally, we assumed he was cheating on Linda with some girl, though we never caught up with the car to see who it was. But Ferguson and Paterson were spotted parking several times later by a cruising policeman.

Linda had realized Robert's preference for members of his own sex probably about the same time he did. They had been going steady on and off since the summer, and she was having trouble holding him. He enjoyed dating her but not, after a time, the intimacy. In fact, Karen learned, he'd been discreetly approached a number of times before by Mr. Ferguson. Now Robert found himself increasingly attracted, though he didn't know for some weeks how deep that attraction would run.

It was in one of their times apart that Linda took me for a ride in her daddy's car. I think she was doing it to spite Robert, although it flatters me to think perhaps she needed sexual satisfaction as well. At the time she had no intention of turning me into a criminal, but that night of lust served her in the end.

Robert had also begun drinking that fall. He was clever about it, choosing Vodka from his father's well supplied liquor cabinet so you couldn't smell alcohol on his breath. And he didn't show the effects--probably a potential alcoholic. But there were times when he drank late into the night and began the next day with the hair of the dog. On those occasions when I had noticed he had bad breath, that was only a symptom of a larger loss of control over his life's routine.

After a while Linda came to the conclusion that the only way to keep her boyfriend was to get pregnant by him. It was a terrible game to play, with risk and consequence. But she was a determined player, possessing, remember, that killer instinct.

Robert's increasing inability to get excited with her, though, made conception a challenge. On most recent dates, when she was being careful *not* to get pregnant, the only way she had been able to turn him on was by showing him her backside and letting him do what some men do to boys. So one night parking on Old Farm Road, a night right in the middle of her cycle, she slid his manhood from one place to another. He was so drunk he didn't even know. A week later, she told him what had happened and said she was carrying their child. She claimed this showed he was not really queer.

He panicked and said it couldn't be. He broke away from her and wouldn't even answer her phone calls. Of course, her claim that she was pregnant was half bluff-- she hoped it was so, but she had not had any tests.

Then she missed a period. Something had to be done. And that's probably when she first decided she could use me, Hugh Noone of Black Street. She was going to claim I had assaulted her, that she was the victim of outrage.

Why she didn't cry "rape" once she made that decision, though, wasn't clear. Perhaps she had some new reason to believe Robert would eventually come back to her. They would marry, and he would accept the child (who may or may not have been mine).

Or maybe she even thought about the consequences for me. Raping a girl from a good family would be a serious crime. So she hung fire with her plan for some weeks, long enough for Cross Rhodes to happen, for Robert to die, and for her to lose the baby. Then there was no need to accuse anyone. There was no need, that is, until her father heard me rambling at the hospital after the crash of Spirit of St. Louis II and he learned about Mr. Ferguson.

Dr. Roy, like everyone else, had accepted Paterson as Linda's seducer, though he had never liked it that this meant his daughter had been sleeping with someone outside of wedlock. He was fiercely moralistic about such matters, like many of Fairfield's elite. Since all involved agreed to keep it quiet, though, he had accepted the shame he felt for Linda's behavior.

Then I practically confessed. And he learned from Mr. Murphy that Robert had been an unlikely lover for his daughter. That unhappy boy was discovering his true desire with a man at the very moment she was conceiving.

Seeking a guilty party, Dr. Roy confronted his daughter, who broke, already unsteady from dealing with the accident, Robert's death, the miscarriage. She fell back on her earlier scheme and fingered me as a rapist, someone from Black Street who wouldn't have the resources to fight such a charge. I was a boy whose stepfather should be fired and whose mother took in laundry. Linda was the daughter of a wealthy dentist, highly respected in town. And Paterson was the nephew of the mayor.

I'd called and called, Linda said, pestering her so that she'd decided the only way to get rid of me was to go out once. She claimed I'd taken the wheel of her daddy's Lincoln, driven her into the country, and forced myself on her. Afterwards, she'd been too traumatized to tell anyone. Dr. Roy believed he could recall signs of shock in her behavior at the time.

To make matters worse, I couldn't deny having had sex with Linda Roy. There was even physical evidence of the act. She had hidden the underwear she wore that night, she confessed, stuffed it in an old clothes bag in the back of her mother's closet. She assumed they would become rags. But they sent me to prison.

Sexual crimes, especially against minors, were tried quietly in those days. If anything was written in the paper, euphemisms like "attack" were used. And the name of the victim was ferociously protected. So anyone who might have helped in my defense didn't even know what I was accused of, let alone the outcome of the trial. One report circulated that I had joined the Army, gone overseas. Only a handful learned I had been convicted of "assault."

Billy Rhodes and Karen Murphy tried to ask my mom what was going on, but she was crushed by my arrest and Henry's death. He'd had the final, fatal attack the very day I was taken into custody. Mom had no one to turn to.

For my part, I believed events were fulfilling a terrible destiny plotted out for me, the left-handed one. I had been doomed from the cradle to travel counter to Route 66. I was a man born in the wrong world who did everything backward.

Remember, too, that I had convinced myself at the time that I was the one controlling events in the back seat of the Roy Continental. Women were not sexually aggressive, so I must have taken the lead in what happened. The sexual revolution and science's expanding study of desire have given me a different view today, of course.

I took my fatalistic attitude into the courtroom, accepted the verdict, went off to the Missouri State Penitentiary without appeal. Only one person believed I was innocent, the person who would become my lawyer. She would try for years to gain access to the court record, sealed when I pleaded guilty. And she would eventually discover the truth, though, until recently, she had no means to prove it in a court of law.

And now I take this record of my life, this revision of what I had believed for a decade, maybe more, and present it to the judge who's hearing my case tomorrow. If it's accepted, and the scientific evidence confirms it, I'm a free man.

In some ways--some very important ways--I don't really care. I know the truth now. And, as we all believe, it's the truth that sets you free. All the same, I think I could do more outside than inside now. I would like to start again.

Epilogue: A Left-Hander on Route 66 at Last

I'm out.

It took a little longer than I thought--anything like this does--but Judge Parker read my story, reviewed the lab reports, and reversed the decision. I'm out.

It was the physical evidence that did the most to prove my innocence. DNA testing showed conclusively that the sperm on Linda Roy's underwear was not mine. Whose it was, we do not know. Robert's possibly. Maybe there was yet another lover in Linda Roy's circle. It doesn't really matter now.

Another fact of the matter is that the panties exhibited as evidence at my original trial were white. For all my bedazzlement in the backseat of the Roy Continental two decades ago, I know Linda was wearing black.

I didn't contest the issue at the trial, didn't even tell my court-appointed lawyer. I had decided that I was doomed, that I'd killed my stepfather, that everyone was against me, that I wouldn't go free no matter how much evidence was on my side.

But now, well, I believe I am meant to be free. So I allowed my lawyer to request that the panties, preserved by the court all this time, be tested.

Not that I think Linda Roy, later Linda Pierson, should take my place in here, if she were still alive. We no longer view teenage sex the way we did in those days. Some kids made a mistake, sure. But they committed no crime that needs additional punishment.

Linda Roy, by the way, went on to college, married an engineer, and moved to California. She died of cancer at the age of 33. The judge hearing my appeal sees no reason to exhume her past and damage that new family. And I have to agree.

If she were alive, it would be hard to prove she'd instigated sex that long-ago night. But I had never made a formal confession, and her father over time changed his view of the case. In recent questioning, he told the judge he'd come to suspect his daughter's promiscuous behavior after several scrapes she'd had at college. He now thought it probable that any sex she'd had with boys in high school was wholly consensual.

The primary facts that someone else was having sex with Linda and that I could not be shown to be the one who had impregnated her, did, then, bring about a reversal of my conviction. The judge has kept the details from the public but announced that scientific findings prove my innocence of the original charge. I write this final note for my own satisfaction, not publication.

My mother might have wanted the public to know the full truth, but she died the year of my arrest, I believe of a broken heart. In heaven, she's been satisfied all along that I, though sentenced to life in prison, am not an evil man. And my lawyer has convinced me that a higher justice prevails in this and all cases.

My lawyer I guess I can tell you now who that is, especially because it appears she's going to be important in the rest of my life. Karen Murphy never gave up on me after the trial. I thought she was just a friend, still living in Fairfield, who came to shop in Jefferson City and was good enough to visit.

She told me at one point that she was no longer dating Billy, that she had decided to quit working with her father at Rexall's, that she would go to college. After a divorce she decided on law school, eventually setting up a practice in Fairfield defending indigent and poor clients. She's come to be viewed as something of a saint by the underprivileged of Phipps County.

Every few months she would pay a visit, the only one who ever did after my mother passed. I built up a whole new life behind bars, and she was my only link to the past, to the outside.

Some years after her own parents died and her practice was pretty well established, Karen bought the house across 10th Street from the former Roy place on Missouri Avenue, one block off Business Route 66. In fact, as I write these final words at her dining room table, I can see across the street to the side yard where I once wrestled the former first seed on the Fairfield High girls' tennis team.

Karen's commitment to fairness was built on religious principles, the fundamentalist faith she'd strayed from for only a brief time in her youth. I regret that I was party to that straying, though I've begun to wonder if even that error wasn't part of a larger plan.

It was a Christian spirit of charity that inspired Karen to reach out a helping hand to the needy and to the unfortunate--to people like me. And sometimes she got hurt in the process.

She carried her message of redemption to me behind bars in Jefferson City, but I assumed for a long time that she talked that way to everyone. And it's true that she witnessed to other jailbirds, often former clients whom she'd defended. In her view God's mercy touched everyone. But her eye rested on me in a special way.

I ignored her appeals for years, though I took back from her the little chain with the cross she'd given me so long ago. My mother had found it in my bedroom before she died, and asked Karen about it. Karen was a regular visitor to the house on Cedar Street in my mother's last months. She promised that I would have it.

Despite Karen's faith, religion made no sense to me in a prison environment. This was a place of punishment, not redemption. When I got past a resigned bitterness, I became a student again, not a religious enthusiast. I took the GED and got the high school diploma I had been only months from obtaining at Fairfield High School. Then I took college courses by correspondence and from the University of Missouri, which sent professors to the prison in the years of flush state budgets.

While I studied the law informally, I never had a desire to become a lawyer or to plead my own case. I did offer counsel to other inmates when I thought their character or their circumstances warranted it.

In my official studies, though, I did something unlike students on the outside at the time, who became business majors, planning lives of making money. Instead, I studied literature, reading the Great Books.

I'm convinced that was a good choice for someone who'd felt the burden of Fate. It's not just that I had no prospect of ever having a job when I was studying, but I really wanted to learn about the human experience. I wanted to know what Ulysses felt far from Ithaca, what Lear did when he was betrayed by all those around him, what David Copperfield dreamed when he worked in the blacking warehouse in the slums of London. I drew strength from their examples.

When did I come around fully to Karen's way of thinking? That's hard to say, as it occurred slowly. For a good while I was convinced that, if I ever got out of the Missouri State Penitentiary, I would emigrate alone to Australia. Down Under I would become the self I had never been, the left-handed twin who might have shared life in my mother's womb. I would find myself in a land where water swirls down drains counterclockwise, the way I approach many of my problems.

But somewhere along the line I came to understand that there was no inverse self, no me-in-a-mirror. I was what I was; left-handed was as good as right-handed; I could live in a right-handed world; I had the same right as everyone else to travel down Route 66 to fulfillment.

I am now convinced that it was the experience of Cross Rhodes that actually marked the turning point of my life, when death laid a heavy hand on Robert Paterson and spared the rest of us. It has haunted me through the years, its meaning emerging slowly. Everything has consequences; it's a serious world.

Of course, I'm also convinced now that there were other signposts along my way, hints that life made more sense with a God in the picture, even a picture that includes tragedy. To endure in a world that includes pain you have to be helped--by the mother who loves you, by good teachers like Miss Timmons, by a fatherly Doc Garnet. And, of course, by Karen.

The same Karen who will be here soon. She called from the courthouse, where she's pleading the case of another lost soul.

I suppose I can cite the date of our marriage, just over eight years ago, when I was still in jail, as the time when I accepted the message she'd had for me since we were children. At the time, I still felt marriage was a foolish gesture on her part. We'd never have a life together.

During that time I also rediscovered joy, the other hand of suffering. Not that I think every life achieves a perfect balance of the two, but no life is all one or the other. Knowing that joy exists gives us something to strive for, something to believe in.

Are Karen and I too old to share the joy of being parents? We're trying to decide. I'm haunted--no, that's too strong . . . I think often of the baby riding in Linda Roy's womb, the child that might have been mine. Have I missed my one chance to continue my family line? Is that lost baby an endpoint for this individual life? Was Cross Rhodes a sign that I took too lightly the mystery of love, the miracle of conception? If so, can my present state of mind cancel out the debt I owe creation?

There's some irony here, to be sure, if I was the one who impregnated Linda. I, who never saw my own father, never saw my child. Deaths mark my biological being like bookends. So maybe I should take the hint and enjoy the rest of this time allotted me with Karen and not ask for more.

But there are other impulses urging me in different directions. And my mind races with the events of the last few days. Writing the story of my life has been exhilarating. I'm a new person, or an old person who's found himself at last.

Karen asked me this morning before she left what I was going to do with this record of my thoughts, which, I suppose, ought to contain somewhere the shape of my future. That future will be the product of my past, I'm sure.

One thing that will come is the restoration of my sailplane, The Spirit of St. Louis II. The damaged glider is in the garage out back, rescued by Karen from Cedar Street, where Billy had hauled it. Soon, maybe tomorrow, I'll begin repairs.

I even have one fantasy in which I fly over the town of Fairfield and along Route 66, me the left-handed flyer. I could scatter the pages of my life's story on the citizens below. Let them have the truth after all.

But, I don't know, maybe not. It will be enough to soar high above Black Street and know that I'm free.

303

Route 66 books by Michael Lund

Growing Up on Route 66 —Michael Lund (2000) ISBN 1-888725-31-1 Novel evoking fond memories of what it was like to grow up alongside "America's Highway" in 20th Century Missouri. **AudioBook** on CD—Growing Up on Route 66 ISBN: 1-59630-021-3 by Michael Lund abridged 6 CD's --7 Hours running time.

Route 66 Kids —Michael Lund (2002) ISBN 1-888725-70-2 Sequel to *Growing Up on Route 66*, continuing memories of what it was like to grow up alongside "America's Highway" in 20th Century Missouri.

Route 66 Spring-- Michael Lund (2004) ISBN: 1-888725-98-2. The lives of four young Missourians are changed when a bottle comes to the surface of one of the state's many natural springs. Inside is a letter written by a girl a dozen years after the end of the Civil War. Lucy Rivers Johns ' epistle contains a sad story of family failure and a powerful plea for help. This message from the last century crystallizes the individual frustrations of Janet Masters, Freddy Sills, Louis Clark, and Roberta Green, another group of Route 66 kids. Their response to the past charts a bold path into the future, a path inspired by the Mother Road itself.

A Left-hander on Route 66--Michael Lund (2003) ISBN 1-888725-88-5. Twenty years after the fact, left-hander Hugh Noone appeals a wrongful conviction that detoured him from "America's Main Street" and put him in jail. But revealing the details of the past and effecting a resolution of his case mean a dramatic rearrangement of his world, including troubled relationships with three women: Linda Roy, Patty Simpson, and Karen Murphy

Miss Route 66--Michael Lund (2004) ISBN 1-888725-96-6. In the fourth novel of Michael Lund's Route 66 Novel Series, Susan Bell tells the story of her candidacy in Fairfield, Missouri's annual beauty contest. Now married and with teenage children in St. Louis, she recounts her youthful adventure in this small town along "America's Highway." At the same time, she plans a return to Fairfield in order to right injustices she feels were done to some young contestants in the Miss Route 66 Pageant **Audiobook** on 5 CD's ISBN 1-888725-12-5

Route 66 to Vietnam Michael Lund (2004) ISBN 1-59630-000-0 This novel takes characters from earlier works in the Route 66 Novel Series farther west than Los Angeles, official destination of the famous highway, Route 66. Mark Landon and Billy Rhodes find the values they grew up on challenged by America's role in Southeast Asia. But elements of their upbringing represented by the Mother Road also sustain them in ways they could never have anticipated. **AudioBook** on 6 CD's ISBN: 1-59630-011-6 Michael Lund's fictional commentary from the viewpoint of a draftee. by Michael Lund unabridged 6 CD's --9 hours running time

Route 66 Chapel Michael Lund (2006) ISBN 1-59630-012-4 Route 66 Chapel, Michael Lund (2006) . When the forces of progress threaten the foundation of smalltown life—a small church—five senior citizens, a mysterious newcomer, and one young couple band together in an unlikely campaign to save it. The embattled meeting point of old and new is Route 66 Chapel, a building curiously linked to America's "Mother Road."

Route 66 Choir-- A Comedy (2010)Michael Lund ISBN 9781596300583   In Route 66 Choir Stanley Measure takes early retirement just before September 11, 2001, and his impulsive decisions participate in an unraveling of confidence in the American way of life. His wife Felicia finds that everything she holds dear is in danger of coming apart: her marriage, her church, her business, and even her country. Who or what can orchestrate the recovery of harmony necessary to sustain the spirit of the Mother Road?

Route 66 Bride (Fall 2010)

BeachHouse Books is an imprint of
Science & Humanities Press

Order Form			
Item	Each	Quantity	Amount
Missouri (only) sales tax 6.925%			
Priority Shipping			$5.00
	Total		
Name			
Address			

BeachHouse Books
PO Box 7151
 Chesterfield, MO 63006-7151
(636) 394-4950

www.ingramcontent.com/pod-product-compliance
Lightning Source LLC
Chambersburg PA
CBHW051239260626
47162CB00002B/518